ASHES TO ASHES

ASHES TO ASHES
HELLHOUND ACADEMY™
BOOK ONE

MARTHA CARR
MICHAEL ANDERLE

DON'T MISS OUR NEW RELEASES

Join the LMBPN email list to be notified of new releases and special promotions (which happen often) by following this link:

http://lmbpn.com/email/

This book is a work of fiction. All of the characters, organizations, and events portrayed in this novel are either products of the author's imagination or are used fictitiously. Sometimes both.

Copyright © 2025 LMBPN Publishing
Cover by Fantasy Book Design
Cover copyright © LMBPN Publishing
A Michael Anderle Production

LMBPN Publishing supports the right to free expression and the value of copyright. The purpose of copyright is to encourage writers and artists to produce the creative works that enrich our culture.

The distribution of this book without permission is a theft of the author's intellectual property. If you would like permission to use material from the book (other than for review purposes), please contact support@lmbpn.com. Thank you for your support of the author's rights.

LMBPN Publishing
2375 E. Tropicana Avenue, Suite 8-305
Las Vegas, Nevada 89119 USA

Version 1.00, April 2025
ebook ISBN: 979-8-89354-703-0
Print ISBN: 979-8-89354-704-7

This series (and what happens within / characters / situations / worlds) are Copyright (c) 2017-2025 by Martha Carr and LMBPN Publishing.

Thanks to our JIT Readers:

Gretchen "Lsai" Cook, C.J. Colaric, David Bowerman, Robert McCollum and Paul Dutton-Sim

CHAPTER ONE

Robin's eyes snapped open as her shoulders broke through the surface of Lady Bird Lake. A ripple of moonlight traced the water, and she realized that she didn't need to breathe. She tried to inhale sharply anyway, and her lungs expanded out of habit, not necessity. That strange fact settled in her mind like a neon warning sign.

She looked down and found a soaked, floral print dress clinging to her skin, the hem bobbing in the water. It might have been someone's idea of church attire, but it was nothing she would have chosen for a midnight swim. Trouble was, she had no idea what she usually wore or where she had come from.

She swam slowly toward shore and stepped onto squishy lake sediment, her bare feet pressing shells and pebbles into the mud. A wave of confusion rolled through her creating a mild panic. Around her, the night stretched in near silence.

The Austin city skyline shimmered in the distance, lights glowing across the dark water. Not a single jogger or dog walker roamed the popular trail that hugged the lake's edge, a detail she found more eerie than anything else.

Robin crawled out of the water and felt a breeze blow across her skin, but she didn't shiver. She stared at her hands and flexed them to be sure they still worked. They did. She felt no pain or cold, no memory either. Fog swirled where thoughts should have been.

What day is it? Who am I?

She grasped at fragments, such as a name or a face, but found only emptiness. The effort sent a phantom throb behind her eyes, a headache born of sheer absence. Last name? Favorite food? How did she get here? Everything was impossibly gone, leaving only the rising tide of panic and the chilling reality that she wasn't cold, wasn't breathing, wasn't alive. "No, no, no, no, no." She shook her head hoping that would help, but nothing.

She muttered a curse under her breath and scanned the shoreline for clues. The moon reflected across the slow moving lake, and in the glow she saw a pair of startled turtles plop beneath the surface. She wondered if fish had nibbled on her while she was down there. The possibility made her stomach twist.

She pressed trembling fingers to her neck. Nothing. Cool skin, no thrum.

"Okay, that's not creepy at all," she muttered, pushing wet bangs out of her eyes. The words fogged in the cool March air, but her breath made no mist. "Creepier. Fantastic."

A dull ache tugged at her left forearm. She rolled her sleeve and found a raised brand the size of a silver dollar of a stylized hound's head with the muzzle snarling, and hollow eyes. The flesh wasn't burned or inflamed; it simply *was*, as if she'd always had it. Robin sucked in another useless breath. "Tattoo artist from hell, noted."

Footsteps pattered on the trail above. Two figures jogged into view, both in charcoal hoodies, jeans, and running shoes that glowed faintly blue along the soles. Under the hoods, faces were half-lit by the screens of their phones. Images—impossible swirling symbols—crawled across the glass like intelligent graffiti.

The shorter of the pair, a woman, stopped five feet away. "Subject acquired," she said into her phone, voice flat as black coffee. She crouched beside Robin and offered a gloved hand. "Robin Sullivan. Glad you made it through the water hazard intact."

"Sullivan," Robin muttered, as if hearing it for the first time. She ignored the hand and pushed herself upright. "Intact is debatable. Who are you? What did you do to my heart? Why is it offline?"

"Your circulatory system's in a managed state. It's temporary." The taller escort, a man, spoke without lowering his hood. "Think of it as airplane mode for your body."

"I'd rather not think of myself as a cell phone, thanks." She stumbled to standing, shoes squishing. "Someone explain—now—or I start screaming, and I'm not above biting."

The woman chuckled. "You won't like the taste of us." She thumbed her phone, and the symbols brightened. Robin's tattoo pulsed in answer—cold, metallic, a tuning fork in her bones. Her knees buckled before she could hide it.

"What did you just do?"

"Verified the bond. You're tethered, Cadet. Congratulations on your resurrection."

Resurrection. The word slapped her harder than the lake water. Memory fragments flashed of rain, headlights, being pulled inside a van—then nothing. She reeled, grasping the deck rail.

"Easy." The woman steadied her. "We'll answer the essential questions in a secure location. Time matters."

"Then move," Robin snapped, yanking free. "But you owe me explanations, receipts, and possibly a therapist."

"That's above my pay grade," the man said, voice half amused. He pointed toward a squat boathouse painted city-maintenance beige. "This way."

They hustled along the wooden walkway. The moon threw silver shadows on the lake, and the downtown skyscrapers rose just beyond the trees. In normal circumstances, Robin would savor the skyline, but tonight everything felt uncanny, as if Austin was a familiar movie set filmed with the wrong lens.

"Name?" the woman asked.

"You just used it."

"Full name. Middle too."

"Robin *Marie* Sullivan. Wait, how did I know that? Why do you need it?" *My brain feels like its been scrambled.*

"Ledger entry confirmation," the man said. "Better you speak it than we rely on a file corrupted by your, uh, unexpected swim."

Robin frowned. Ledger. Files. Swim. So many clues without any real answers.

At a boathouse the escorts stopped before a padlocked

steel service door. A large wooden sign out front read Waller Street Boathouse in large blue letters.

The man pressed his phone to the lock as symbols spilled across the metal like hot circuitry making the shackle popped open. Robin blinked. No flashy sound effects, no sparkles—just old hardware obeying arcane Bluetooth.

Inside, mildew and motor oil scented the dark. The escorts guided Robin down a staircase barely wider than her shoulders. Each step groaned. She counted to sixteen before landing on concrete. A single bulb came on, triggered by who knew what. The corridor beyond stretched straight and narrow, ribs of limestone forming walls and ceiling. A faint vibration thrummed underfoot.

"Underground?" Robin asked. Her voice bounced in the tunnel.

"Austin's full of surprises," the woman replied. "Keep up."

Robin did, though a rebellious part of her cataloged every turn and doorway. If she needed to break out later, she'd want the labyrinth memorized.

The trio reached a junction where three steel doors waited. The escorts stopped at the center door—matte black, no handle—while the man tapped his phone again. The symbols danced, and a peephole eye slid open, scanning them with a red beam. Robin half expected it to hiss, "Welcome to Jurassic Park," but it stayed blessedly silent. A lock released with a soft *thunk*.

Before stepping through, the woman faced Robin. She pushed back her hood, revealing a face that might have been pretty if it weren't worn paper-thin by exhaustion.

She had olive skin, a freckled nose, and short dark curls. "I'm Sarah. That's Mateo. You'll meet plenty of other staff soon, but we're your first handlers."

"Handlers," Robin echoed. "How comforting."

Sarah's mouth twitched. "Here's what you actually need to know *now*. Your second chance isn't a free ride. You train, you follow orders, you protect the city. However, break core protocol and the ledger recalls you."

"Recalls. As in…" Robin made a throat-slitting gesture.

"As in your current…animation ends." Mateo shrugged. "It's cleaner than your first death, or so I'm told."

Robin swallowed hard. "And if I cooperate, I get to keep—what? Existence?"

"You get time," Sarah said softly. "Time you didn't have yesterday."

The phrasing chilled Robin more than the lake. Yesterday. How long had she been gone? "My family—do they know? Do they *remember* me? Who are they?"

"That answer is above our clearance." Mateo gestured at the open doorway. "Welcome to Hellhound Academy."

Names slammed together in Robin's mind. 'Hellhound' echoed the brand on her arm. 'Academy' conjured images of plaid uniforms and cafeteria trays, but she doubted anybody inside was trading SAT scores. She sucked a steadying breath—pointless but comforting—and stepped through.

The door sealed behind them with a vacuum hiss. Inside lay a reception area cut straight from a spy thriller. There were graphite-gray walls, LED strips, and a desk of frosted glass. "No windows," whispered Robin. A half-circle emblem glowed on the far wall—a hound's head over crossed keys. Beneath it, tidy lettering of *Vita Secunda, Urbs Prima*.

Sarah peeled off her damp hoodie, revealing a charcoal tee with the same emblem. "Life second, city first," she translated, catching Robin's eye. "It'll grow on you."

Mateo produced a towel from a supply locker. "Dry off. You'll meet with June for intake in a minute and she hates puddles."

Robin accepted the towel, scrubbing her hair and face. "You two sticking around for my 'intake'?"

"Bodies to collect elsewhere," Mateo said. "We're night-shift escorts. Spoiler for you. You came through cleaner than most. Nobody, or nothing, tried to eat you."

"Eat me?"

Sarah smirked. "Ask June." She pulled a slim card from her back pocket and pressed it into Robin's palm. Blank except for the glowing hound emblem. "Key to your dorm once they assign one."

Robin glanced at it, the brand on her forearm tingling when skin met card. A soft heartbeat *thump* echoed in her ears, then vanished. *False alarm.* She was surprised at the twinge of sadness that passed through her.

"Until orientation." Sarah tapped two fingers to her brow in a casual salute. The pair turned and left through a side corridor, laughter trading between them like siblings in on a prank.

Robin stood alone. The silence felt heavier inside these walls, as though the concrete remembered every secret whispered against it. She inhaled through her nose, tasting ozone and floor polish.

"City first, huh?" She studied the emblem again. The

hound's head reminded her of old myth sketches. It was Cerberus minus two heads. "Appropriate, given my undead status."

She paced with every step squeaking on polished epoxy, echoing. The towel dripped steadily. Time stretched. Her brain, freed from immediate terror, started listing priorities:

1. *Figure out who killed you. The memories hovering beyond reach needed coaxing.*
2. *Understand the ledger. They wielded it like a cosmic leash.*
3. *Locate exits. Because captivity—even cushy, undead captivity—was still captivity.*
4. *Do not die again. Preferably for a very long time.*

A shiver went down her spine, but it was from fear and not cold. "Dead, how am I dead?"

The side door slid open with a soft whir. An older woman strutted in, gray streak blazing through black hair twisted in a severe bun. She wore a navy blazer over fatigue-style cargo pants and looked like she ate chain-of-command for breakfast.

"I'm June," she said, her voice a precise instrument. "And you're late for being dead, Ms. Sullivan. Let's expedite."

"I've always been an overachiever," said Robin, attempting levity.

June didn't smile. "Follow me. Intake is three minutes, sanitation two, fit-out five. Ask questions on your own time. That begins… never."

Robin blinked. "So…be quiet, stand still, and keep breathing air I don't need?"

"Excellent comprehension." June handed her a plain black duffel. "Change. Your briefs are vacuum-sealed—we maintain hygiene standards. Mud and memory loss are no excuses."

Robin peeked inside and saw dark sweats, sturdy boots, and toiletries in biodegradable sachets labeled *courtesy of Hellhound Academy*. "You have some creepy corporate swag."

June pressed two fingers against the hound brand. Pain—white, electric—spiked up Robin's arm. She hissed, letting out an involuntary growl.

"Biometric imprint verified," June said, unfazed. "The mark ties you to the city's lifeline. Consider it a pacemaker for undeath."

"And if I peel it off?" Robin growled.

June met her gaze, unblinking. "Peel off your arm while you're at it. Results will be comparable."

Robin clenched her jaw. "You people really need a customer-service seminar."

"Duly noted. You're not the first to point that out. Or the hundredth. Shower station's through there." June pointed to a frosted door. "Water is warm. Enjoy it while you can." She turned on her heel and exited.

Left alone again, Robin exhaled—a habit refusing to die with her body. She tapped the hound brand. It felt like smooth stone, pulsing faintly under her fingertips.

"Not yours forever," she whispered. "One way or another, I'm getting my life back." She looked around and whispered, "When I can remember it."

A faint echo from the door sounded suspiciously like a scoff, but Robin chalked it up to the building's guts settling. She squared her shoulders and headed for the shower, her mind already plotting escape routes.

Find the truth or claw it out of whoever's hiding it. The vow beat in her head, replacing the absent heartbeat, and for the first time since surfacing, Robin Sullivan felt at least a kind of alive.

CHAPTER TWO

Robin emerged from the steamy shower stall smelling faintly of industrial citrus and borrowed soap, heart still stubbornly silent in her chest. The tactical sweats from June's duffel fit like they'd been tailored—black, breathable, a subtle Kevlar sheen woven into the threads. Someone had taken her measurements *before* she died, which was unsettling on at least three philosophical levels.

June reappeared the moment the locker door clicked shut, as if keyed to Robin's every move. "Efficient," she noted, looking over Robin's damp ponytail. "We'll make a soldier out of you yet."

"I don't know what I used to do," Robin replied. "But I'm feeling confident my résumé did not include 'soldier.'"

"Congratulations on the spontaneous skill expansion," June deadpanned. She gestured toward a rolling medical cart that hadn't been there a minute ago. An autopod unfolded from its center, bristling with syringes, diagnostic lenses, and one ominous bone saw attachment Robin hoped was ornamental.

"Quick vitals and spectral scan," June announced. "Stand on the pad, arms out."

"How about dinner and a movie first?"

"You don't eat in the traditional sense. Consider yourself spared the cafeteria meatloaf."

"So many upsides," Robin muttered but stepped onto the glowing circle. Cold light crawled up her body, painting her skeleton in a ghostly outline on the ceiling. Numbers scrolled by on a screen. **TEMP—ambient; HR—null; SOUL SIGNAL—stable**. Robin's eyebrows rose at the last metric.

June followed her gaze. "The soul leaves a signature. Yours is registering at ninety-three percent integrity. Minor trauma from your death and then the resurrection lag, but nothing training won't reconcile."

"Good to know my soul is slightly scuffed but serviceable." The cart beeped completion, retracting the scarier tools. One needle jabbed her arm, depositing what felt like ice chips under the skin. "Vaccine?"

"Nanite mesh," June said. "Accelerated repair matrix. Unless you're fond of limbs reattaching slowly."

"Can't say I've ranked preferences for limb reattachment speed." She swallowed hard. "Am I a zombie now? Wait, let me say it. It's above your pay grade."

A vent overhead hissed, releasing a flutter of ebony feathers. A crow emerged, diving in a lazy spiral and landing on a perch attached to the cart.

June offered a finger, and the bird nipped it lightly.

"Phoenix will be your familiar. You're one of the lucky ones."

Up close, Phoenix was bigger than Robin expected—raven-big, with shimmering feathers that shifted from black to midnight blue. His eyes burned an eerie ember red.

"Great, a babysitter from the dark side." Robin raised her forearm. The hound brand glowed faintly, resonating with the bird's stare. A pulse of pressure bloomed behind her eyes—like déjà vu mixed with feedback static—and an image flashed in her mind. It was a map of Austin with crimson dots marking bridges and water towers. Then it was gone.

"What was that?" she gasped.

"Bond initialization," June said, unbothered. "Visual data packets. You'll get used to them."

Robin rubbed her temples. "Do the packets come with Tylenol?"

"You no longer process analgesics. Headaches are motivational." June tapped a wrist tablet, and a translucent screen projected academy schematics. "Orientation continues with a facilities tour. Walk and absorb."

They left the intake bay through sliding panels into a main corridor lit by soft bioluminescent strips embedded in the floor—an eerie river of pale teal guiding the way. Phoenix flapped to Robin's shoulder, the wings settling into place. Robin pursed her lips and took a sidelong glance at the large bird, not sure what to do.

"Left is the Armory," June narrated. Through a blast door's tiny viewport Robin spotted racks of sleek weapons. Not guns but staffs, blades, and odd crystalline slingshots humming with energy. "You won't touch those for weeks. Maybe months."

"Motivational headaches and delayed weapon access. Truly paradise."

"Try sarcasm on the instructors," June advised. "See how that goes."

They paused at a wall alcove displaying portraits. Each frame held a cadet in modern combat gear, face half hidden by a stylized hound mask. Beneath, brass plaques read RETURNED TO SOURCE. Dozens of them.

"Graduates?" Robin asked.

"Failures," June corrected. "Cadets recalled by the ledger back to the underworld. Reminders of consequences."

A chill rippled over Robin's skin. The portraits—all so young—made the corridor feel like a Millennial mausoleum. Phoenix shifted uneasily on her shoulder.

At the end of the hallway, they entered an atrium with a retractable ceiling showing stars beyond tinted glass. A giant kinetic sculpture hung overhead, made up of three interlocking rings of tarnished silver that were rotating silently. Each ring was etched with more of those animated symbols.

"The Orrery," June said. "It tracks incursion probability. When the outer ring glows red, we mobilize."

"Incursion meaning…?"

"Things that should not cross into this plane but routinely try. Demons, wraiths, budget tourists from limbo."

"Lovely. And we, the freshly revived, stop them?"

"With supervision." June's gaze went to a balcony where two figures in plain clothes watched. One, a wiry man with salt-and-pepper stubble, drummed fingers on the railing; the other, a woman in fatigues, carved the air with hand signals Robin didn't understand. "Command staff," June said. "They'll grade your first assessment tomorrow."

Robin waved up at them. The man raised an eyebrow as the woman's lips curved in something not quite a smile.

Beyond the atrium, stairs descended to what June called "The Quad"—a broad subterranean arena lined with crash mats and holographic emitters. Cadets in black and gray sweats sparred with fully realized holograms. There were smoke wolves, a skeletal boar, and one enormous manta-ray shape that glided overhead like a nightmare kite. Barked commands from the instructors bounced off the concrete walls.

"We train any time the ledger is calm," June explained over the din. "Adrenal responses remain intact post-mortem, so drills are effective. Pain teaches."

"How humane," Robin observed. A cadet yelped as a holographic talon raked his side. Medical drones zipped in, spritzing blue foam. Seconds later the wound knitted closed.

"See? He's learning. He won't forget the experience." June ushered her on. They passed a glass wall overlooking a server farm—rows of crystalline coffins filled with violet light.

"Data cores housing the ledger's neural substrate," June said. "Only Archivists access them."

"Let me guess—Archivists outrank you."

"Everyone outranks someone until they don't. Focus on your lane."

They reached an elevator and June scanned her tablet,

causing the doors to part. Inside, soft jazz played. The sudden music was abrupt and bizarre given the setting. Robin cocked an eyebrow.

"Elevator company sponsorship," June offered. "They insisted."

"Commercials even among the undead. Because nothing says 'secret undead barracks' like elevator jazz."

The elevator rose smoothly. Transparent walls revealed additional levels with dormitory tiers, hydroponic gardens glowing emerald, and a library wreathed in floating lights. Robin leaned closer for a better look. Books, hundreds of them, lined up tight on shelves. The novelty of paper drew another pang of nostalgia.

"You'll get two hours a week in the archive," June said, noticing. "You can earn bonus hours by not getting sent back."

Robin saluted with two fingers. "Understood, ma'am."

The elevator deposited them outside a door stenciled *CADET SERVICES*. Inside, a half-moon desk was staffed by a barrel-chested young man wearing a cheerful smile and neon-green headphones. A name tag read *Kip – Logistics Wizard*.

Kip took off the headphones, letting them rest around his neck, and grinned. "Fresh meat! Don't look so grim. You survived dying, everything else is downhill."

"Encouraging," Robin replied.

"You need your dorm key, meal chip, and sim-band." Kip produced a slim silicone bracelet pulsing faintly. "Tracks your location, vitals, and wisecracks for quality assurance."

Robin slid it on beside the brand. The two glows synced, emitting a satisfied chime.

"Cute," she said. "And totally not Big Brother."

"Big Brother works upstairs," Kip joked, thumb jerking skyward. "Big Sister lives in the walls. You'll meet her when the fire alarms sing. Fire is not your friend and can send you back early." He handed over a hexagonal coin. "Meal chip. Don't lose it; the vending goblins get testy without payment."

"There are goblins?" Robin asked.

Kip winked. "Only on taco Tuesdays."

"I thought I didn't need food?"

"It passes the time, and you can still taste. You can finally eat whatever you want without gaining an ounce. This is it. Whatever you left the living with, you're stuck with," he said, patting his ample belly.

"You're dead, too? Is everyone undead down here?"

"Almost everyone."

June glanced at a slim wristwatch. "Your schedule uploads in four minutes. Let's finish the bond."

Robin followed her into a small chapel-like room paneled in black glass. A single podium held a leather tome the size of a suitcase. The *ledger*. The cover bore the hound emblem in embossed silver.

June snapped her fingers and Phoenix hopped from Robin's shoulder onto the podium, his claws clicking on metal. The bird croaked once, and the ledger opened itself, pages riffling before settling near the middle. Names glowed in columns—hundreds of them.

June handed Robin a stylus tipped with quivering light. "Sign. Full name, intent line below it."

"What if I refuse?"

"Then the ledger refuses you, and you return to the lake the slow way."

Waterlogged lungs flashed through Robin's memory. She shivered. "Fine." She scrawled *Robin Marie Sullivan*. She hesitated and then, beneath that she wrote: *To uncover the truth and protect the innocent.*

The ink flared a gold hue, sank into the paper, and vanished. The hound brand on her arm warmed pleasantly. Phoenix cawed his approval.

"Clever." June's eyebrows lifted. "Intent guides power. Protecting innocents scores you cosmic brownie points."

"I'm fond of brownies."

"Kitchen is level three—but no sugar rush after curfew." June closed the ledger with a decisive slap. "Orientation complete."

"That's it? No secret handshake?"

June actually considered. "Shake Phoenix's wing."

Robin extended a finger; the crow brushed it with a primary feather. A pulse of calm and reassurance rolled through her, unexpectedly warm.

"Report to Dorm Delta-Nine," June said, handing over a data card. "Sleep cycle starts in thirty." She strode away, echoing heels announcing authority.

Robin exhaled, alone again except for Phoenix. The crow tilted its head, eyeing the corridor.

"Lead on, feathery Fitbit."

Phoenix launched, gliding ahead as Robin followed through hushed hallways that smelled of cedar-cleaner and recycled air. Lockers lined one wall, each tagged with a cadet's last name: Alvarez, Blake, Chen...Sullivan. The locker door clicked open at her approach, a set of dim lights snapping on inside. A matte-black training pack waited with the embroidered initials R.M.S.

"Nice to feel welcomed for once," Robin said. She slung the pack over a shoulder, ignoring how her arms were no longer tired. "So, this is my *afterlife*. Wonder if it comes with dental."

Phoenix croaked what sounded like skeptical laughter and winged toward the dorm level.

As she trailed him, Robin replayed the night of water, branding, and a spooky ledger. Somewhere in that twisted chain lay an explanation of her death—and maybe her salvation.

Another fragment of memory suddenly popped. A large blade and a sharp pain in her chest that was only a memory, but still made her double over for a moment. A snarling face too close to hers and hot breath on her face.

"What the hell? Who was that?" She gritted her teeth and caught up with the crow, who was circling back to check on her. "I will find you," she whispered to whatever shadow had ended her first life. "Count on it."

Phoenix cawed agreement, and together they stepped into the cadet wing—the next chapter of an existence that had already run out of chapters once.

CHAPTER THREE

Robin unlocked Dorm Delta-Nine and confronted a space that wouldn't have passed a halfway-house inspection. It was twelve feet long, seven feet wide, with bulkhead-gray walls that still smelled of primer, and a single metal bunk bolted to the floor. Someone had jammed a desk and chair into the far corner, forcing the bed to sit diagonally like it was trying to escape. A ceiling vent rattled with recycled air that was probably forty-percent confidence and sixty-percent freon. "I suppose it doesn't matter for most of us what that is."

Phoenix fluttered in behind her, perched on the overhead sprinkler, and issued a satisfied *caw* that echoed like judgment.

She dropped her training pack, testing the mattress with a shove. The springs squealed in protest. "Luxury accommodations, Mister Crow. Five stars if I lose all feeling in my back."

A knock—two quick taps—sounded at the partially open door before Robin could start cataloging further grievances. A petite girl slid through the gap as if she'd rehearsed slipping past wardens her entire life. Bubble-gum-pink pixie cut, oversized gray hoodie, and leggings printed with tiny jack-o'-lanterns, like Halloween refused to leave her closet. Big brown eyes took in Robin, widened with something between relief and caffeinated panic.

"Hi!" the newcomer whispered so fast the word almost disintegrated. "I'm Ashley. Newish. Memory-free. Totally freaked. They said knock if I needed anything, but I thought maybe you needed something because first night and all." She hugged a steel travel mug to her chest as though it were a therapy cat.

Robin blinked at the barrage, then forced a weary smile. "Robin. Also newish, mostly memory-free, moderately freaked." She jerked her chin toward the mug. "Coffee?"

Ashley grimaced. "Wish. Cafeteria sludge. But it's *warm* sludge, which helps when your circulatory system is running on ghost credits." She thrust the mug forward. "Share?"

Robin accepted and took a cautious sip. The liquid tasted like scorched chicory and burnt caramel, but the warmth seeped into her bones. "You're a saint."

A tall silhouette filled the doorway. The man ducked under the jamb, his lanky frame folded into plain tactical sweats. Thick black curls spilled over thoughtful eyes the shade of river stones. He carried a tablet tucked beneath one arm and a cardboard box that rattled ominously.

"David," he supplied before Robin could ask, in a rich drawl that might have once belonged to Louisiana. "Saw the welcome wagon cruise past. Figured you'd need the starter kit." He set the box on the desk and opened it. Inside were two bottled waters, protein-nut rectangles masquerading as energy bars, and a fist-sized orb that glowed faint turquoise.

Robin raised an eyebrow. "And that is...?"

"Night-orb." David tossed it gently in the air. The sphere hovered, shedding a soft light that banished hospital fluorescence. "Turns itself off when you fall asleep. Or when you flatline—again, whichever comes first."

"Cheery feature." Robin rotated her forearm, letting the orb illuminate the hound brand. Ashley extended her wrist, revealing an identical mark, smaller but no less defined. David followed suit. Three matching badges of forced enlistment.

"Guess that makes us teammates," Ashley said, voice dipping toward sincere. "Or cellmates."

"Prefer *friends*," David murmured. His gaze lingered on Robin a heartbeat longer than polite. Robin was certain he felt confused, like déjà vu scratching at a locked door. He recovered with a shrug. "Tomorrow's combat assessment tends to forge quick alliances."

Robin set the coffee on the desk. "Speaking of, which of you two mines of information wants to brief me on Academy survival?"

Ashley hopped onto the edge of the bunk, cross-legged. "Rule one is don't mouth off to Instructor Jude unless you're okay with spontaneous sparring. He fights with an illusion blade that leaves *phantom* bruises. They hurt worse than real ones."

"Rule two," David added, leaning against the wall, "never miss curfew headcount. The halls reconfigure at zero-two-hundred, and if you're not in your dorm, you end up on Sub-Level Seven."

Robin tilted her head. "What's on Sub-Level Seven?"

Ashley and David answered in unison, "Laundry." Their shared shudder told Robin laundry involved more than detergent.

"Rule three." Ashley ticked each one off on her fingers. "Cafeteria breakfast is edible if you smother everything in the green salsa. The red salsa is—" She hesitated, searching for an adequate trauma descriptor. "—sentient. Don't."

Robin laughed despite herself. The tight coil in her chest loosened an inch. "Okay, life hacks noted. What about tomorrow's assessment?"

David tapped his tablet, sending a tactical map onto the wall via a micro-projector, displaying a rectangular arena dotted with glowing nodes. "There are nine obstacles, all time-gated. We're graded on teamwork, adaptability, and 'manifestation control,' which means keeping your undead quirks from melting your squad."

"Undead quirks," Robin echoed. "Examples?"

Ashley bounced a shoulder. "I can see kinetic energy trails—where people just moved—which sounds cool but mostly gives me migraines."

"Intuitive pathfinder," David explained, tapping a node that brightened in Ashley's color. "Helpful in obstacle mazes. I hack memories—short-term only," he added quickly, as Robin's eyes widened. "Pull surface thoughts if I'm touching someone. It's...disorienting."

Robin swallowed. "And you think we'll be a squad?"

David shut off the projection. "Intake groups usually

stick together for the first month. Safety in shared ignorance."

"Great." Robin tugged at her ponytail. "Because my special talent seems to be making sarcastic comments while technically deceased."

A throaty *caw* drew all eyes upward. Phoenix dropped from the sprinkler and landed on the desk, talons tapping a staccato rhythm. The bird cocked its head at Robin, then at the protein bar box, and finally at the door letting her know he was feeling impatient.

Ashley frowned. "That's his 'incoming message' posture."

"You know this bird?"

"We've seen him around but you're the first cadet he's bothered to hang around."

David looked inside the box and was startled to find a small scroll, a parchment that was wax-sealed with the hound emblem. He offered it to Robin. "Looks like Phoenix already raided the tube system."

"How did he get it in there?"

"That bird is full of tricks."

Robin broke the seal and unrolled the note. Neat block letters read:

CADET SULLIVAN – REPORT TO OBSERVATION DECK 11:45 P.M. – COME ALONE.

There was no signature.

She checked the wall clock: 11:32. Curfew was midnight. "You two ever gotten after-hours summons?"

Ashley shook her head so hard the pink strands

blurred. "Nope. And 'come alone' is horror-movie phrasing. Decline!"

Phoenix pecked the desk once, decisively. David studied the crow, then Robin. "You have to go. Trust Phoenix. The Observation Deck is top-level. There's a quick route through Stairwell C. I can map it for you."

Robin folded the note. "June said breaking curfew is bad karma. But ignoring secret messages sounds worse."

Ashley chewed a thumbnail. "If you're going, take backup. Preferably *us*."

"Message says alone." Robin's eyes narrowed at the bird. "Phoenix will tattle if we break instructions."

Phoenix gave an innocent ruffle.

David exhaled. "Then at least wear this." He dug into the starter kit and handed over a slim baton. At her puzzled look, he pressed the base, and a translucent blade of pale cobalt energy snapped to life with a low hum. "Training saber. Nonlethal. Mostly."

Robin weighed the baton. Light, balanced. She turned it off and clipped it to her waistband. "Thanks."

Ashley hopped off the bed. "We'll wait in the hall. If you're not back by 12:05, we raise alarms and maybe stage a daring rescue."

Robin's chest warmed with gratitude, quickly mixing with trepidation. "Deal." She grabbed a water bottle, took a swig, and headed for the door.

Observation Deck turned out to be an elongated mezzanine ringing the inner atrium where the Orrery still revolved, its rings throwing shifting constellations onto concrete. Robin arrived with two minutes to spare, breathing steadily despite the six flights of stairs. Apparently, being undead came with cardio perks. Phoenix glided ahead, settling on a railing post, becoming silent and still.

A figure stepped from the shadow between support pillars. It was Instructor Jude, the drill sergeant June had name-dropped. He wore civilian jeans and a long sleeved t-shirt, his arms crossed, every inch a relaxed menace. A holographic practice blade dangled at his hip.

"Cadet Sullivan," he greeted, voice like gravel on asphalt. "You disobeyed the note."

Robin's pulseless heart stuttered anyway. "I came alone."

Jude looked at Phoenix. "Alone means without the bird."

"Phoenix goes where he pleases." Robin squared her shoulders. "Why summon me?"

"Because tomorrow you'll lead your squad through the gauntlet." He stepped closer. "Leadership is chosen, not assigned. I wanted a look at the merchandise before I stamped it."

Robin's laugh came out brittle. "Merchandise? I'm not a product."

"Everything's a product. Some just have a better warranty." Jude's gaze dipped to the saber at her hip. "David's handiwork. Good. You'll need it."

He paced to the railing, staring down at cadets still drilling in The Quad. "City needs protectors who can improvise. You woke up improvising when you crawled out of the lake, demanding answers, and didn't accept illusions."

"Because illusions don't change facts," Robin snapped. "Someone killed me."

"You have memories?"

Robin hesitated. "Some. Only bits and pieces."

"Keep that to yourself. The higher ups don't like to hear that. They don't like the idea of someone chasing their old life and exposing the Academy to the living. And that anger keeps you sharp," Jude conceded. "Harness it. Point it outward, not inward, or the ledger will reclaim you."

He turned, suddenly inches away. Robin fought the urge to step back. Jude's eyes were moth-wing gray, ancient despite his thirty-something features.

"You want the truth," he said softly. "Prove you can handle it. Survive the gauntlet. Keep your team breathing—or whatever counts as breathing for you lot. Finish top tier and I'll answer one question."

Robin's jaw clenched. "Any question?"

"Any."

He paused, then added, "You're not the first cadet to come back with gaps that don't add up. But you're the first one I've seen who might actually dig deep enough to expose why."

Robin narrowed her eyes. "You think someone's hiding something?"

"I think this place tells half a story, and most cadets never ask for the rest. The ones who do… don't usually last long."

"Why can't you figure it out?"

"The undead can do things that those of us who still have a beating heart can't."

"You're still alive," Robin said with a gasp.

A siren chimed midnight, distant but clear. Jude tilted his head. "That's curfew. Return to dorms before security drones find you." He stepped backward and vanished into the shadows and must have triggered a hidden door because no footsteps echoed.

Phoenix launched, circling twice before settling on her shoulder. The crow's warmth grounded Robin. She exhaled, rubbing its glossy feathers.

"Top tier," she murmured. "Guess we'd better form a team by breakfast."

Ashley and David were exactly where she'd left them. They were leaning against opposite corridor walls trying, and failing, to appear casual. Relief flooded their expressions.

"Well?" Ashley burst out.

"I got homework," Robin replied. "We're a squad. Assessment at oh-eight-hundred. Our goal is to finish first."

David's mouth quirked. "Ambitious and on your first day."

"Non-negotiable." Robin looked between them. "So, friends?"

Ashley beamed. David extended a fist and Robin bumped it.

Inside the dorm wing, a night orb dimmed automatically, casting long shadows across the empty common room as they peeled off in different directions. Ashley muttered something about setting a triple alarm before slipping into her room and shutting the door with her foot. David gave a quiet nod, clutching his tablet of bunker schematics, then disappeared down the hall. Robin stepped into her own room alone, the hush settling over her like a second skin. She stretched out on the bunk, eyes locked on the ceiling vent where Phoenix was perched, feathers fluffed as he preened in the soft glow of the night orb.

The brand on her arm pulsed a steady rhythm of a mock heartbeat. She placed her other hand over it, savoring the phantom thump. *Survive tomorrow, earn a truth.*

A smile tugged her lips. "Challenge accepted," she whispered, and finally let the night orb wink out.

CHAPTER FOUR

Robin awoke at 05:30 to the soft glow of the night-orb brightening by degrees, mimicking dawn even though they were several stories underground. Phoenix let out a single croak that sounded like an alarm clock's snooze button finally giving up. A schedule notification scrolled across her sim-band. Gauntlet Briefing – 06:15, Mess Hall B.

She threw on a charcoal workout tee, compression joggers, and a pair of new boots that had been left in her room, then went to find Ashley and David.

She headed for Ashley's wing first, the hall still echoing with early morning throat clears and the hiss of locker doors. A cadet yawned so hard he almost walked into her, mumbling something about simulated bacon.

Ashley's door was slightly ajar. Robin knocked once and pushed it open.

Her friend and teammate was already half-dressed, jacket shrugged on over a tank, and her boot laces still undone. She had one brow arched and was sipping from a dented thermal mug labeled *NOPE*.

"You read the schedule?" Robin asked.

Ashley held up the mug like it was self-explanatory. "Already bracing for it. What's the call?"

"Gauntlet briefing. Mess Hall B. We're rolling in as a squad."

Ashley drained her cup, grabbed her jacket, and followed without another word.

They turned down the west corridor toward David's room. The air smelled faintly of recycled citrus, the overhead lights still warming up. They passed a pair of instructors whispering over a sim pad and a cadet quietly crying into a protein bar.

Robin gently elbowed Ashley and leaned in to whisper, "What's that about?"

Ashley shook her head, and they were about to turn back when they saw an instructor lead the cadet away.

Robin watched till they turned a corner and then rapped twice on David's door.

He opened it fast, appearing dressed, groomed, and gear already slung over one shoulder like he'd been expecting her. "Didn't think I was getting a wake-up knock."

"You didn't," Robin said. "But you're on the hook anyway."

"Then lead the way."

They hustled past other half-dressed cadets who were wobbling toward caffeine. Everyone was wearing some combination of sweats, hoodies, and trainers in shades of black, gray, and the occasional neon accent.

Mess Hall B resembled a tech-start-up cafeteria mashed with a college dining commons with steel countertops, touchscreen order kiosks, and rows of tables bolted to the floor. ⁸Digital screens ran motivational slogans over B-roll of Austin landmarks. Robin grabbed trays for her new squad while David poured three cups of sludge coffee, adding precisely one sugar packet to Ashley's because, apparently, that prevented her energy-trail headaches.

Instructor Jude appeared on a raised platform at 06:14 on the dot. He wore dark jeans, a graphite utility jacket with the Academy logo complete with mantra, and a headset mic. The lighting overhead dimmed, and a 3-D schematic of the Gauntlet expanded in mid-air. Nine zones appeared, forming a twisting corridor full of rising walls, collapsing floors, and holographic enemies color-coded by threat level.

"Cadets," Jude began, voice carrying without feedback. "You will enter as squads of three. Finish in twenty minutes or less to qualify for lunch. Finish top three and you earn an honest answer to one question from the instructor of your choice." He did not look at Robin, but she felt the weight of the promise he'd made to her last night.

Kip, wearing a Friends-themed apron over his logistics tee, zipped between tables, handing out wrist patches that pulsed with squad colors. Robin, Ashley, and David received a cobalt-blue emblem. Phoenix peered down from an overhead beam, eyes burning like twin LEDs.

"Zone one tests agility," Jude continued. "Zone two, puzzle logic. Zone three, manifestation control—watch your quirks. Zones four through nine escalate from there.

We're broadcasting live to the Command balcony. Make it entertaining."

Ashley's hands trembled until Robin slid a water bottle into them. "We've got this," she said, keeping her tone calm but brisk. "Follow my lead, call out anything you see in energy trails, and David—keep your hands free in case you need to yank a memory shard."

He nodded. "And you?"

"I improvise." She flashed a grin that tried to be confident.

By 07:55 the squads lined up outside a massive set of steel doors painted with the hound logo. A countdown hovered over the archway. First up was Team Crimson. The doors parted, the timer began, and the squad sprinted into neon fog.

A jumbotron replayed their progress through wall runs, swinging beams, and a laser pit. They stumbled but finished in nineteen minutes forty-two seconds. The hall erupted in applause. Robin's stomach tightened.

"Team Cobalt, you're next," an overhead voice announced.

David adjusted his sim-band. "Sensors sync in three… two…"

Phoenix fluttered down, landing on Robin's shoulder, and pecked the hound brand once, like a referee starting a match.

The doors opened as Robin inhaled, charging ahead.

The first stop was Zone 1 and the Incline.

A conveyor belt angled skyward at twenty degrees, plates popping up like malicious Whac-A-Moles. The floor lurched beneath them.

"Red flare—left!" Ashley shouted, eyes blazing with kinetic trails only she could see.

Robin cut left, landing on a secure plate. "Green arc—two strides right!"

David matched her movement, muttering, "Who designs treadmills from hell?"

"Someone who hates cardio," Robin grunted. Plates slammed down behind them as momentum threatened to throw them back, but they hit the summit in forty seconds. A pressure pad hissed approval, and mist swallowed them into the next chamber.

Next came Zone 2 and the Cubes.

A grid of floating blocks waited in frigid air, each cube muttering half-formed phrases in digital static. Above, a glowing outline rotated slowly.

David closed his eyes, fingertips brushing a cube. "They're arguing about prime numbers and…cheeseburgers. Focus, guys." He moved three cubes into position, the outline adjusting slightly.

Ashley hopped to another cube, pushing it with her foot. "Trail shows this one belongs right of center."

Robin steadied the final cube overhead. "Last piece of the burger puzzle—done." The outline flashed teal, then disintegrated, revealing a sliding door. A surge of confidence warmed her belly.

David exhaled. "Puzzle solved in fifty-three seconds. New record?"

"No time to brag," Robin said, already running.

She immediately launched into Zone 3 and Drone Alley.

The corridor erupted with whirring disks that spat

darts of stinging light. Robin ignited her training saber; the cobalt blade thrummed as she batted a hail of darts aside. "Look at what I can do," she said, amazed and curious.

"Top rail—checkpoint light," Ashley called, sprinting up a curved wall. She tagged the beacon, turning every drone crimson.

"Crimson means hackable," David said, pressing his palm against a passing drone. Graphs of data scrolled over his iris implants before the drone veered off and kamikazed two of its friends.

Robin pole-vaulted a half-pipe, slicing through the last drone. Warning klaxons whooped and the exit lit emerald.

Ashley landed beside her, breathing hard but grinning. "Zone three cleared in one-thirty. We're flying."

Next came Zone 4 and the Razor Crawl.

A tunnel no wider than their shoulders stretched forward, studded with spinning light blades. The catch was that the blades only moved once sensors detected panic.

"Stay chill," David whispered. "Heart rate false-zero, remember?"

Robin crawled first, regulating her breathing. A blade spun inches from her ear, burning ozone. She kept her tone light. "Camping trip, anyone?"

Ashley snorted. "Your camping trips suck." The blade slowed. They crawled, calm, deliberate, surfacing at the far hatch without a single cut. "Over there. Zone 5. The Vertical Dive."

The hatch opened onto an eighty-foot shaft split by a central column pocked with handholds that retracted at random.

"Phoenix—spot me," Robin called. The crow soared

upward, cawing twice whenever a grip threatened to retract. Robin leaped, fingers catching rubberized metal. Ashley followed, calling energy-trail shifts: "Left grip retracts, three seconds!"

David nearly lost his grip when a hold snapped away. Robin shot her free hand down, gripping his wrist. He steadied and they scrambled up, slapping the finish sensor in unison.

At the top landing, David wheezed, "Definitely filing a safety complaint."

"No time. Go!" They headed into Zone 6 and the Resonance Platform.

Three discs hovered over a glossy pit. Turrets lined the walls, each muzzle glowing.

"Separate platforms," Robin noted. "Stay connected, no matter what happens."

They stepped onto the nearest platform as turrets fired synchronized bursts. Gold energy struck Ashley, flooding her vision with prismatic speed lines, and violet beams hammered David with competing memories. A white pulse hit Robin, sending thunder through her bones.

"My head is a rave!" Ashley yelped.

"Too many voices—need an anchor," David gasped.

"Focus on each other," Robin said, gripping her arm over the tattoo as if it were a rosary. "Ash—count down from five. Dave—repeat with her."

"Five…four…" Ashley's voice steadied, David echoing her words. Robin matched the cadence, latching onto their rhythm. The discs glowed emerald, stabilized, and a bridge extended.

The turrets powered down as Ashley massaged her temples. "That was brutal."

"We're still alive. Well, a version of it," Robin noted. "Next."

She wasted no time getting to Zone 7 and the Mag-Float Maze.

Gravity vanished beneath them. They drifted in a chamber of magnetic anchors the size of shoeboxes.

"Swim through the air and get yourself to anchors," Robin said. She hooked a boot on a magnet, used it to hurl herself toward the opposite wall.

David laughed, relieved. The weightlessness was working wonders on his vertigo. He used momentum to slingshot Ashley toward a distant anchor. She squealed, pink hair streaming behind her.

They ricocheted across the maze, tagging the exit pad with a perfectly timed group grab that spun them upright just as gravity switched back on, dropping them back to the platform.

Zone 8 was Mood Tiles. A corridor of floor panels glowed soft blue. The moment Robin's irritation at the sudden gravity spike rose, a panel flipped to red and dropped six inches.

"Keep calm," David warned. He inhaled slowly. "Talk about something boring. Teamwork is the key to all these tests. Have you noticed? That's the lesson here. Nothing can be accomplished alone."

"Tax codes," Robin offered, forcing a relaxed grin. "I have no idea why that's still a memory."

Ashley grimaced. "Filing status single…deductions… paperwork." The floor stayed level. They coasted through while chanting the least exciting topics they could imagine—laundry, DMV lines—until the final threshold.

Next came Zone 9 and the Chimera Arena. A cavernous gym lit in alternating blue and orange strips. Columns rose unevenly as a lion-headed chimera roared into existence.

"Charge tiles are blue," Ashley reminded. "Reset orange."

"Target needs coordinated strikes," Jude's voice echoed. "Each blue panel empowers the saber and each orange resets turrets."

David sprinted to an orange panel, absorbing the memory imprint of prior runs. "The tail strikes every seven seconds!"

Ashley saw the energy wake a beat before the chimera lunged. "The left side is opening after the next swipe!"

Robin took the cue, landed on a blue panel that charged her blade white-hot, then launched herself off a column. She slashed through the chimera's shoulder, the light shards scattering. Ashley tagged another blue panel with a thrown baton, super-charging the attack. David lobbed an emp puck he'd swiped from the puzzle cubes, freezing the tail mid-strike.

Robin finished with a decisive upward cut. The chimera dissolved just as a spotlight bathed Team Cobalt, and the final timer stopped at 18:07.

Damp with sweat but exhilarated, Robin traded high-fives with Ashley and David as cheers filled the hallway outside.

Robin stepped out of the training hall, sweat still clinging to her neck despite the chill in the air. She took a deep breath, as Phoenix landed silently on the railing beside her, something small pinched in his beak.

Robin blinked. "Is that trash in your mouth? You shouldn't eat so many of those things."

The bird opened his beak and let go of a crumpled taco wrapper that fluttered down, landing at Robin's feet.

She picked it up, eyebrows drawn together in concern and wonder. After all, everything in this place was suspect. The inside of the wrapper was smudged with a familiar grease, but there were also faint pen marks. Lines. Arrows. Circles.

"Is this supposed to be a map?" she muttered.

Phoenix gave no response, just stared at her with his usual maddening stillness.

Robin folded it carefully and tucked it into her back pocket. "Fine. I'll play along."

This seemed to satisfy the crow and he took off, circling overhead, triumphant, while the digital leaderboard updated to Team Cobalt – 1st place. And somewhere above, on the Command balcony, Jude watched, and one promised answer awaited Robin.

CHAPTER FIVE

Adrenaline pounded through Robin's newly resurrected veins as Team Cobalt burst from the Gauntlet exit into the observation hallway. A roar went up from cadets leaning against guardrails, and the leaderboard hovering overhead pulsed in victory blue.

Team Cobalt – 1st Place, 18:07.

David punched the air with both fists. Ashley squealed loud enough to earn a cheer of her own and wrapped her arms around her teammates in one exuberant squeeze. Phoenix dropped into a tight spiral above their heads, then settled on the leaderboard rail like a proud track-coach, puffed chest reflecting the scrolling lights against his dark feathers.

Instructor June intercepted them with military efficiency, thrusting silver hydration pouches into their hands and pressing blister-cold protein gels against bruised forearms. "Acceptable performance," she announced, the faint upward pull of her mouth ruining the stern effect. "Auto-med diagnostics in five. Debrief follows on Deck Four."

Robin ripped the top from a pouch and gulped blueberry electrolyte fluid that tasted like melted ice-pop. "Where's Instructor Jude?"

"Command balcony," June replied in a tone that suggested, *of course*. She pointed to a bank of translucent cubicles where drones already hovered, misting disinfectant. "Station Three."

David's sim band chimed, confirming her instruction.

DIAGNOSTIC QUEUE – STN 3 PRIORITY. He led the squad inside the auto-med alley.

Glass doors hissed shut behind them. The room smelled of antiseptic citrus and ozone. Four spidery drones descended, scanning each cadet from boots to hairline. Cool foam spritzed across Robin's ribs where a drone sting had tagged her earlier. Another unit projected her vitals in a 3-D ribbon.

TEMP—ambient, HR—null, SOUL SIG—94%.

A faint cheer rose from beyond the glass as another squad finished their run. "My soul is one percent better," she said with a shrug.

Ashley winced when a drone dabbed foam along her collarbone. "Feels like someone stuffed snow into my skin."

"Quit complaining," David teased. "It's artisanal liquid nitrogen. A premium spa treatment."

The drone responded with a burst of air down his neck, making him yelp. Robin chuckled, tension bleeding away on a tide of endorphins.

A diagnostics tech in medical scrubs stepped in with a tablet. "Symptom check?"

"No dizziness," Robin said. "Just the usual pulseless nausea."

The tech nodded as if that were entirely normal—which, in Hellhound Academy, it was—and dismissed them with a quick thumbs-up. Their soul-integrity bars ticked higher on the hallway display as they stepped out into the hallway.

"Next stop, the lounge. We earned a victory lap," said David.

They followed animated floor arrows to Deck Four, spilling into a lounge that looked like a cross between a sports bar and an eSports arena. Curved couches were clustered around holographic replay screens. A snack bar served neon drinks, and cadets lounged with ice wraps and animated bragging rights.

Team Crimson—today's former champs—rose from a leather sectional. Their leader, a broad-shouldered girl named Elsa, offered an exaggerated bow. "All hail the new speed demons. You squeaked past us by ninety-five seconds."

"Seventy-five," Ashley corrected, grinning. "But who's counting?"

"We are!" called another Crimson member, raising a mock protest sign. *REMATCH PLS*. The good-natured ribbing evaporated as Kip emerged from behind the smoothie bar, neon-green headphones perched like antennae.

He brandished three frosty cups with biodegradable straws. "Victory tastes like mango-mint-matcha, heavy on the mint." He handed them over, each cup already printed with their names and a pixel-art hound.

Robin eyed him over the lid. "You printed these before we ran."

"I saw Ashley and David's training footage yesterday," Kip said, winking. "Odds were solid. You were the risk, but I had a good feeling."

Before she could retort, the lounge lights dimmed. Every holo-screen froze on the academy seal. The debrief was commencing. A hush rolled across the room, broken only by Phoenix's satisfied croak.

Instructor Jude strode in, civilian utility jacket traded for a charcoal blazer and slim black jeans. He carried no blade—he didn't need one. A silence came over the room.

"Top performers," he said, his voice smooth as paved asphalt. His gaze swept the room before anchoring on Team Cobalt. "Today's benchmark stands at eighteen-oh-seven. Respect."

Ashley visibly shook with barely contained glee. David managed a cool nod, his hands on his hips. Robin clasped her hands behind her back, her fingers entwined, willing her nonexistent heart to calm.

Robin dropped onto the common room couch, her boots still wet from the Gauntlet. Ashley handed her a water bottle and collapsed next to her.

"Tell me this gets easier," Ashley said.

Robin didn't answer. She was too new to know, but she had a good idea of the answer.

Her mark had been aching all afternoon, like it was trying to tell her something she hadn't figured out yet.

Jude thumbed a remote and Zone Six footage appeared mid-air. He froze the moment Robin's branded tattoo blazed white-hot. "Cadet Sullivan demonstrated advanced stabilization of resurrection energy. It was commendable but volatile. You will report to Archivist Evangeline tomorrow at 09:00. Non-negotiable."

A ripple coursed through the lounge. Archivists were rumored to spend entire decades bathing in data streams, but face-time with one by a cadet was rarer than a day without drills.

Jude advanced to the chimera fight from Zone Nine. "Team synergy showed impressive improvisation. However, verbal confirmation lagged." He met Robin's eyes. "Instinct is a blade, but technique sharpens it. Train both."

"Understood, sir," Robin answered, determined not to break eye contact. She wanted something from him, but she wasn't going to grovel.

He closed the footage and held up three metallic coins, the hound logo glinting. "Question tokens. Redeem with any Instructor for one free unfiltered answer. They activate at curfew so choose your midnight wisdom carefully." He bent his wrist, and the coins arced through a ray of light. Robin, Ashley, and David snagged them out of the air.

An immediate chorus of what-ifs rose from the crowd.

Jude allowed one finger to the cadet cluster near the front. "Cadet Yoon?"

The lanky boy swallowed. "If a question breaks operational security, do you refuse to answer or...?"

"I answer," Jude said, "and you carry the burden. Knowledge is weight, and you are expected to grow strong enough to lift it."

A girl from Team Elm raised her hand. "Could I ask *why* any of us were chosen?"

"You may," Jude replied. "Whether the truth satisfies is another matter."

The room buzzed with nervous anticipation. Robin closed her fist around her warm coin. It was heavy already.

"Dismissed," Jude said, and the lights returned to daytime brightness.

On the way out, cadets dissected hypothetical midnight questions. Robin caught snatches of them.

Is the ledger sentient? Who funds us? How long until we decay? How did I die? Where is my family?

Each query felt like an echo of her own restlessness.

June blocked her path near the stairwell. "Archivist appointment at 09:00 sharp." She tapped Robin's brand with a stylus, and a reminder popped onto the sim-band. "Bring the crow. Evangeline likes witnesses."

"Wouldn't dream of going anywhere without him," Robin said. Phoenix jabbed her shoulder with his beak, seconding the sentiment.

Instead of heading straight to the dorms, David suggested a victory detour. "We need to celebrate," he said, smiling. A rare gesture from him. They followed a service corridor into the academy's hydroponic garden where there were tiers of leafy greens under pink grow lights, and the air was humid with basil and ozone. There were no cameras in this corner, just soft hums and chlorophyll.

Ashley plucked a cherry tomato and tossed it skyward. Phoenix snatched it with a snap, the fruit disappearing in two gulps.

"To first place," David toasted, raising his smoothie.

"To surviving cardio from hell," Ashley amended.

"To answers," Robin said, clinking cups. The blend of mint and mango coated her tongue with a familiar taste she knew she liked. It was a promise of better things.

As they stepped into the lounge, Phoenix fluttered down from a ceiling vent and landed on the back of the nearest chair. With a soft rustle, he dropped something onto the table. Robin reached for it—an old Polaroid, its edges frayed, the image slightly overexposed. Three figures stood on the lakeshore, the middle one unmistakably her, laughter frozen mid-breath. On one side was David, his face half turned to the camera. But it was the third person that made Robin's chest go tight. A girl about her age, her arm casually slung across Robin's shoulders.

The girl's face was slightly blurred, but something in the posture pulled at her gut. A knowing tilt of the head. A warmth that felt earned. Robin couldn't place the name, but the ache it stirred told her the person mattered.

Sister? Friend? Something more?

Robin turned the photo over. Nothing. No name, no date. Just the ache of something lost. She tucked it into her pocket beside the taco wrapper map Phoenix had delivered earlier. One cryptic artifact was strange enough. Two in a single day? That felt deliberate.

"Who's feeding you this stuff?" she muttered to Phoenix. The crow only stared, his head tilted like he understood more than he let on.

Maybe someone in the underworld didn't want her to forget. Maybe someone *wanted* her to dig.

She looked again at the picture. Those broad shoulders and casual lean on the right were unmistakably David. In that instant, she understood she hadn't faced that final night alone. Her friends had been there beside her. No wonder David's touch had sent a ripple through her—he'd shared that moment, too.

Robin swallowed hard, and tucked her hand over the photo, feeling the paper's cool edge beneath her fingertips, and met Phoenix's expectant gaze. "Hold tight," she whispered. "We'll figure this out, together."

Back at Robin's broom-closet-sized dorm room, evening mode from the globe cast a warm amber light along the walls. Ashley collapsed onto the swivel chair and spun slow circles, while David sat cross-legged on the floor, his token balanced on his knee. Robin perched on the bunk, studying the Polaroid. In the background, Lady Bird boardwalk lights glowed, and the Austin skyline shimmered like a circuit board.

"You look happy," Ashley said softly. "I wonder if I'm a part of this."

Robin ran a thumb over the photo's edge. "Whoever took this didn't expect me to see it again." She wasn't going to mention what memory it was trying to bring back. Not yet.

David glanced at his token. "We could combine questions—trade answers."

"Tempting," Robin said, "but tokens are single-use. We'd be gambling three questions for one truth."

"Worst casino ever," Ashley muttered.

Robin tucked the photo into her journal alongside field notes from training. She added a heading of *Connections?* and underlined it twice.

Phoenix flitted to the overhead duct. His scarlet eyes dimmed to embers as the curfew alarm chimed 23:00. Time for all the undead to pretend to sleep. The dorm doors instantly sealed with a hydraulic whisper.

The hound brand on Robin's arm pulsed in soft, steady beats—her borrowed lifeline. She closed her eyes and listened to one silent second, then another. In the hush, she made a promise as fierce as any vow she'd spoken alive. *I will unearth the truth, and I will not let Hellhound Academy or death itself stall me again.*

Below, Ashley murmured a prayer to no one in particular, and David hummed an old melody that stirred the back of Robin's missing memories. She drifted on that sound until the night-orb dimmed to black, her coin a warm circle of possibility pressed tight in her palm.

CHAPTER SIX

Robin's eyes snapped open at 07:13, three minutes before her sim-band's vibration setting was due to buzz. The night-orb above her bunk had already brightened to a gentle gold, but it couldn't soften the churn of nerves in her stomach—if undead guts could churn. Today was Archivist day, the appointment Jude had stamped into her future like a date with destiny and, possibly, a jackhammer.

Phoenix cawed from the overhead vent, reminding her that showers and caffeine were still things the quasi-living enjoyed. She slid from the bunk, tugging on black joggers and a slate V-neck tee that hugged her shoulders—no robes, no capes, just practical fibers that could survive a chase. Ashley snored softly in the swivel chair, knees hugged to her chest, curls neon-pink against the hoodie she'd used as a pillow. David slept on the floor mat, his token still clutched like a poker chip he refused to fold. "You guys are gonna have to go back to your own beds," whispered Robin, trying not to disturb them.

Robin's token lay on the desk, glinting in a pool of night-orb light. She tapped it once, but there was no warmth yet. The curfew latch would keep it dormant until midnight. She locked it in the top drawer and scribbled a note for Ashley and David.

I've got a date with my brain. Archivist at 09:00, sharp. See you at training—wish me luck.

She tucked the Polaroid into her journal's inside pocket and headed into the corridor with Phoenix riding shotgun on her shoulder.

Hellhound Academy felt different before eight a.m.. The corridors were quieter, and the usual bark of drill sergeants was replaced by shoe squeaks and the soft hum of ventilation. The bioluminescent stripes in the floor were somehow turned down and ran at half-brightness like dimmed runway lights.

Robin passed maintenance bots polishing anti-scuff panels and a yawning logistics cadet pushing a cart stacked with breakfast burritos. "Food as a cure for boredom," she muttered as she passed the cart. "I could get behind that."

She ducked into Mess Hall A long enough to grab a protein wrap and a to-go mug labeled *HOUND FUEL*. The coffee was still sludge, but it was hot sludge, and she liked feeling the warmth inside her chest. It helped her feel not so dead for just a few seconds. Phoenix eyed the burrito until Robin took one and tore off a corner, offering it to the crow. He gulped it with a delighted *clack* of his beak, then fluffed his feathers in contentment.

A final floor arrow directed her to a pair of brushed steel doors etched with the hound emblem and the words *ARCHIVIST ACCESS ONLY*. The doors read her tattoo. A thin, green scanner beam swept across her forearm, tickling her skin, and unlocked the doors with a sigh, rolling back to reveal a cylindrical elevator with transparent walls.

The lift ascended through levels she hadn't seen yet. There were vast data vaults stacked like honeycomb, conduits glowing with electric veins, and a greenhouse of server towers sprouting cooling fins like metallic leaves. Finally, the elevator docked against a glass mezzanine bathed in morning sun filtered through skylights she hadn't known existed. Austin's skyline peeked beyond them, jagged and defiant.

It felt good to be near the surface again.

Archivist Evangeline was waiting behind a floating workstation that was shaped like a crescent of luminous glass. She wore a burgundy blazer over slim charcoal slacks, and her salt-and-pepper braids were coiled into a crown. If June radiated military precision and Jude simmered with a weird, friendly menace, then Evangeline exuded outright authority—quiet, but immovable.

"Cadet Sullivan," she greeted without looking up from the glowing sheets of data orbiting her desk. Her voice reminded Robin of the first note from a cello. It was warm, resonant, and impossible to ignore. "And Phoenix, of course. Punctuality suits you both." She took a closer look at the crow. "I see you've been visiting the underworld again, crow. I can always tell."

Robin jerked her head around and studied Phoenix but couldn't see anything unusual. "How can you tell?"

"It's one of my quirks. A kind of knowing. The bird likes to travel and can go from here to there," she said, swirling a finger in the air. "No one knows how he does it or has ever seen him do it, and yet, we all know he does. You're a lucky girl to have him as your familiar. As one of your quirks."

"He's a quirk," she whispered. Robin swallowed the last of her burrito and tried to match confidence with humor. "Dying leaves a person extra appreciative of calendars."

Evangeline's mouth twitched. "Sit." She indicated a low recliner that looked suspiciously like something from a private dental lab. It was sleek, with white leather, and a headrest sprouting electrode stems.

"You'd tell me if this was a bad idea," whispered Robin, as she took a seat. The bird bobbed before taking flight and circling the room. Phoenix finally fluttered to a perch on a tray beside the station and gave a few more encouraging bobs. The Archivist handed him a small silver wafer, which he accepted with his beak like a gentleman accepting a canapé.

"Before we begin," Evangeline said, "understand that the memory bridge is voluntary. But first, you have to learn the five ironclad laws of undeath." Her eyebrows rose, wrinkling her forehead as she made a steeple with her fingers. "Break them and the ledger yanks you back to the grave."

She lifted her index finger. "Rule number one. Keep your soul-integrity level above eighty-five percent. Two consecutive days below that line and the indicator turns red, and you're recalled. Hydration, steady emotions, and electrolyte balance will keep the number green."

A second finger joined the first, slowly undoing the steeple. "Rule number two. Your heartbeat is null," she said, patting her chest, "but pain is very real. You can't bleed out, but your nerves can still scream. Listen to them."

Robin's mouth opened into a perfect 'o', but she didn't say anything, trying to imagine what it would be like to be dead and in pain.

Evangeline raised a third finger. "Rule number three. Food is comfort, not fuel, but water is mandatory. Two liters a day or the brand or what most cadets call, the tattoo, starts itching like fire ants."

"Strange how I don't remember much, but I can still remember fire ants," said Robin.

"That's very common. Fire ants make an impression." Up went the fourth finger, peeling away a side of the steeple. "Rule number four. Watch your adrenaline budget. Every surge super-charges your resurrection energy. Too many spikes and your memory strata will fracture. First-month cadets get two sanctioned combat events per day, and your Gauntlet already counts as one."

"Are you saying I could lose the few memories I've still got?"

"And be left with nothing but a fondness for fire ants." Finally, Evangeline stuck out her thumb like she was hitching a ride. "Rule number five. Pay attention to curfew. You can only take ten hours of natural light a day, maximum. Past that, cell degradation triples and your soul-tether frays."

"I can molt and die at the same time. Lovely."

Evangeline folded her hands. "Memorize them—super glue them on your body if you have to." She leaned back and studied Robin for a moment. "Now, tell me. What do you want to know today?"

"I want a simple truth," Robin replied. She sank into the

recliner, pulse ghosting faster. "I want to remember whatever or whoever took my life."

"Be careful what you ask for." Evangeline gestured, and that was enough to make sensors descend, attaching themselves to the brand on Robin's arm, her temples, and the base of her throat in quick succession with cool, rubber suction cups.

The workstation dimmed, re-lighting as a three-dimensional waveform. Robin looked up to see her soul-signature hovering above in a hologram. Streaks of cobalt and gold danced along a central axis.

"Your stabilization rate rose overnight," Evangeline observed. "Ninety-five point one percent. Purpose does wonders."

She introduced a soft hum into the room in a frequency only slightly louder than breathing. "Find the rhythm of the tone," she instructed. "Four-count inhale, six-count exhale. Anchor yourself to the present. Trust me and follow the instructions if you want this process to work."

Robin followed the cadence. On each exhale, the hum seemed to resonate through her bones. Her peripheral vision faded until all she saw was the waveform, pulsing like a colorful, exotic jellyfish.

"Now," Evangeline murmured from somewhere beyond the hum, "trace the echo signature braided around your own. The violet thread. Guide me there."

Robin closed her eyes, drawing her focus inward. Everyone carried an echo signature—their magical fingerprint. It held fragments of their strongest emotions, and memories, and even of how they died. Hers shimmered inside her like a quiet hum of who she used to be.

But this time, something else was there. A thin violet thread, soft and sharp at once. Violet threads were rare. They were tracers of foreign magic that had bonded deeply, often left behind during powerful moments of loss, protection, or sacrifice. It wasn't hers. It pulsed gently, like it was alive, or like someone had left it there on purpose.

"That's not mine," Robin whispered. "It's... reaching."

The thread carried something else with it. A sorrow that wasn't her own. A call, maybe. Or a warning.

Whoever had touched her this deeply had left a mark behind—for her to find and follow. Echo signatures weren't just echoes—they were guides. Tools that, when traced correctly, could lead back to the origin of a magical event or reveal the truth buried inside it.

Robin reached, mentally, and brushed the foreign strand with what felt like a flow of energy leaving her body to seek out the answer. Ice skated across her nerves. Images erupted, piling together and then straightening into a linear memory.

Rain slanting across a downtown crosswalk. Headlights slicing puddles into shards of silver. A rushing horn. The smell of wet brakes and cedar mulch from planters. A hand gripping her jacket, rough and desperate.

She jerked her head in surprise, mingled with a slight feeling of panic, but the sensors held firm. Evangeline's voice steadied her. "Stay with it. Describe what you see."

"I'm downtown at Eighth and Brazos, near a taco trailer," Robin whispered. The scene became clearer, and she could see a neon *Los Güeros* sign reflecting in a pool of water. "It's late and I have somewhere to be." She shook her head, trying to force an answer. "I...I don't know where, though."

"Let that go and let the memories guide you."

"Someone grabs me from behind. It's a man. He's taller than I am and wearing leather gloves."

Phoenix croaked once, his wings spreading as he stuck out his chest, balancing on the perch.

"Continue," Evangeline urged.

The memory abruptly jumped to something new. She stood under a pedestrian bridge, the river churning below. The stranger's face remained obscured by shadows and a soaked gray hoodie. He said a single word—"Sorry"—before a surge of sorrow and light slammed into her chest. Pain, weightless and total, took her body. She toppled, hitting water that swallowed any sound. Then there was nothing but darkness.

Robin gasped, her eyes snapping open. Tears she couldn't explain burned and flowed down her cheeks. Evangeline offered a glass of water. "You surfaced at the critical node. You were at your death stroke. That is enough for today."

Robin's voice shook. "I didn't see his face clearly enough. I didn't recognize him," she wheezed, feeling a little desperate for more.

"Memory requires acclimation, patience, and time," the Archivist said. "Breakthroughs often arrive in fragments, then cascade later when you're doing something else." She pulled up the waveform again. The violet thread now pulsed brighter, details coalescing into a partial print of the initials *M.K.*

Robin leaned forward. "Is that—?"

"An identifier," Evangeline confirmed. "We'll run cross-references. Meanwhile, context matters. You were walking in front of the Los Güeros taco trailer. That location closed eighteen months ago. It's no longer there."

Robin frowned. "But I've only been dead... a few weeks?"

"Seventeen days," Evangeline confirmed. "Which means someone recreated that site, or your memory latched onto symbolic cues. I suggest you investigate both avenues." She frowned, pursing her lips. "Hmmm, seems you have another quirk. Did you know you can channel the resonance from one being to another? That could come in handy."

"I'm not even sure I know what that means."

"It means you're a kind of channeler, but for energy, simply put. That could come in very handy." Evangeline peeled the sensors off, offering antiseptic wipes. "Session two will be tomorrow night. Drink plenty of strong green tea and stir up minimal adrenaline until then. Here, start with this," she said, handing Robin a paper cup of lukewarm tea.

"Oh sure, no adrenaline in Hellhound Academy," Robin quipped, taking a long sip of the bitter brew. Her mind was a galaxy of tangled tangents. *What does MK, a hoodie, and a waterlogged apology all add up to?*

She didn't know how yet, but she was determined to figure it all out.

As Robin stood, the doors whisked open and Jude stepped inside, his hands jammed in his blazer pockets. Unlike most instructors, who were themselves returnees, Jude was unmistakably alive. Robin had already heard the rumors around the dorms. Cadets swore that his heart still beat the old-fashioned way and always had, making him one of the very few truly breathing souls at Hellhound Academy. Robin had wondered why anyone who was still alive would want to spend so much time hiding underground with the undead. A zombie groupie.

"How'd the mind-dig go?" he asked, his tone casual but his eyes sharp. He was always trying to pull off an aloof, tough guy, but Robin could sense that inside the persona was something more.

"Progress," Evangeline answered before Robin could say a word. "And it's not your concern until I release the report."

Jude nodded, but the muscle in his jaw twitched. "Sullivan's squad hits the field lab at 14:00 for urban incursion drills. Clear?"

"Clear," Robin said, matching his coolness.

"No love lost there," muttered Robin, carefully watching them both.

Jude leaned closer to Robin, his voice dropping to a whisper. "Careful what memories you drag back across that bridge. Some doors shut for a reason. Training begins in five minutes. Don't be late." Then he left as silently as he entered.

Evangeline snorted softly with a whisper of amusement. "He practices menace the way some people practice yoga. Inconsistently with a hint of drama." She handed Robin a sleek data stick. "Those are your breathing algorithms for tonight. And Robin, trust your crow. Familiar bonds anticipate danger better than even logic, and crows are particularly good at both."

Phoenix responded with a regal bob of his head.

The cadets were all lined up against the wall, watching Robin and a handful of other cadets battle a mythical beast that wasn't real but could still cause real pain.

Robin plunged in with her fists, startled to realize that her undead strength let her hit harder than she ever would have expected in a normal life. Ashley clung to her side, terrified but determined, until she managed to hurl her own protective shield at a beast that was about to slash Robin's back. Robin met Ashley's amazed look with a lopsided grin, feeling a spark of camaraderie. Even so, Robin's mind kept wandering to the memory gaps that haunted her, and it frustrated her that the Academy's demands offered no time to investigate her own murder.

Jude supervised from behind a metal railing, occasionally barking suggestions on how to flank an enemy or watch for certain movement patterns. His snappish tone riled Robin, but she gritted her teeth and complied for the sake of progress.

From his perch above, Jude narrowed his eyes, watching Robin weave between the illusions with controlled aggression.

"She's not just another resurrection," he muttered under his breath. *"If we follow her trail, we might finally see who's rewriting the rules."*

Another instructor snapped at a cadet for freezing up, shouting that the projections were bound with necrotic sparks and could knock them flat. Robin jabbed and pivoted, using her momentum to drive a fist into a snarling beast's chest. It burst into sparks as she turned to face the next.

She wasn't just learning how to fight. She was learning how to survive this place—and hopefully find the truth buried under it.

By the time the final round of illusions dissipated, the air in the training bay felt dense with ozone and old sweat. Cadets panted out of habit more than need. A junior instructor made a final circuit around the mats, tallying performance notes. Robin flexed her scraped knuckles, not sure if the ache in her muscles was real or phantom.

Jude stepped down from the railing, clipboard in hand, eyes still fixed on Robin. He said nothing, just logged something in his notes.

A younger instructor sidled up beside him and lowered their voice. "You watching her for a reason?"

Jude didn't glance over. "Call it a theory."

"What kind of theory?"

He snapped the clipboard shut. "The kind that might finally explain why some of them come back wrong—and others come back *angry*."

"Meaning?"

"Meaning with the wrong ones, something is *off* about their resurrection. Maybe their soul is unstable, or their memory is scrambled beyond the norm, or their behavior is distorted. They might malfunction, unravel, or snap and then are quickly recalled. While others, like Robin Sullivan, show up angry. These cadets retain a spark of willpower, rebellion, or clarity that the Academy doesn't expect or want. They question, they dig, and they fight. Their anger is focused, not chaotic."

"You need to keep that to yourself unless you want to get put six feet under."

"I need answers."

The instructor hesitated, then gave a wary nod and backed off.

Jude turned to study Robin one more time as she helped Ashley to her feet. The girl had no idea what storm she was circling, or how close she already was to cracking it wide open.

Robin met Ashley and David in Mess Hall B, snagging three brisket tacos and a pitcher of the least-burnt coffee on tap. They claimed a corner booth beneath a mural of grackles in sneakers. Phoenix perched on the faux leather seat-back, eyeing the guacamole.

Between bites, Robin relayed everything about the memory fragment, the initials M.K., and the taco trailer clue. "I mean, none of it makes sense. What if I go through the torture of trying to remember and nothing adds up? I might be worse off."

Ashley bounced on the bench. "Evangeline was wrong. Los Güeros reopened last month, but on the southeast side, near Riverside. Maybe the killer hangs there? But why were you there?"

"Another good question."

David had his tablet out before she finished, his fingers flying across the keyboard. "Permit lists a *Martin Kling*, an

M.K.! "Says he's age forty-two, ex-military, and the founder of Kling Security Consulting." He nudged the tablet toward Robin. "Could be our guy."

Robin studied the file, pulse quickening. "Could it be this easy? Security consultant means he knows how to hide footprints. Figures."

"It can be if I'm the one doing the research." David hesitated, thumb resting on the corner of the screen. "There's something else." He lowered his voice so it barely carried over the lunch crowd. "When I pulled your wrist at the vertical climb yesterday I got a flash, and not just surface thoughts. You and me were alive and sharing coffee under a neon sign that said, *Los Güeros*. The same place as your memory."

Robin's breath caught. "No, why would we be thrown together? You're certain?"

"The signal felt like déjà vu and static at the same time." David's gray eyes held hers. "I think we knew each other, Robin. Before all this," he said, raising his arms and looking around the room.

Phoenix crooned, like punctuation, bobbing his head.

Ashley leaned in, being whisper-level serious. "If Command finds out we're digging this deep into our pasts without clearance, they could yank our pulses. Sent back to the dead, no appeals."

"Then they won't find out," Robin said, her voice steady. "We keep this circle tight." She tapped the taco-wrapper maps Phoenix had dropped earlier with the same coordinates both times. "Your room this time, David. Tonight, before curfew."

David nodded, but tension tightened his shoulders. "I'll

keep pulling records, but I'll scrub my digital trails in case the ledger audits our queries."

Ashley exhaled. "Stealth detectives. Just what I signed up for when I got resurrected." She managed a shaky grin. "Let's try not to die twice anytime soon."

The trash can at the end of the aisle dinged at capacity, startling them, just as a mechanical voice summoned Team Cobalt to Urban Lab Two. Robin gathered the wrappers. "First, we ace whatever simulation Jude throws at us. Then we hunt a ghost."

Ashley cracked her knuckles. "Alive, undead, whatever. It doesn't matter. We've got each other's backs no matter what rises out of hell next."

Phoenix pecked Robin's pocket, nudging the hidden maps with his beak, and gave a decisive flap.

Urban Lab Two resembled a chunk of post-apocalyptic Austin sealed in a warehouse. There were half-collapsed walls, graffiti neon under UV lamps, and abandoned e-scooters strewn like metal bones. Drone cameras buzzed overhead recording everything and giving the instructors a full view. Jude waited at a portable command table, tablet in one hand, and what passed for coffee in the other.

"Your objective," he began, "is to extract a data drive from a hostile sector within thirteen minutes. Hostiles are holographic but the injuries will bruise. Map knowledge and teamwork will decide your survival."

Robin buckled her chest strap, still tasting the Archivist's tea. "Data drive located where?"

Jude activated a holographic map. A glowing red dot pulsed on a replica of the Riverside taco trailer. "Creative coincidence," he said, lips curving.

Ashley blinked. "Seriously?"

"Is he playing with us or trying to help us?" Robin flexed her hands, ready to go.

"Life loves irony," David replied. "Let's move."

The countdown began with a loud *tick, tick, tick*, that echoed against the walls.

They sprinted through the illusion of a derelict alley, David rerouting security codes on a smart door while Ashley spotted heat signatures through cracked windows. Phoenix scouted, returning with three sharp caws—enemy drones ahead. Robin vaulted dumpsters, landing behind a holographic guard. One silent takedown later, they breached the courtyard.

A neon sign reading LOS GÜEROS buzzed overhead. The trailer door hung ajar, light spilling.

"Two hostiles inside," Ashley whispered, eyes tracking glowing trails. "One back door."

"On my mark," Robin said. David palmed the lock as Ashley lobbed a flash pellet. Robin dove through smoke, her saber humming. In seven furious ticks of the clock, the guards disintegrated into pixel dust.

The data drive was sitting unguarded beneath a salsa shelf. She pocketed it, her breath shallow even if she wasn't alive.

"Extraction point," David called, pinning a waypoint.

But before they could move, a new hologram materialized. This time it was a hooded man, his face hidden. It was all a pattern eerily matching Robin's memory. A glowing M.K. tag floated above his head.

Ashley inhaled sharply. "Boss, do we fight already?"

Robin's stomach clenched. "We finish this."

The hooded figure produced a shock baton. His movements were calculated, skillful, like he did this for a living, or at least got paid by somebody. Robin parried a strike, her saber casting white arcs. Ashley darted around, peppering him with kinetic pulses. David hacked the environmental controls, blasting the illusion of M.K. with a gust of vented cold air that slowed his reflexes.

Robin caught the advantage, sweeping his legs. She pressed the saber to his throat, pixels sizzling at contact. The figure looked up, his face still hidden under the hood, but a single word escaped his codec-voice.

"Sorry."

Exactly the way he'd said it in her death memory. Robin almost dropped her saber, her hands shaking. "What kind of sick joke?" She swore under her breath, angry tears pricking her eyes.

The scenario froze as the ticking stopped. The simulation was complete.

Jude approached, tapping his tablet. "Completion time was twelve minutes and thirty-two seconds. Impressive. But you, Sullivan, froze mid-combat at the end for three seconds."

"I recognized him," Robin said, voice steady but ice-cold. "That was the same man from my death moment."

"That's why the sim was chosen," Jude admitted. "The

data drive contains a location file that holds the coordinates of tonight, in southside Austin, at half-past midnight. It always syncs to your token at curfew. Consider it your first field assignment. Find the man. This place could use some transparency."

"What does that mean?" asked Ashley.

"You will need to find that out for yourselves."

David's brow furrowed. "Is this an authorized mission or a trap?"

"Yes," Jude said, which sounded maddeningly like both. He turned on his heel, leaving nothing but coffee steam still floating in the air.

"Why are you helping us?" Robin asked, but he was already gone, and she wasn't sure he was actually trying to help or get them recalled.

Back in the dorm, Robin queued Evangeline's breathing file. A soft ocean hush filled the room, washing over the bunk. Ashley tuned her guitar-app earbuds while David traced route options on a holo-map.

Robin practiced the four-in, six-out pattern. With every breath the memory settled, losing its shard-edge. M.K. felt less like a phantom and more like a person she could face.

At 23:59 the tokens beeped awake. Blue glyphs swam across the metal surface. Robin's coin projected coordinates two blocks from the real Los Güeros trailer. Beneath, a single directive was printed in bold letters that read, ***ASK THE RIGHT QUESTION***.

Ashley and David exchanged looks. "We're in," Ashley said.

"We do this carefully," Robin cautioned. She pocketed

the coin, the Polaroid, and the data drive—three keys to one puzzle.

Phoenix fluttered to her shoulder, claws firm, ready. Outside, Austin's night lights blinked an invitation. The real world, her old world, waited beyond Hellhound's tunnels. And somewhere near Riverside, a man in a hoodie might still be there.

Robin smiled—a thin, determined smile, and just a little wicked. "Let's go make an inconvenient truth uncomfortable."

The dorm lights dimmed behind them as Team Cobalt slipped into the service corridor, on their way to rewrite the story that had ended at Lady Bird Lake and begun again five stories underground.

CHAPTER SEVEN

The service corridor exhaled a breath of recycled air as Robin, Ashley, and David stepped out of Hellhound's subterranean world and into Austin's humid spring night. Overhead, the city's lights glittered just like a field of bioluminescent spores. Alive, oblivious, and painfully normal. Phoenix rode Robin's shoulder for exactly three seconds before he launched skyward with a sharp *caw* that echoed between the parking-garage pylons.

"Does he always do that?" Ashley whispered, craning her neck as the crow vanished into the darkness.

"Phoenix travels," Robin answered, tugging her hoodie's hem low. "Evangeline says he can hop between here and... wherever the ledger parks the afterlife buses. No one knows how he slips the lines."

"Or why he comes back," David added, fast-marching beside them. "But he always does."

Robin hoped that remained true tonight. The crow had carried messages, coordinates, even a Polaroid no living soul remembered taking. If anyone could scout the underbelly of Austin—and whatever lay beneath—it was Phoenix.

They crossed South Congress and headed down Riverside Drive, their shoes slapping against the pavement in sync with Robin's undead pulse—that phantom throb she only felt when her adrenaline spiked.

Have to stay calm. Can't let the adrenaline spike too much more tonight.

The coordinates projected by her question token painted a blue arrow in her peripheral vision, guiding them past shuttered food trucks toward the revived Los Güeros trailer.

Ash-gray clouds dimmed the moon, turning every streetlamp into a lonely island. Robin noted vantage points, alley choke-points, and shadow pockets where a security professional might lurk. Martin Kling's dossier trailed through her mind. He was ex-military, decorated, and went private five years ago. There was nothing about murder on his résumé.

David flicked his wrist, using his quirk to mute the map feed and pull up a decrypted city-cam. "Last public footage of Kling puts him near the boardwalk fifteen minutes ago, headed in this direction."

"Then we're on schedule," Robin said.

Ashley shivered with fear, zipping her jacket. "We're sure we're ready? If this turns into a trap, Command will bury us—literally and probably face down for good measure."

"Command can try." Robin squeezed Ashley's shoulder. "Tonight is about answers." She tapped the token in her pocket—the metal felt warmer the closer they drew to the glow of Los Güeros' neon grinning pepper.

"You realize we're taking a huge risk trusting Jude this much." Ashley walked faster to keep up with their pace. "He's leading us straight to your white whale without a lot of explanation."

"It doesn't matter. I have to know." Robin stopped and took Ashley by the shoulders. "Look," she said gently, "if you don't want to go any further, I understand. You can go back, and we're cool. I can tell you all about it later."

Ashley shook her head, her pink bangs falling in her face. "No, we stick together. Let's keep going."

They got to their destination and saw that the once-derelict trailer looked brand-new. The silver panels were polished, and the order window looked brightly trimmed with LED fairy lights. Yet no customers stood in line or were milling about, and the posted hours sign read *CLOSED FOR PRIVATE EVENT*. Robin's skin prickled, somewhere on a scale between the itch of adrenaline and the ledger's phantom ants.

David scanned the trailer's wifi. "There's a secure network ping, an unmarked SSID with a strong encryption. It's Kling's brand."

Robin nodded. "Ash, you circle left and watch the alley. David, you're with me." She flipped her gray hood up, feeling the cool night kiss her cheekbones.

They walked toward the sound of music drifting from a portable speaker inside. It was an old Willie Nelson ballad. Through the window, Robin saw a man wiping down the countertop. He was tall, with broad shoulders, and salt-and-pepper stubble. He moved with military precision despite wearing a casual plaid shirt and jeans.

"Martin Kling," Robin called, sure it was the same silhouette from her memory. *You can do this.*

He didn't startle. Instead, he simply turned, his eyes already assessing the situation. "You have ten seconds to explain why three academy cadets are trespassing after curfew."

"You know about the Academy?" Robin rested a hand on her saber hilt but didn't ignite it. "I'm here because you killed me seventeen days ago."

Kling's jaw clenched. "You're leaving out that I saved the city."

"From what, a food-truck shortage?" David retorted.

Kling reached under the counter and Robin tensed, ready to strike. But he only produced an old Polaroid camera sitting atop of a cardboard box. "Memories distort. Pictures don't." He set it down and slid the box toward them. "There's your evidence."

Robin glanced inside and saw a ledger page with her name highlighted, a USB drive, and a patch bearing the Hound logo crossed with a key. "What is this?"

Kling leaned on the counter, fatigue shadowing his features. "Hellhound's founders made some rather serious mistakes with their grand plan. Resurrection tech may have given the city guardians, but it also opened doors to things that shouldn't cross. You were infected by something we don't have a name for yet. I neutralized it."

"By stabbing me through the chest and dumping me in Lady Bird," Robin said, her voice low. She was gulping in air, just trying to calm herself but it wasn't having the same affect now that she was dead.

"I slowed the entity's merge. The academy grabbed you out of the water before it re-manifested." He pointed at the box. "That USB holds diagnostics proving the infection remains dormant. If the ledger sees that data, they'll recall you for 'containment.'"

Robin's phantom pulse stuttered. Ashley, listening near the alley, hissed through the comm bead, "Two SUVs inbound—no plates."

Kling heard it too, and his eyes turned flinty. "That'll be ledger enforcement. They don't like outsiders like me meddling." He lifted the box. "Take the box, ask your crow to deliver the proofs to someone you trust. I'll stall the suits."

Robin weighed her options. She could fight Kling, trust Kling, or flee. Phoenix was still gone—maybe in the underworld, or maybe overhead. *Underworld*, she thought. He would have come closer, let her know something if he was close by. She grabbed the box. "Why help me now?"

"Because death didn't stop you," he said quietly. "Means you might succeed where others failed."

"Failed to do what?"

"Stop the demons from pouring in, and the infection." He snapped a photo, the flash blinding them, and then quickly crossed the space between them and shoved the new Polaroid into Robin's pocket. "For your memories. Now go."

Robin sprinted to Ashley as headlights sliced the street and black SUVs with tinted glass swung to a stop, doors flying open. Instructors in tactical black uniforms poured out, equipped with stun rifles.

"That's ledger enforcement," whispered David. "We need to get out of here if we want to stay in the game."

"Cadets!" a bullhorn boomed. "Stand down and relinquish contraband."

"Not happening," Robin muttered. She ignited her saber, and the white blade hissed. David triggered a drone battery from his wrist launcher, sending shimmering decoys darting skyward. Ashley lobbed a flash pellet, saturating the alley with star-white light.

They dove behind dumpsters, Robin still holding tight to the box. Stun bolts crackled overhead, sparking against brick.

"South exit!" David shouted, pointing to a chain-link gate.

Robin nodded—just as Phoenix appeared, dropping out of nowhere to land on the gate's padlock. His talons glowed silver, making the shackle clatter open. He flapped his broad wings once, scattering motes that smelled faintly of river fog. It was proof he'd hopped back from the underworld exit ramp, somehow.

"Thanks, crow." Robin shoved the gate open, letting the trio quietly slip through.

The friends navigated a maze of back-lot paths, Phoenix leading, as they ran past people here and there sleeping next to a shopping cart piled high or a dingy pop-up tent. The bird darted ahead, then backtracked with impatient caws, swooping down occasionally to nip at Robin to hurry along. Twice they heard the enforcement team fan out, their radios crackling, but Phoenix always took a turn that put dumpsters, fences, or thick clumps of bamboo between the trio and their pursuers.

Finally, they ducked into an abandoned laundromat lit only by a single red EXIT sign. Phoenix perched on a broken washer, feathers shimmering with dew that evaporated into wisps of grey smoke—the underworld still clinging to him.

Robin tore open the evidence box, her mouth dry. She listened for any sound of the squad nearby, but there was nothing. The ledger page on top listed her and twenty-six other "subject IDs" flagged with the status *PENDING RECALL – INFECTION RISK*. Three names were already crossed out with the word, *RECALLED.*

Ashley read over her shoulder, hand flying to her mouth. "They've been erasing cadets quietly. Not because of anything that they did, either."

David plugged the USB into his tablet. Strings of code scrolled, showing waveform readings with violet interference identical to Robin's memory echo. Eight other cadets' signatures showed the same anomaly.

"We need to get this to Evangeline," David said. "She might protect us."

"Or report us," Ashley countered.

Phoenix hopped between them, a glint of something metal in his beak. It was a key made of old-fashioned brass with the Hound emblem on its bow. He set it neatly at Robin's feet.

"Where'd you get that?" Robin whispered.

Phoenix just stared, unblinking, unreadable, then abruptly vanished. One blink he was there, and the next he dissolved into drifting motes of cinder and feather, like a reverse snow globe. He'd hopped worlds again, this time right in front of them, leaving them with the key.

David examined it without picking it up. "This crest matches the patch in the box." He flipped the ledger page and on the back was a hand-drawn map of the academy's sub-levels, a star marking Sub-Level Seven, *LAUNDRY*.

Ashley groaned. "I knew the laundry rumors were bad."

Robin picked up the key and slid it into her pocket. "Kling wants us in that laundry. Looks like the underworld's mailing route is stranger than we thought."

"Is that good news or bad?" asked Ashley. "We still don't know who's sending us messages."

"Kling has pointed us toward Sub-Level Seven because that's where the truth is. It's not a punishment, it's a clue, a mission. For all his gray morality, he's trying to help us uncover what's really going on at Hellhound Academy."

"The man did still end your life." David put the ledger page back in the box.

"Yeah, that's going to take a lot more explanation, but not now."

Outside, sirens wailed. This time, it was the Austin city PD, which would slow the ledger enforcers. Robin turned off her saber. "We lay low till dawn, then infiltrate Sub-Level Seven. Whatever the infection is, we find the answers before the ledger recalls us."

David glanced at the crow-shaped shadow Phoenix had left the dusty tile. "And hope our feathered courier comes back with reinforcements."

They crashed in a half-renovated hostel on East 4th, paying the night clerk with a prepaid debit card Evangeline had slipped into Robin's bag "for emergencies." Robin spent the dawn hours reviewing the USB data, cross-referencing each infected cadet. Ashley drafted a stealth route into the laundry sub-level. David wiped their city-cam trail, though ledger forensics might still piece it together.

By 08:30, pale morning sunlight crept across the hostel's floor. Robin drew the curtain. Ten hours of daylight maximum, Evangeline's rule reminded her. Curfew would come quickly.

David's tablet chimed with an encrypted academy push-notice. He decrypted it and whistled low. "New mission ticket for Team Cobalt, two nights from now. Congress Avenue Bridge, 23:00. Spectral incursion flagged as a Class-Three banshee."

"We got a mission assigned to us? The ledger doesn't know who they were chasing. How is that possible?" asked Robin.

"It's a guess, but I'm thinking your familiar has something to do with it."

"Phoenix, or whoever is on the other side."

Ashley bit her lip. "The mission is on the Congress Avenue bridge where the bats live? This time of year, there will be tourists everywhere."

"Not at eleven p.m.," Robin said, reading over David's shoulder. "The bats will have moved on along with the lookey loos." The mission parameters scrolled down the screen: Contain, neutralize, minimize civilian exposure. Short and to the point. "A live field test. We'll be babysitting a screaming spirit in the middle of downtown."

David tapped a sub-note. "There's a side objective. We are to retrieve an echo stone for archivist study. That's new."

"Evangeline wants data," David guessed. "I read that a banshee's echo stone could map to the infection interfering with cadets. Makes sense."

Ashley nodded, her eyes bright despite fatigue. "We handle a banshee, we can earn more leverage."

David set the tablet aside. "Then step one—get through laundry sub-level alive."

"I wonder if *laundry* is code for cleaning up their mess," said Ashley, chewing on her lip.

Robin checked the portable med kit, ensuring extra ear filters—banshees could shatter skulls with their wail. Plans for tomorrow, plans for the bridge all spiraled in her head.

She closed her eyes, breathing Evangeline's four-in, six-out cadence, letting the hush of the hostel mimic ocean surf. Somewhere between breaths she drifted to sleep, token warm in her fist, key heavy in her pocket, and a plan charted in the midnight ink of determination.

CHAPTER EIGHT

Robin sat on the edge of her bunk, tapping a foot, her fingers drumming on the bed. The rest of the room was quiet in that fragile hour before curfew broke and drills resumed. Phoenix preened silently on the vent above, feathers twitching with unreadable thoughts. Ashley and David had gone to their own dorm rooms, for once.

She pulled the Polaroid from her jacket pocket—creased, worn, but still echoing with unfinished things. Robin, David, and the girl with the familiar smile, an arm slung around Robin like they must have done it a thousand times. That blurred face had haunted her since the moment Phoenix dropped it in front of her.

She didn't know why she did it, but she closed her eyes and let her thumb trace the edges of the girl's outline. A warm shiver rose from somewhere deep. It wasn't pain. It was longing.

And then the name rose, uninvited and unshakable.
Wren, my sister. My older sister.

Images popped inside her head. A violin bow slicing

through the air in a living room. A laugh that danced just outside the memory's edge. The way her older sister used to press her forehead to Robin's and promise they'd outrun whatever shadows came next.

She gasped, the recognition sharp enough to fold her inward.

Wren. Not just someone from before. She was the person who anchored Robin to who she used to be.

The ache that followed wasn't hollow, it was electric.

"I remember you," Robin whispered, pressing the photo to her chest.

Phoenix rustled, watching. He tilted his head once and croaked, quiet and low.

Robin stood, her breathing steady for the first time in days. "She's out there," she said to the crow. "And I'm going to find her."

Footsteps echoed from the corridor until David's silhouette filled the doorway.

"You ready?" he asked.

Robin tucked the photo safely into her inner pocket and nodded. "More than ever."

It was 00:47 a.m. in the Academy Service Tunnels. David's guess had been right. No officials were searching for them once they managed to slip back inside.

Robin's eyes adjusted to the sodium-orange gloom of Hellhound Academy's lowest corridor. Concrete walls sweated humidity, and somewhere overhead the night-shift ventilation rattled like a distant subway. Robin,

Ashley, and David moved single-file, following the hand-drawn map Kling had supplied them. Take four rights, one left, then a dead-end hatch that wasn't on the official blueprints.

June had caught them leaving the dorm wing earlier and delivered her dry, two-sentence warning. "Field trainees, remember, linger among the living too long and the ledger flags you for recall. Command expects you back by sunrise. Don't be late."

The translation they took away was sneak, succeed, and return before anyone notices. Mixing with civilians—or getting caught out after curfew—could wipe their soul-signatures for good.

Robin had nodded, feeling uneasy, then pressing on.

Phoenix was riding on her shoulder, his feathers still faintly rimed with an underworld frost. Every few minutes, the crow vanished through a hairline shimmer in the air, gone for seconds, sometimes minutes, before snapping back into view with a frustrated *caw*, as if scouting between realms for threats no living, or undead, eyes could see.

Ashley tapped her wristband, muting the LED glow. "Map says the hatch is behind those water pipes."

David knelt, unscrewing the access grate, exposing a lock. "You have the key ready?"

Robin produced the antique brass skeleton key that Phoenix had delivered. The Hound-and-Key crest gleamed beneath her night-orbs glow-mode. She slotted it into the tiny lock hidden beneath decades of paint. Tumblers clicked into place and the panel slid sideways, revealing a spiral staircase corkscrewing down into darkness.

"Sub-Level Seven," Robin whispered. "Laundry of doom."

Stale heat wrapped around them as they descended. The staircase terminated in an industrial cavern of humming boilers and conveyor belts carting heaps of academy uniforms through automated pressers. But at 1 a.m. the machines slept, leaving only the clank of distant pipes.

Phoenix flew upward, weaving between ductwork, before vanishing again with a sound like wind sucking through a keyhole.

"Some crow," Ashley muttered. "Can teleport but refuses to do laundry."

"I don't know that anyone is doing a lot of laundry down here." David scanned for thermal signatures. "Nothing hot except those dryers, but there's an energy spike dead-center."

They followed the spike to an unmarked service door sealed with biometric glass. "Open sesame." Robin held the ledger page to the reader, creating a violet interference that danced across the pane, making the door hiss open. Inside lay rows of tall cryo-capsules, thirty at least, each filled with a cadet suspended in blue gel. Hound brands still glowed amber on their wrists.

Ashley pressed a hand to the glass of the nearest pod. "They're...alive? Or whatever counts as alive."

"A third version." Robin found a data plate and read it, her eyes wide. *Subject 14 — Status: Containment / Infection Risk.* The name matched one of the eight anomalous waveforms.

David uploaded the pod's logs to his tablet. "Soul-integrity dipped under eighty-five percent, and the ledger forced stasis," he read. "They've been down here for months," he said, with a gasp.

A soft footstep echoed behind them. They spun, their sabers half-drawn, to find Instructor Jude emerging from the shadows, hands raised in a faux surrender. "Easy, Team Cobalt. I'm tonight's chaperone."

Robin narrowed her eyes. "And you just happened to follow us?"

"Command tracks keycards, Sullivan. You're lucky I caught it and was able to scramble where you were wandering off to. Sub-Level Seven isn't on the tourist map." His gaze swept the pods. "You wanted proof that the ledger recalls cadets. Here it is."

Ashley swallowed hard. "Why keep them in cold storage?"

"Because the infection hitches a ride on resurrection energy," Jude said. "The cryo-gel dampens that current. Safer than letting them roam in either world."

Robin stepped closer. "Kling said containment equals execution once Command decides it's safe and convenient."

"That depends on results." Jude's voice stayed calm, but tension framed every word. "Evangeline believes there's a cure buried in the echoes. I believe stopping this infection means throttling its gateway, in Austin and in the underworld."

Phoenix reappeared mid-air, dropping a silver memory wafer that clanged off Jude's boot. The disc shimmered with embedded code—compressed echoes harvested from the field. Robin recognized it as one of the tools Phoenix had used before, storing residual memories from near-death spaces. The crow circled once, landing on a pod, and fixed Jude with an intense glare before dissolving again.

"Crow courier service. Figures. Your familiar is growing bolder." Jude retrieved the wafer, scanning its hologram. "Looks like Phoenix pulled this from the Candle Factory," he added, angling the disc toward the light. "Residual echoes—emotional imprints, magical traces. If the energy under the bridge matches this, we'll know we're on the right trail.

He pocketed the disc. "Listen, you three. Tomorrow night's mission to stop a banshee under Congress Bridge isn't random. Banshees ride spectral currents similar to your infection's signature. Extract the echo stone, and maybe we can triangulate the origin."

David crossed his arms. "Why us? Why not Enforcement?"

"Because Enforcement shoots first, interrogates never." Jude reached inside his coat and produced three slim ear-filters and a skyhook grapple. "And because Phoenix picked you. Familiar bonds carry weight with things on the other side. That makes you more useful even when fighting the darkness pouring into this side."

Robin held Jude's gaze, determined. "We'll get the echo stone. But we're not leaving these cadets to rot."

"We're leaving them where they are for tonight," Jude countered, voice softening. "But bring me that stone, and Evangeline will petition to thaw the pods."

Robin looked down the aisle of silent capsules. Faces floated in blue suspension that were hopeful, afraid, and frozen mid-blink. She touched the glass, silently promising Wren she'd never end up here.

Alarms pulsed in the distance—Enforcement was sweeping the upper tunnels. Jude ushered them back toward the staircase. "You still have to beat sunrise, remember?" He shot a pointed look at their wristbands. "Ledger curfew ends at 06:00."

They retraced steps, key-panel sealing behind them. At the tunnel junction, Jude paused.

"One more thing." He leaned in, eyes steely. "Living civilians, the normies, can tolerate your presence a few minutes before anomalies register. Banshee crowds are worse. Get in, contain, extract, and fade. Overstay and the ledger will recall you on the spot. Understood?"

Robin nodded. "Understood."

"Good." Jude faded into the opposite corridor; the sound of his steps swallowed by the humming ducts.

They reached her dorm with six minutes to spare. Phoenix was waiting atop the night-orb, feathers finally free of underworld frost. He hopped down and dropped a tiny chalk-white fragment onto Robin's pillow. It was part of a bat skull, polished smooth.

"Reminder for tomorrow," Ashley guessed.

Robin pocketed the shard beside the key. "Bats at the bridge. Phoenix never sends souvenirs without purpose."

David collapsed onto the floor mat, mental exhaustion fogging his brain. "We relaxed for zero hours. We risked cryo-revenge. And tomorrow we face a screaming ghost. What's next, a dragon rodeo?"

"Don't jinx us," Ashley yawned, curling up on the chair.

Robin pulled out her journal, writing on a new page, *BANSHEE OPS*. She sketched Congress Bridge, marking bat exits, vantage walkways, and civilian clustering points taken from their ops instructions.

Phoenix fluttered down, tapping the page at a point beneath the bridge's central arch. Robin penciled a star. "Echo stone likely there?"

The crow answered with a low rumble that felt like agreement and disappeared again, leaving only a drifting feather that smelled faintly of cedar smoke and river water.

Robin exhaled, letting her undead pulse settle. Tomorrow they'd wade into banshee song and hope their ear-filters and courage held. She thought of her sister again. Wren needed to know Robin hadn't just vanished. That she was fighting her way back.

Lights dimmed to curfew level. Robin stashed the key, bat fragment, map, and Polaroids in her lockbox. As a kind of sleep claimed her, she pictured Phoenix slicing between realms, gathering secrets like seeds in his beak. Seeds that, if planted right, could grow into the truth that set all of them free.

Somewhere under the academy, thirty cadets slept in cold blue light, waiting. On the surface, a banshee sharpened her cry. And Robin vowed that come tomorrow, both the living and the undead would hear her answer.

CHAPTER NINE

Time was marked at 23:04 at the Congress Avenue Bridge, on the North Embankment. Tall hotels lined the far side of the bridge.

The balmy night smelled of river water, bat guano, and distant food-truck smoke. Robin crouched behind a concrete balustrade while tourists above her strolled the bridge, oblivious to the mission unfolding under their feet. A street musician strummed carefree chords, and the swirl of headlights painted lazy stripes across the Colorado River. Austin felt alive, painfully alive to Robin, and Team - Cobalt had no heartbeat to spare.

Phoenix perched on the balustrade, feathers ruffling in the warm wind. A shimmer rippled over his wings. It was a telltale sign Robin had learned that he might hop dimensions any second. Robin scratched his beak. "Stay nearby, featherbrain. We need your two-world GPS tonight."

The crow let out a low croon, acknowledging the plea, or ignoring it. With Phoenix, both sounded the same.

David clipped an ear filter into place. "Remember Jude's

warning. You have ten minutes tops among the living before the ledger's anomaly detectors ping."

Ashley unslung the skyhook grapple Jude had issued them for the mission. "We get in, get the echo stone, get out. Simple." She glanced at the throng of tourists lining the rail for the bat-flight show. More than a million bats would fly out at once in a winged cloud at dusk. "As simple as ghost-hunting under a city landmark."

Robin checked her watch. Showtime. "Let's move."

They slipped through a maintenance gate, descending metal stairs to the service catwalk that ran the bridge's length underneath. Sodium lamps sputtered overhead. Cheap bulbs that cast sickly halos on the water below. Robin's undead pulse, the phantom throb she felt in her tattoo brand, quickened. Adrenaline budget be damned. Tonight demanded speed.

Halfway across, Phoenix vanished with a *pop* of air and no sound. Ashley frowned. "Hope he comes back before something screams."

"He will," Robin said, with more certainty than she felt.

At the bridge's midpoint, the catwalk widened into a platform used by city maintenance crews. Cold air leaked through rusty grates. David's thermal scanner lit red. "We have a temperature drop of ten degrees. The banshee's nearby."

Robin nodded. She drew her training saber but didn't ignite it yet. There was a risk the sparks might spook tourists topside. "Ear-filters in. Remember, the banshee cry fractures bone at five meters and disorients at twenty."

Ashley clipped her second filter. "The echo stone forms at the heart of the wail, located right under her throat."

David unslung a handheld sonic dampener. "We have sixty seconds of suppression max. After that, we're deaf or even more dead."

The river's surface was glassed over, wind dying to a hush. From the shadows rose a figure draped in spectral tatters. The banshee's hair was whipping in a nonexistent storm, her eyes hollow voids. She hovered a foot above the platform grates, her mouth parted in a silent sorrow.

Robin felt the temperature nosedive, and frost kissed the metal railings despite the time of year. Normies overhead shivered, some moving along, oblivious to the true cause of their discomfort.

The banshee regarded Team Cobalt, her sorrow swiftly deepening into rage. Her mouth opened wider, pausing before the onslaught of sound.

"Now!" Robin barked. David thumbed the dampener. A pulse of counter-sound rippled outward, muffling the first note of the banshee's cry.

Even suppressed, the half-wail made Robin's teeth ache. Her ear filters vibrated, absorbing the frequencies.

Robin leapt, saber sparking to white life. She slashed at the air as Ashley launched the skyhook. The grapple bolt shot past the spirit, anchoring in the steel arch beyond. Ashley clipped the line to her harness and zipped through the banshee's periphery, a blur of gray hoodie and courage.

The spirit lunged after Ashley, which was exactly the plan. Robin pivoted, struck the banshee's side with her saber as the blade hummed and sliced ectoplasmic cloth. The spirit shrieked, a soundless noise, thanks to the dampener, and spun away, finally exposing her throat.

David rushed forward, his extractor gauntlet glowing.

He plunged two prongs into the shimmering banshee flesh. The echo stone coalesced, releasing a fist-sized crystal gleaming with swirling grief.

A hairline fracture spidered along David's ear filter. His suppression system was failing. "Stone still forming, fifteen percent!"

Ashley hit the far arch and reversed direction, zipping back with the line taut behind her. She tossed a kinetic mine, watching it latch to the spirit's ankle, humming.

"Detonate on my mark!" Robin called, blocking a claw swipe with her saber. Her arm was rattled numb from the force.

The banshee's next wail slipped through as the dampener sputtered. Even filtered, the sound stabbed like ice picks. Robin saw stars and felt a pressure behind her eyes.

David gritted his teeth, the extractor at ninety percent. "Almost—"

Pop! Phoenix reappeared above them in a blur of feather and shadow. He spiraled once, dropping something small and metallic onto the banshee's head. It was a simple bell etched with runes. It rang with a soft *ting*, and the wail faltered.

"Mark!" Robin shouted. Ashley triggered the mine. A concussive blast of kinetic force blew the spirit back into David's extractor. The device pinged full capture. The echo stone solidified, falling into David's palm like a crystallized scream.

It was none too soon. The suppressor was dead, but the banshee had dissolved into mist, even though her residual scream was still echoing up through cracks in the bridge.

"Not good," muttered Robin. Tourists overhead gasped

at the intrusion of noise, and several smartphones peeked over the railing.

"Clock's ticking," David warned. "Anomaly detectors will trigger any second."

Robin sheathed her saber. "Extraction route B."

Ashley recoiled her grapple. "Route B is street level."

"Exactly—looks normie." Robin unclipped a flare marble from her belt. She tossed it downriver, and it detonated in a flash, drawing onlookers away from their catwalk exit.

Team Cobalt didn't hesitate and climbed emergency rungs to the pedestrian path. Robin plastered on a half-panicked expression. "Did you see that explosion? Someone call 9-1-1!"

A pair of tourists rushed to the rail, giving the trio enough cover to slip into the Austin nightlife crowd.

Phoenix circled once overhead as if keeping watch, then vanished. Returning to courier duty.

The trio regrouped on an abandoned rooftop garden lit by twinkling fairy lights. David gently set the echo stone on a planter table. It pulsed blue-white, soft but insistent.

Ashley removed her filters, massaging her ears. "Ledger detec-timers?"

"Ten minutes before automatic sweep," David answered. "We beat it by two."

Robin ran a hand over the stone, feeling the banshee's raw grief pulse. "Let's get this to Jude, and Evangeline before it pops."

Phoenix re-materialized, dropping an academy envelope. Inside was a single sentence in Evangeline's neat cursive. *Bring the stone to the old music hall at 00:30.*

David checked the address. It was an academy-owned property only two blocks away. "That's doable."

Robin pocketed the note. "Wren used to sneak into that hall for acoustics. Said the echo made her violin sound like a cathedral." Her mouth hung open in surprise at what had popped out of her mouth. The memory had surfaced crisp, no coaxing needed. It was proof that contact with the echo stone might be strengthening her recollection.

Ashley grinned. "Then let's play a cathedral."

The red-brick hall loomed silent, its marquee dark. Inside, dust motes drifted through moonbeams reflecting off broken windows. Evangeline waited onstage amid rows of empty chairs.

Jude stood beside her, his arms crossed, and his expression unreadable. Behind them, the air wavered in a thin curtain of light. There was no frame, no machinery around the veil between this world and the next. Just a raw seam where reality felt stretched, shimmering like oil on water.

Robin placed the echo stone on a pedestal dotted with runes. Evangeline almost smiled as she slipped sensor bands over it. "Excellent work, Team Cobalt."

Jude tossed Robin a data badge. "Pods in Sub-Level Seven are being set aside as we speak. Your success bought them time."

Ashley loudly exhaled relief. David leaned forward, watching the readings climb. "This stone's resonance matches the infection signature."

Evangeline nodded. "Phoenix brought us confirmation." She gestured as the crow hovered over the iridescent seam. "He walks both realms on a treaty older than the ledger. He ferries what truth he deems necessary."

"How old is he? You know more than you're saying about the other world, and Phoenix." But Evangeline ignored her. Robin frowned and tried again. "Why does the crow help us?"

The shimmering seam rippled. A child's laugh drifted through. A familiar sound. A memory with Wren? Robin's heart, or its ghost, lurched. Phoenix cawed, wings spanning both sides of the gate.

Jude rested a hand on Robin's shoulder. "Because he guards the border, and something crossed that shouldn't be here. The infection wants hosts. Phoenix wants balance."

Evangeline's instruments pinged. "The stone is already decaying. I must transcribe the resonance now."

She kept her elbows pinned to her side, but turned her hands out, palms up, and let out a deep breath. Blue-white energy channeled into a crystal lattice as data symbols spiraled.

Robin watched, her mind reeling. Was that Wren's laugh? Maybe it was just a coincidence, or an echo from the past? She took a step toward the opening that was forming in the veil—

Jude blocked her path. "Not tonight."

The echo stone cracked, releasing a tremor through the hall. Evangeline ended the capture, sweat dotting her brow, strands of hair clinging around her face. "Got it."

She handed Robin a thumb drive, pressing it into her palm. "There's a memory strata of the infection on it."

"Will this cure the pods?" Robin asked.

"Perhaps. Or reveal how deep the infestation goes."

A distant siren wailed, startling everyone. The academy enforcement was sweeping the area. Jude hurriedly ushered them backstage. "Go out the alley door. Phoenix will cover your retreat."

The crow dropped onto Robin's forearm, talons cool against her skin. His eyes glowed ember red as he dissolved into a mist that spread across the hall like ink in water. Just like that, the lights shorted, leaving a darkness that masked their exit.

The group threaded different alleys, making their way toward the campus tunnels, the adrenaline draining. Robin clutched the drive. "We saved thirty cadets tonight."

"And maybe ourselves," Ashley said.

David sighed. "One banshee down, entire ledger to go."

Phoenix re-formed atop a dumpster, brandishing a new offering. It was a tiny brass violin charm. Robin's chest tightened. A memory flashed of Wren practicing in a parking lot, playing old country ballads for tips.

That's Wren's. "Thank you," she whispered to the crow and pocketed the charm. "We're not done. Next step, we have to expose whoever sanctioned those pods."

Phoenix cawed an agreement that was sharp, triumphant, and unknowable, before he vanished back to whichever realm cared for crows who guarded the line between the living and the dead.

Robin led her squad toward the service tunnel, sunrise nowhere in sight but already ticking like a deadline. Balance might be Phoenix's goal, but justice, that belonged to Robin Sullivan, undead or not, and she intended to claim it before the ledger claimed her.

CHAPTER TEN

00:45 a.m., Evangeline's Midnight Workshop

Her lab was a glass-walled loft suspended between academy towers. It was a shark tank of data swirling in holographic streams. When Robin, David, and Ashley entered, the archivist looked up from her crystal resonator, eyes bright behind silver-rimmed glasses. Phoenix sat atop her console as a silent guardian who only left Robin's side to travel to the dead, now that a bond had been forged.

"Good," Evangeline greeted them, her voice low and urgent. "We have minutes before the ledger enforcement scrubs this sector. Let's begin."

Robin stepped forward, her heart, or the souvenir jolt of her brand, thrumming. She carried the thumb drive, while David cradled the echo stone in a levitation cradle, and Ashley balanced two flask vials of cryo-gel extract. Between them lay a holographic schematic of the cryo-pod array, now flickering with thaw alarms.

"First," Evangeline said, "we isolate the echo resonance and map the infection signature. Then we administer the targeted antidote to our thawing subjects in the pods and use Robin's quirk to move the energy. Time is of the essence."

Evangeline placed the echo stone on a plasma-charged platform. She adjusted nano-filament probes, each as thin as a spider's thread, until the stone's pulse matched the cadets' soul-integrity readouts.

"Dr. Kling's diagnostics are accurate," she murmured. "The infection signature derives from spectral trauma. A banshee frequency mixed with necrotic code. We must reverse-engineer it."

David tapped his comm-band. "Running memory-synch algorithm. Shall I patch my console into yours?"

Evangeline nodded as David waved a hand, and his console instantly mirrored hers. He initiated a memory scan on the echo stone, picking up on unused energy rippling through his gauntlet's interface.

"Now," he said, eyebrows raised, "watch this." He placed his palm near the platform and closed his eyes. His mind rewound to the banshee encounter. To the suppressed wail, Phoenix's bell, and the kinetic strike that captured the crystal.

A translucent waveform appeared above the stone, annotated with David's subconscious markers. "I see it," he said. "The banshee responds to empathic pulses. If we encode an emotional anchor of joy or love, it destabilizes the infection."

Robin exchanged a glance with Ashley. "So, Wren's

laugh recorded in the hall might do the trick?" she whispered.

Evangeline's lips curved into a satisfied smile. "Precisely. Collective positive resonance can sever spectral tangles. Now let's craft the antidote."

Ashley donned protective gloves and hovered over the cryo-gel extract. "Temperature-stabilized gel infused with echo-stone sonics," she recited, measuring two precise milliliters into a diffuser vial.

Robin watched as Ashley triggered her kinetic-trail vision with an iridescent haze around each movement. She positioned the vial under an ultrasonic resonator, and the gel vibrated in time with the echo waveform.

"Now," Ashley said, flipping a switch. The gel shifted colors to a pale violet that melted into a warm gold. "Emotion code locked."

David sealed the vial with a resonant cap. "Antidote ready." He tagged the data drive to the construct. "Evangeline, push the deployment protocol."

Evangeline tapped a command sequence. "Injection drones synchronized. In two minutes, the thawed pods will receive the cure." She turned to Robin. "You remember the first rule of undeath?"

Robin pressed a hand to her brand. "Keep soul-integrity above eighty-five percent."

"Use that bond to help them," Evangeline urged. "Channel your anchor, Wren's laughter, into the network to reinforce the antidote."

The arched window of the lab swung open, and a shimmering seam of air slicing the veil was visible, but only when the light hit right. Phoenix hovered at the edge of the seam, head tilted, as if he understood. Robin lifted her hand, closed her eyes, and remembered Wren's bright, off-pitch giggle as she taught Robin to dance in their mom's kitchen. The memory echoed through the lab as soft and unbroken.

Across the hall, thirty cryo-capsules hissed open. Nano-drones slipped inside, delivering the golden gel into each cadet's wrist-brand veins. The echo resonance filled the room, rippling outward in a translucent wave.

One by one, sleeping cadets stirred. A chestnut-haired girl flexed her fingers, and a boy opened his eyes, blinking at the fluorescent lights as if waking from a dream. Phoenix flapped into the chamber, swooping low as if surveying his flock.

Robin watched as the soul-integrity bars rose from brown to amber, then amber to green, settling above ninety percent. Evangeline exhaled. "They're waking. Your emotional anchor stabilized the resonance."

David tapped his gauntlet. "Cure efficiency is ninety-eight point six percent. Only two pods need a second pass."

Ashley smiled. "We're saving lives."

A sudden intrusion alarm rang out from Evangeline's console. A blinking icon showed a civilian presence at the lab's rear entrance. Someone had slipped inside. It was likely a courier or enforcement.

Evangeline's eyes narrowed. "Too much mixing has alerted them. Get back to Delta-Nine. I'll cover the cleanup."

Robin grabbed her saber. "We'll need to explain to Jude why civilians were pounded by a sonic burst."

David slid the data badge to her with a grim nod. "This won't help with that. It's an encrypted log, internal data only. No civilian IDs were captured. Whatever happened out there, sonic burst included, it won't show up in the official records."

Ashley touched Robin's arm. "Remember June's warning. If you linger with the living, the ledger will recall you. Move."

They retreated through service hallways, Phoenix darting ahead in bursts of shadow, re-materializing to guide them.

Delta-Nine's door sealed behind them. Phoenix perched on Robin's desk, ruffling into a neat row as if satisfied. Ember red eyes met Robin's.

Robin knelt, placing a gentle palm on his feathers. "Thank you for everything."

The crow crooned and tapped her wrist as the brand flared warmly.

"Guess this bond goes both ways," she whispered.

Ashley dropped onto the bunk, exhaustion finally catching up, even for the undead. "We did good."

David sank onto the chair, wiping sweat from his brow. "And set the academy back on course."

Robin stood, pocketing the thumb drive and the violin charm. She closed her journal to the *Wren* tab, the memory of her sister's laughter safe inside. For the first time since awakening, she felt closer to truly living, and to saving the people she cared about.

Somewhere beneath the city, the infection had been pushed back. Above, Austin's pulse beat on. And in the seam between realms, Phoenix waited as the guardian of gates, bearer of secrets, and proof that even the undead could still choose love. Still choose life.

There was still more work to be done. Robin was still determined to stay among the normies, and that wasn't going to be easy.

CHAPTER ELEVEN

A low, amber glow filled the training gallery as Robin Sullivan awoke for the first time since their mission under the bridge. The night orb above her bunk dimmed to coax in the artificial dawn.

The night before, Ashley and David had slipped quietly into their own dorms instead of crowding into Delta-Nine with Robin. No late night gear checks in the hallway, no whispered strategy sessions under one roof. There had been just the soft click of their own doors shutting behind them. It was a small grace, a chance to rest alone before the next tide of missions swept them back into the breach.

Robin swung her legs off the narrow bed as the notification scrolled across her sim band:

MISSION BRIEFING – 07:15 – BUNKER ROOM C2 – ASSIGNED TEAM: SULLIVAN, ROMERO, LIN.

Another mission, but this one came with a twist. The briefing notes said they were heading above ground to investigate reports of a local musician named Malachi. He was currently playing late sets at Antone's and might be showing signs of ghoul possession. Just rumors for now, but Evangeline had flagged it as credible. If the possession was real, they'd need to act fast, before the thing inside him took root.

Robin eased herself upright and slid into tactical joggers and a fitted tee, made of modern fibers that would survive anything the underworld threw her way. Phoenix, ever her sentinel, fluttered from the desk and landed on her shoulder, heavy talons pressing into the echo scar of her brand.

She padded across the tile floor to where David's tablet glowed on the desk, just as there was a knock at the door.

"Morning," she whispered, letting David into the cramped room.

He closed one eye, smiled wryly. "Slumber's for the truly alive."

"True that," Robin muttered, rubbing her temples as she touched the brand, which pulsed in sync with the crow's blink. "Ready for round two?"

"I'm up." Ashley wandered into the room, yawned and stretched, knocking over a stack of holo maps. They fanned across the floor like a flock of startled birds—the banshee site, and fresh schematics with the cryopod array laid bare in phosphorescent blue.

"What do we do with our downtime?" Ashley asked, gathering the maps. She folded them into neat squares.

David sat up, planting his feet. "Research. Training. And maybe a little mech therapy." He tapped a holo-button and the cryopod blueprint whirred to life, revealing hidden service conduits and access panels.

Robin watched Phoenix preen, shifting half-invisible into the seam that rippled across the ceiling vent—blink and later he'd reappear somewhere else. "What's downtime? We need to dig into our next mission. It's already assigned, and we gear up for it tonight."

Ashley's grin took on an edge. "I'll recalibrate the kinetic mines for water resonance. If another banshee sings at the lake…"

"No banshees this time. Something different, a ghoul," said Robin.

David waved her off. "Let's not get ahead. Right now, we help to stabilize the pods on level seven and finish what we started."

They slipped into the long glass hall leading to Evangeline's workshop. Gurgling servers lined the vault below where strings of light were pulsing like neural pathways. The archivist stood at a crescent console, silhouetted by data symbol motes drifting overhead.

"Back so soon?" Evangeline's voice was like the first note of a cello—low and resonant. "Two of the pods need another dose of the antidote. Just a quick test before you leave on the next mission."

She gestured to her holo-grid, where she could see three pods on Sub Level Seven lit up in amber. Seven, twelve, and unexpectedly, nineteen.

"Pod 19 dipped without warning," she said. "The move

may have damaged something. But your imprint reverberated through the others. The echo stones carried the resonance farther than expected."

Robin glanced at Ashley, uneasy.

Evangeline tapped a console key. They could watch on the screen, two of the pods hissed open, their nano-gel interiors releasing with a soft whoosh. Inside, the cadets, suspended in a glowing gel, were transferred onto mobile gurneys. Skeletal drones hovered at each side, their mechanical arms tipped with injector nozzles ready to deploy.

David raised his holo-map. "I'll tag the brands with the emotional anchor code. Ready."

Robin leaned in. The sight of the pods still made her stomach twist. They held more than mystery—they held a reason for her death. Some of the mystery was explained, but not all of it. "We need to figure out what else the Academy's hiding," she said under her breath. "All of it."

Ashley clipped a kinetic stabilizer cuff onto the first gurney. "Gel's primed. Resonance filter is set to banshee harmonic inversion." She met Robin's gaze. "Your turn. Use your quirk."

Robin pressed Wren's pick to her temple, letting its frequency settle deep in her bones. "Let's bring them back."

The drones buzzed, injecting a thick, golden fluid. The gel rippled through their veins, then cracked just under the skin, like ice under pressure. One by one, the cadets' chests lifted with wet, shuddering gasps.

"Stabilization at ninety-eight percent," Evangeline reported, watching her holo-meters. "Pods 7 and 12 are green. Pod 19 is holding at ninety-five. I'll need to monitor that one more closely."

Robin exhaled. "Thank you, Archivist."

Evangeline inclined her head. "Your bonds saved them. But don't forget, every undead is a ledger entry. Keep them out of stasis if you want our work to stay hidden, and for now, we do."

The doors hissed open behind them, and Phoenix gave a sharp caw.

Jude stood in the corridor, his arms crossed. He was dressed in field gear wearing a charcoal jacket, black tactical boots, and a data visor pushed up on his forehead. "Field briefing. Let's go."

They followed him through the corridor and down a side stairwell that bypassed the usual cadet routes. No cadets were milling around. No idle chatter. Just the hum of unseen systems and the distant rattle of industrial fans.

"Rainey Street Depot," Jude said over his shoulder. "You already got the basics. This is the rest."

He keyed open a secure room near the weapons lockers. A holo-table bloomed to life with a 3D schematic of the Rainey Street transit station's underworks. A beehive of cracked tiles, rusted grates, and a labyrinth of sealed tunnels like arteries long gone cold.

"There's a breach," Jude said, pointing to a blinking red point beneath the old switch house. "An energy spike is reading a partial overlap with some familiar resurrection resonance. It's not identical but close enough to make the Archivists nervous."

Robin folded her arms. "So not just a demon squatter?"

Jude looked at her. "If it were that simple, I'd send someone disposable."

"Good to know we're not disposable." David frowned. "You're saying this is connected to the pods?"

"I'm saying the pattern matches your energy signature from Pod 19." He let that sit for a second. "So, whatever's down there, it's pulling from the same current."

Ashley shifted uneasily. "What's the objective?"

"Twofold. Confirm the breach origin and shut it down before it mutates. But there's a catch," Jude said, voice tightening. "The breach isn't just a crack in the veil. It's already taken a host in the form of a local musician named, Malachi Price. You have the mission directive. He is playing at Antone's on 5th Street this month. Everywhere he goes, he draws a decent crowd, nothing flashy." He ran a hand through his thick hair. "A week ago, he collapsed midset and got back up, but he was singing lyrics no one recognized. Since then, the ghoul's been bleeding through more and more. It's a subtle possession, using Malachi as an anchor. Malachi's still in there, but barely. Your job is to extract the parasite without alerting civilians." Jude cut through the air with his hands. "You are to use resonance suppressors to weaken the tether, then isolate the ghoul, and if possible, contain it. We want it alive, for study. If containment fails, you end it clean. And if Malachi goes down with it... make sure no one sees."

"And what is secondary?"

"If there's someone, or something, trying to replicate resurrection, I want it intact. For questioning."

Robin's voice was flat. "And if it can't be questioned?"

Jude's stare sharpened. "Then it doesn't walk out of there."

"Poor Malachi," whispered Ashley.

Jude tapped a control on the table and brought up their loadout assignments. "Your gear will be in locker Delta-Seven. You've got a few hours before the mission. Take a break and don't use up your adrenaline stores. When the mission starts, Phoenix will scout ahead and transmit visuals. I want eyes on everything before you step through the first hatch."

Phoenix flapped once, circling the room like he approved.

Jude looked at each of them in turn. "You made top marks on the Gauntlet and performed well with the banshee. Let's find out if that was luck, or instinct."

Robin nodded, her pulse steady. "Either way, we'll handle it."

"Good," Jude said. "Because as usual, if you screw it up, no one gets a second chance."

By midday, they decamped to the terraced lounge where there were floor-to-ceiling windows overlooking the hydroponic gardens below. Phoenix roosted on a statue of a hound, ruffling his feathers at the artificial midday humidity.

They spread holo-tables on a cloud soft couch. "Our

next mission is about a possessed artist named, Malachi." David loaded snippets of Malachi's last Antone's set: the banshee echo peaks, crowd soul bar dips, network glitches. Ashley clicked through the kinetic flow data, highlighting hotspot clusters.

Robin pulled out the Polaroid showing herself with Wren and David at Lady Bird Lake, and then she felt it. It was a ripple in her memory. Not of drowning but of dripping lockers, gloved hands, and that blade at her throat. The memory had come to her once before of someone inside the Academy killing her. Now the echo of that internal betrayal was intertwined with the external threats.

Ashley paused her map drawing. "You okay?"

Robin blinked, pressed a hand to her brand. "Just... remembering. The killer wore an Academy sleeve."

David closed his tablet. "That seal was well hidden. It could be any instructor."

"Or archivist," Robin whispered. "Evangeline had access that night."

Ashley's eyes narrowed. "We will dig deeper. But first, we train."

They convened in the underground Quad to get in some practice, mindful of Jude's warning about adrenaline. Kinetic blankets covered synthetic rubble and holographic beasts. June punctuated a flurry of cadets sparring with smoke wolf constructs, and her eyebrows arched on seeing Team Cobalt.

"Cadets, clear the field," she barked. "Your next mission

relies on finesse, not brute force." She eyed Robin. "Eye on the inside threat as much as the outside."

Robin saluted. "Understood, ma'am."

June handed her a slender baton tipped with resonant crystal. It was another proof-of-concept echo stave. "Use this to trace spectral leaks. Let sound guide you."

Ashley strapped on reactivegrip gloves. "I'll map residue trails."

David angled a sonic scanner. "I'll triangulate the tremors."

Phoenix set on a perch overhead, preening a midnight black wing.

At June's signal, the team sprinted through a loop of obstacles of zero-G slides, echo pulse walls, and finally a static corridor rife with hidden spectral nodes. Robin's baton hummed as she swept it along the floor, detecting muted after tones. All signatures that matched the cryopod echoes and Malachi's banshee wail.

They converged at a holo-barrier. David toggled a code, as Ashley triggered a pulse, and Robin slashed her baton in a precise arc. The barrier sang, dissolving like mist.

June's approving nod awaited. "Solid work. Your harmony matters more than your hits."

Back in the sub workshop, Evangeline's lo-fi arsenal gleamed on steel racks. Echo staves, kinetic dampeners, and sonic sashes were neatly lined up. Phoenix hovered among the spare gear, tilting his head at each piece, like a curator inspecting relics.

Evangeline handed Robin a new device. A glove threaded with crystalline nodes and slim resonance channels. "Echo-lure," she said. "Designed to funnel spectral frequencies. It'll pull a possessed entity's attention toward the strongest memory anchor you project."

Robin slid the glove on and flexed its fingers. The embedded crystals caught the light. "I'll test it with Wren's laugh tomorrow. See what pulls."

She hesitated, glancing down at the glove. "It was this light, quick thing she used to do. Just before she said something smart that got us both in trouble." Her voice tightened. "If that one, little memory's strong enough to catch a ghoul's attention, we're all in deeper than I thought."

Ashley picked up a kinetic pulse grenade. "It's tuned to disrupt low level spectral cohesion. Should jolt a ghoul out of a host long enough to trap it."

David leaned over his gauntlet, a multifunctional piece of wearable tech or armor that he was wearing on his forearm. It was a high-tech bracer or cuff that David was using for scanning, hacking, in defense, or storing data modules. He was soldering a new module into place. "Upgraded sonic dampener. Wider pulse, tighter control. We'll need it if the host starts broadcasting."

They gathered around a battered cardboard box Evangeline had pulled out, marked *Project Blackfinch*. Inside lay dozens of brass Ferryman's keys—identical to the one Phoenix had dropped after the last mission. Each was etched with faint runes that shimmered under the workshop lights.

Evangeline's lips curved, but it didn't reach her eyes. "Encrypted access tokens courtesy of your crow. He's full of surprises. Phoenix selects which one to deliver, and to whom. He doesn't always explain why."

Robin picked up a key and turned it over in her palm. The weight felt old. Intentional. An energetic hum buzzed across her skin.

Evangeline ran a finger along the rim of the box. "Blackfinch was our first attempt at threshold tracking. We were mapping ghoul movement between tether points. It worked," she said, uncomfortably clearing her throat. "Too well. We lost two cadets to cross surge resonance. The program was shelved after that." She paused. "Phoenix insisted we keep the keys."

"I get it." Robin closed her fingers around one of them. "And this is how we cross into places we're not supposed to go."

Robin broke away to the gallery's north corner, to the only spot where the Archivist told her she was sure to find the veil shimmering against the wall. Phoenix fluttered in, coming to rest on her arm, his talons hovering inches from her tattoo brand.

She pressed the new key against the seam. The air rippled, but the seam didn't open. Instead, she felt a pulse and Wren's whispered, "Be brave," from years ago, tangled in the echo from the key. The memory surged even clearer, and Robin felt Wren's hand gripping her own, with music playing in their mother's kitchen.

Robin closed her eyes, tears pricking the corners, almost overwhelming her. "I'm ready," she murmured.

Phoenix fluttered close enough to coo, warm against her ear.

Then the seam faded, leaving only the glow of a night orb and the distant hum of servers. But the memory remained bittersweet and defiant. "Just like us," murmured Robin.

Her comm band suddenly chimed with a single message: Antone's Bar 23:00. She rushed to gather her gear and meet one last time in the war room with the others. Jude eyed their gear and their faces, which were tougher now, worn but determined.

"You're prepared," he said. "You've already saved lives, healed the betrayed, and reshaped the Academy's dead. Tonight, you heal the living." He paused, looking at each of them. "Trust each other. Trust Phoenix. And remember why you fight."

"To not get sent back," said Ashley, not looking away when Jude glared at her.

"She's right, you know," said Robin. She slid Wren's violin pick into her palm. Her heartbeat when she had none. Phoenix clicked his beak against her brand. Ashley and David formed a silent pact with a nod.

As they strode into the corridor, gear shifting on their backs, Robin whispered, "Onward. Undead or not, we have a purpose."

Phoenix led the way while three dots blinked on Jude's holo-map heading toward Antone's side door.

The trio slipped through the alley behind Antone's entrance. The marquee out front cast colorful reflections on slick pavement. Tourists and locals queued at the wide, double doors, while bouncers nodded hello to familiar faces.

Through a barred window in the back, Robin heard Malachi's baritone humming a slow, mournful riff that vibrated the gravel under her boots. She crouched beside a dumpster and tuned into her quirk. "Energy signature's through the roof. The same as the banshee frequency harmonics."

Robin knocked three times and waited. A barmaid unlocked the side door as planned. An acquaintance of Jude's that he didn't care to explain. Phoenix rematerialized on the windowsill and pecked the latch. The barmaid was already gone, and they easily slipped inside, unnoticed by the normies.

The club's interior was a cathedral of old brick and polished wood. Smoky amber light pooled on tables, and the stage was set like an altar. Malachi stood in the center, his guitar strap over his worn denim jacket. The strings glowed with spectral filaments only the trio could see, rippling with every bend and slide.

Patrons were gathered in a clump in front of him, captivated. Some clutched their chests as tears welled. Even a bartender leaned in, their eyes glassy.

Ashley activated her goggles and her quirk. "Kinetic trails show audience resonance is drawn to the guitar's headstock. He's siphoning emotional energy with sound."

David scanned the room for surveillance. "Academy

sensors are being overridden by local EM interference. We're on our own."

Robin inhaled the smell of smoke, stale beer, and sweat. She needed help. "Phoenix?"

Phoenix glided in through a cracked window and perched on a speaker stack. His feathers trembled from the vibrations. A shimmer of underworld frost was coating his wing tips. The swaying audience didn't seem to notice. They were completely focused on Malachi and his voice.

Robin approached the stage's right side. "We'll need a literal cue."

"I'll be back." Ashley crept to the soundboard, quickly adjusting faders and then sabotaging the echo feedback loop. The guitar's resonance faltered, causing Malachi to pause mid riff.

The crowd stirred, momentarily free from their hypnotic state as confusion rippled through them.

Robin stepped onto the stage's wing and extended her hand. "Mr. McKee?"

He turned to face them, eyes wild and voice trembling. "You don't understand, there's something inside me. It sings through me. And I can't stop it. The blues don't lie."

David stepped onto the stage slowly, his saber still clipped to his belt. "We just need your attention for one minute, Malachi. That's all. Then you can walk out of here or keep playing. It's up to you."

Malachi's fingers trembled over the strings. He strummed a low, aching chord, but the note twisted in midair, distorting into something raw and wrong. The sound fractured, like glass under pressure, its spectral resonance slicing through the air in shards only the undead could sense. A chill swept the stage.

Robin took a careful step forward and pulled Wren's pick from her jacket. "Music holds memory. Let me remind you who you are."

She slipped the pick gently onto his E-string. Behind him, Ashley deployed a kinetic pulse just above the stage floor, aimed not at Malachi but at the space tethered to his back where the ghoul's presence was clinging. The shockwave sent a ripple through the possession, momentarily destabilizing the tether.

David was up next and activated his sonic dampener, creating a field that deadened the ghoul's influence, cutting off its control over the sound.

Malachi staggered. His hands faltered. For one brief moment, the noise inside him seemed to hush.

Robin saw her chance and strummed a single note—clear, bright, and true. The pick glowed at her touch.

A tremor shuddered through the guitar, then through Malachi. His eyes widened. A choked laugh escaped his mouth. It was frayed but real. Human.

The ghoul shrieked in response. It ripped free from his back in a storm of smoke and shadow, an emaciated silhouette of clawed fingers and sunken eyes, all wrapped in grief and hunger. It lunged at the undead group, mouth stretched too wide, teeth like rusted knives.

Ashley reacted first, her kinetic vision flaring. She launched an energy burst straight into the specter's center mass. The impact staggered it midair.

David dropped to one knee, pressing his gauntlet to the floorboards. He yanked a memory imprint from the room.

It was Malachi's last clean thought, his grandmother's lullaby. It bloomed into a soft harmonic field, and he hurled it at the ghoul. The melody tangled with the creature, slowing it down, confusing it.

Robin moved behind Malachi, catching him as he sagged. "Stay with me. Focus on the sound, just the sound."

She strummed again. This time three chords from Wren's favorite concerto, reshaped into a tethering melody. The resonance pierced through the ghoul's shriek.

Above them, a fracture in the air began to glow. The portal shimmered, unstable, but widening. Phoenix swooped down from the rafters, his talons gleaming. There were tiny bells on his legs ringing in counter harmony. The ghoul twisted in midair, its form unraveling as Phoenix passed through it.

With one final screech, the entity was yanked into the light, sucked backward into the breach. There was a pop of displaced air, and the stage fell quiet.

Malachi collapsed into Robin's arms, breath hitching. "Thank you... God, thank you..."

David scanned the stage, his focus landing on a jagged crystal bloom forming around the headstock of the guitar. He spotted the residual echo stone. He snapped it free and handed it to Robin. "The ghoul's anchor. Another piece of the puzzle."

Ashley wiped sweat from her brow. "You think the crow's got another breadcrumb for us?"

Phoenix cawed once and dropped a folded piece of parchment at Malachi's feet.

Robin bent to pick it up. The message was simple:

Well played. Next rendezvous: Lady Bird Candle Factory. 02:17.

She looked to her team. "Ready for the factory?"

"Nobody thinks the bird is writing these, right?" asked Ashley, tucking a pink curl behind her ear.

Malachi sat up slowly, his eyes clearer now. "I'm okay. Whatever that thing was… it almost took everything. You saved my sanity."

They left Malachi backstage and slipped out through the stage door while the club stirred back to life. Most of the crowd had barely registered what happened. Their minds were already fogged by spectral interference. Outside, car horns and neon lights filled the gaps where memories had frayed.

Robin paused under the marquee. She touched the warm brick wall, remembering Wren's whispered dream to one day perform here.

Phoenix landed beside her, cocking his head. The pick in her pocket pulsed once, gently, acknowledging the memory.

David and Ashley were already halfway down the alley, gear slung, talking about the new message.

Robin followed, humming the chord she'd played. The one that bridged memory and survival. Somewhere between life and death, it rang out still.

CHAPTER TWELVE

The night air was still thick in the surrounding block with the lingering energy of the confrontation with the ghoul. The spirit was gone, but its effects remained palpable, like static electricity clinging to their skin. Robin, David, and Ashley watched from a distance as paramedics arrived and loaded the still-dazed musician onto a stretcher. His fingers twitched, grasping at invisible guitar strings while they wheeled him toward the waiting ambulance. When the vehicle pulled away, its red and blue lights painting the street in eerie hues, Jude appeared beside them. His face was a mask of calm authority as he surveyed the scene.

"We narrowly escaped the Academy's scrutiny for becoming a spectacle," said Robin, adjusting her pack.

"That doesn't mean you're safe. Stay alert." Jude brushed imagined dust from his sleeves and stepped back, adjusting the collar of his jacket. "We'll handle the rest of the cleanup. The Academy will send someone to fix the crowd's memories or at least muddy them enough that no official story sticks. You three did your part."

Robin tensed. "I'd prefer we stay and see how the musician recovers." She hated being shoved aside, but Jude gave her a thin-lipped stare that said not to push her luck.

David cleared his throat. "We could observe from the sidelines to make sure the cover story is consistent."

Ashley tucked a stray wisp of pink hair behind her ear. "We should also confirm the ghost didn't leave anything behind," she said softly, "No energies or items that might cause another disturbance."

Jude's expression hardened. "Fine, but do not blow our cover." His gaze skimmed over Robin with the usual friction. "If any more weirdness flares up, let me handle it. You mingle or get caught, you know what happens."

Robin nearly rolled her eyes. "Sure, boss," she said, giving a half salute. The truth was she felt half grateful he had stepped in to stabilize everything.

Relief pulsed in her chest. No more random stabs from a possessed fretboard tonight. She and Ashley stood near the entrance, their gear still on their back. David joined them, watching the final half dozen spectators drift away, grumbling about the snafu that killed the vibe.

"I feel bad for the spirit," Ashley said. "But it was messing with people. That can't go unchecked."

Robin pressed her lips together. "I know."

David set the disruptor by his feet and leaned against the wall. "At least nobody died tonight." He hesitated, studying Robin's face. "You seem distracted."

She shrugged. "Part of me wonders if I'd have ended up the same if the Academy had never recruited me. I might have wandered Austin, hopping from one body to another, desperate to hold on."

David's brows knitted, and he looked as if he wanted to reach out. "No way." He said, "You have more sense than that."

She forced a smirk. "Sense, sure. Morals, maybe. Hard to tell which side of the line I stand on these days." Robin peered inside. The lounge staff ushered the last patrons out. Someone fiddled with a cracked mixing board and turned off the house speakers that had carried the spirit's wail. The overhead lights dimmed, easing the pounding in Robin's head.

Jude drifted over. "We're good here. Let's regroup outside. The Academy will handle the rest. Try to look normal as we leave."

Robin snorted. "I'll need a good definition of undead normal."

He rolled his eyes but said nothing. They slipped into the alley. Nighttime traffic hummed along the street, and the breeze still felt thick with leftover tension. She scanned the shadows, half expecting the spirit to lurch out and moan for another encore.

Phoenix, her feathered familiar, swooped from a rooftop ledge and landed on a crate. His glossy feathers shimmered, and he eyed her as if scolding her for taking risks.

"Thank you for the assist, buddy."

He cawed once, fluttered upward, and vanished into the gloom. Robin exhaled. Sometimes she wished he offered more than an occasional squawk and a cryptic message. She was reminded of the sealed note lying in her dorm drawer. She still had not opened it, and she knew it was not a task to tackle alone. David would have to help sooner or later, but he was already digging through Academy records on her behalf. She refused to put him in more danger.

Ashley rubbed her arms. "We're sure it's gone, right?"

David nodded and slipped the disruptor into a hidden pocket. "That spirit is not coming back. We blasted it into whatever final rest it refused before. Let's hope it finds some peace now."

Jude's gaze swept over them. "Academy wants a debrief. We can handle that tomorrow." He tapped the side of his jacket. "We're shelving this job for now. Keep your heads down, and don't brag about your little heroics."

Robin crossed her arms, ignoring the twinge in her sore shoulder. "I don't brag. At least not about this."

A tight silence fell among them. She could not shake the memory of the ghost's final shriek, its raw heartbreak. Part of her wanted to laugh off the entire event, while another part wanted to scream. She settled for giving Ashley and David a weary smile. "We did well," she said, though her words felt hollow. "Kid's free from that possession. That's what counts."

Jude gave them a resigned shrug. "There's a transport waiting down the street. Let's go."

Robin lingered a moment. She glanced at the lounge sign overhead, neon blue letters blinking. A dormant energy still vibrated in the air, as if someone might turn the volume back up and the spirit's song would echo one last time. But it was gone.

She slipped away from the stage door, stepped onto the

sidewalk, and rejoined the others. Every so often, she noticed a straggler reeling out of the lounge, phone clutched in their hand, but she already knew no footage would ever surface. The Academy had ways of smothering that sort of evidence.

As they wandered away, Robin caught her reflection in a blackened window. Her face looked pale, her hair slightly dishevelled, and her expression said she was running on fumes of adrenaline. She had never asked for this job, but it was hers now.

The city remained too busy with its usual chaos to pay them much attention. Headlights swept across the street, and bursts of traffic noise cut through the hush of the evening. She reminded herself this was her second chance. She might not understand every factor that brought her back, but she would not become another spirit latching onto a living host out of desperation. "I have standards," she muttered, a shiver going down her spine. "At least, I hope so."

A reluctant smile tugged at her lips as she fell in step beside Ashley and David. They had saved a life. That was enough for the night.

Robin stepped out of the stairwell and into the night air. The buzz of Sixth Street hit her all at once. The music bleeding from open doors, laughter from a rooftop bar, or a line of girls squealing in sync as they stepped out of a rideshare. She paused, letting it all swirl around her.

Then her eyes landed on someone across the street. A woman was standing under the sharp glow of a neon taco sign, her hood pulled up halfway. Her shoulders were hunched, head tilted like she was listening for something the rest of the world couldn't hear.

Robin's heart hit her ribs hard. The sidewalk vanished beneath her. *Wren.*

The image crashed into her. She thought of the Polaroid, the laugh with her head tilted back, the whispered memory in the quiet of her bunk. Foreheads pressed together. That look, that *feeling*.

She wasn't imagining it. This wasn't a trick of the banshee or another glitch in her fading death.

"Wren?" she breathed.

The woman turned, catching her gaze. Her mouth opened slightly. She shook her head once, deliberate, like a warning. And then she bolted down the alley.

Robin surged forward. "Wren!"

Jude's voice cut through behind her. "Robin, don't!"

But Robin was already running.

"Robin!" Jude's voice cracked like a whip in the narrow space. He ran after her, catching her by the elbow. "What the hell do you think you're doing?"

"I saw someone," Robin began, but Jude cut her off.

"I don't care what you saw. You never, ever run off like that." He loomed over her, face twisted in anger. "Pull a stunt like this again, and I'll see to it that you're sent back to the underworld. You can lose this second chance faster than you can blink."

The threat ignited something in Robin. Anger surged first, sharp and fast, but it tangled quickly with something deeper. Desperation. She stepped forward before she could stop herself. "You don't understand. This could be my chance to get my memories back."

Jude paused mid-step. Something in Robin's voice, how raw and real it was, seemed to stop him cold. The usual sharpness in his eyes gave way to something else, something older. He turned, slower than usual, and his brow furrowed in something that looked more like concern than confusion. "What did you say?"

Robin hesitated. Too late to backtrack now. "I meant... I've been remembering things. Flashes. People. Places."

He crossed to her, slower this time, and laid a hand gently on her shoulder. Not the grip of command, but something almost... protective. "You've been remembering? Like actual memories? Not implanted fragments?"

Robin nodded, pulse picking up. "It's her, Jude. The woman I saw, it was Wren. My sister. I know it. I felt it."

Jude let out a long breath and looked away, rubbing the back of his neck. "Robin... there are things the Academy doesn't explain. Not because they're secrets, but because most cadets wouldn't understand. Or couldn't handle it."

"Try me," she said, lifting her chin.

He gave her a half smile, the tired kind that said he'd been down this road before. "That demonstration during orientation? It wasn't just to scare you. It's real. Every cadet who breaks the rules risks unraveling everything holding them here. The mind doesn't like loose threads."

"But this isn't a thread," she pressed. "It's a rope. And I'm ready to climb."

Jude smiled, dimples appearing that Robin had never seen before, then he grew quiet again. He looked back toward the alley where Wren had vanished. "If it really was her... you're not the only one whose past has unfinished business. Just... don't go after it alone. Not again."

Robin blinked. "Again?"

But he was already walking away, softer this time. Not disappearing into the shadows, just giving her space.

She turned back to where she'd seen Wren, her heart thudding out of habit. That hadn't been a maybe. That had been her sister. Alive.

The others waited by the curb. No one spoke as Robin climbed into the van. Ashley sat quietly, twisting a bracelet around her wrist. David stared straight ahead, his jaw tight. Jude rode up front, still and unreadable.

As the city blurred past the windows, Robin clutched the edge of her seat. The same curve of Wren's cheek. The same posture. Her sister was out there. And now, more than ever, Robin needed answers.

The van came to a stop at the boathouse. The building's paint was peeling under the glow of the moon. Jude unlocked the hidden panel, revealing the narrow cement stairs that led underground.

Robin followed the others in silence. The moment her foot crossed the threshold, the cool air from below wrapped around her like a second skin. This place never let her forget what she'd lost, or what she might be able to get back.

Jude caught another instructor near the entrance. Their conversation was hushed but urgent. Robin lingered just long enough to catch fragments. "Unexpected complications... needs more time."

The instructor nodded, then turned to the cadets. "You're dismissed. Debrief tomorrow."

Robin didn't need to be told twice. She turned toward

the dorms, her steps light despite the weight in her chest. David caught up.

"You good?" he asked.

She gave a tight nod. "Yeah. Just processing."

He hesitated. "Feel like doing something reckless and questionably legal?"

A small smile crept across her face. "Always. Lead the way."

They slipped through the dim corridors, their undead status letting them glide under the radar. The hallways were mostly quiet. There was just the low hum of pipes and the occasional creak of settling stone.

David picked the lock of a rarely used office with practiced ease. The room inside was cluttered but quiet, filled with files, old tech, and faint traces of magic.

He got to work at the terminal while she searched the room. Nothing obvious, but the air felt charged.

"Here," he whispered. "Metadata. Training files. Look at this name—W.S. Sullivan."

Robin froze. "Wren. That's Wren."

Before they could say more, footsteps approached. They ducked under the desk just as the door creaked open. A figure entered, poking through the clutter.

Robin barely breathed. Every sound felt magnified. Then, finally, the door clicked shut.

They waited a full minute before crawling out.

"We should go," David said, his voice low.

Robin nodded, looking back only once.

As they crept back through the halls, he grabbed her elbow.

"Jude's hiding something, isn't he? About Wren. About you."

Robin didn't answer. She wasn't ready yet. They split up near the dorms.

In her room, Robin dug out the note she'd hidden days ago, still unopened. It was time.

She sat on the bed, heart pounding. Jude's softer tone, the fear in his eyes, the recognition she'd seen in Wren's. It all added up to something.

And she was ready to find out what.

"Hang on, Wren," she whispered to the dark. "I'm coming."

CHAPTER THIRTEEN

Robin lay on her narrow bunk, eyes wide open in the near dark. The dorm wing of DeltaNine was unnervingly quiet. Just the occasional shuffle of someone turning over or the hiss-click of a ventilation cycle switching modes.

Her SimBand buzzed: **23:28**.

Ashley snored softly on the mattress she'd dragged in from her room. David's breathing was steady from across the way. Robin moved like liquid shadow, slipping off her bed without a sound. She shoved her feet into her boots and pulled her hoodie over her head in one practiced motion. Phoenix, perched on the overhead light fixture, cocked his head at her and ruffled his feathers.

She held a finger to her lips. "Five minutes," she mouthed.

He launched silently and followed.

The Candle Factory mission was next. Phoenix had dropped the new missive hours ago, waxy paper and all. They were supposed to be on quiet time until the briefing.

But Robin needed something before she faced the unknown. She needed more of Wren.

She slipped through the maintenance stairwell and down two levels to the edge of the lab wing. The hall was dimmed for night hours. A night orb bounced gently at the end of the hall. Most cadets gave this floor a wide berth after curfew. The walls hummed with old tech and sealed secrets.

The lab door still looked like a wall, unless you knew what to say. Robin pressed her palm flat against the panel and whispered the phrase Evangeline had murmured once, half in jest. "Red Rover, Red Rover." The wall opened with a low hiss.

Inside, Evangeline sat on a tall stool, her back to the door, sipping from a chipped mug. A dull blue light shimmered off the array of coils behind her.

"You're early," she said, not turning.

"Okay, so you knew I'd figure out how to get in without you. I'm not staying long. We're being sent out."

"Candle Factory?" she asked, finally looking over her shoulder.

Robin paused. "Yeah. How did you—"

"I hear things." She turned fully, her sharp eyes scanning Robin. "You're here for memory work. About Wren."

Robin nodded. "I saw more. It felt different. Like she was trying to show me something."

Evangeline stood and gestured to the neural coil chair. "Strap in. We'll go deeper, but only until the clock hits 00:15. You miss briefing, I take the fall, and I don't fall gracefully."

Robin climbed into the chair. The coils lowered, the hum began, and the world fell away.

She was younger. Wren was crouched in front of her, hands on her shoulders.

"You're stronger than you think," Wren said, her voice soft. "It's not about how hard you hit back. It's about knowing when to stand."

Flash.

Running through an alley. Wren pulling her along. Behind them, someone shouting.

Flash.

A dark room. Wren whispering through tears. "They're not telling you the truth. If I disappear, don't stop looking."

Flash.

Robin gasped and jerked upright.

Evangeline steadied her. "That's it. That's all we've got time for."

Robin blinked against the rush of images. "She's trying to help. She's not hiding from me. She's protecting me."

"I figured you'd come to that conclusion."

"She said something's coming."

"It always is."

Robin stood, breath still short. "Thanks."

Evangeline held her gaze. "You get one more midnight visit before I start charging. Go suit up."

Back in the corridors, Robin made a split-second decision. She turned left instead of right. Toward the dorms would mean suiting up. Toward the far atrium? She was hunting answers.

Phoenix appeared and swooped low to follow.

It wasn't hard to find her way outside. A trick door behind the janitor's supply zone still bypassed the outer alarms. It spit her out into the shadowed south quad.

The city beyond glittered faintly, indifferent. Robin kept to the edge of the perimeter wall and crossed the park just outside the training field. A figure moved in the distance.

Robin froze. It was Wren.

She was leaning against the old wrought iron fence like she'd been waiting. Her hands were tucked into the sleeves of a well-worn hoodie, the kind Robin remembered suddenly borrowing years ago during late movie nights and cold mornings. Memories were overtaking her, jumbling together. For a second, Robin couldn't move. Her brain refused to process what her eyes were screaming was real. She wasn't seeing a ghost or a memory fragment. Wren was flesh and blood. Breathing. Watching. *I really do have a sister.*

Robin walked slowly toward her. "You're real."

Wren smiled. "So are you. Still making terrible choices after dark?"

"I needed to see you. I didn't want it to just be a dream."

Wren nodded, then looked toward the city skyline. "Things are shifting. There's movement underground. It's political, magical, dangerous. You've seen pieces. You're going to see more."

Robin stepped closer. "Why not tell me everything?"

"Because you're not ready to carry it. And because if you say the wrong thing at the wrong time, it gets both of us flagged. Just know this, not everyone giving you orders has your back."

Robin blinked. "The Candle Factory?"

Wren nodded slightly. "It's not sanctioned by who you think. And someone is hoping you won't come back."

Robin's stomach turned.

"I'll be near," Wren said. "When you need me. And when you're ready, I'll tell you the rest."

Robin's breath caught. Her heart was racing, questions clawing their way up her throat. "You don't seem surprised to see me like this. Undead. Half back, or however they define us at the Academy."

Wren's expression darkened. "I knew the moment it happened. I felt it. That hollow tug in my chest like someone ripped a thread out of my life. And I knew it wasn't permanent. Not with what they've been working on."

Robin frowned. "You knew about the resurrection program?"

Wren hesitated, then nodded. "In pieces. I didn't understand the full scope until I tried to come back for you, and they blocked me. Said you were gone for good. But I knew better."

"So, you've been what, following me? Watching from the shadows?"

Wren looked down at the pavement. "Yes. Watching. Listening. Trying to figure out how far they'd go to erase what happened to you. And why."

Robin took a shaky breath. "Why did I have to die?"

"That's the part I haven't figured out. I don't think your death was an accident, Robin. You were getting close to something. You always had that edge and they must have seen it as a threat."

Robin folded her arms, the night air suddenly colder. "You're talking about the Academy like they're the villains. They brought me back."

"Yeah," Wren said. "But did they bring back all of you?"

Robin didn't answer. She wasn't sure she could.

"How are Mom and Dad? Who are they? I don't have any memories of them," she asked, pressing her lips together. "Do they even know I'm—alive?"

Wren's shoulders dropped. "Yes, we have great parents. The best." Wren glanced at the ground, her brow furrowed. "They moved. There were too many memories in the old house. They're safe, but... they were told you died. Real death. No coming back. They never got the choice to know the truth. I wanted to tell them. I did. But every step I took toward them triggered a watcher. Someone's monitoring them. Probably to keep you isolated."

Robin's fists clenched. "Why? What's the point of bringing us back just to lie to us?"

"It's not about you. Not entirely. You're part of a test group. Returnees who still retain critical thinking. Emotional memory. You're dangerous because you remember who you are."

Robin shook her head. "You're saying I'm part of an experiment?"

"Yeah. And someone doesn't like that you're ahead of schedule."

"What about the infections?"

"That's a glitch."

"I got your violet thread." Robin bit her lip, so many questions swirling in her head.

"I didn't know if it would work," Wren said, voice low. "But I had to try. I poured everything I had into that thread—grief, memory, all of it. I hoped it would find you. I figured it out on my own, little by little.

"How did you know to do that?"

"We always had something in us, even before all this. You don't remember, but Mom used to call it 'the pull'. She said we were born tuned to each other. I didn't understand it growing up. Not really. But when you were gone, it woke up in me. Not all at once. It was more like a steady hum in the back of my ribs, or a tug behind my heart. I'd dream in colors I'd never seen before, feel drawn to places I couldn't name." Her hands moved through the air as she talked. "It was like part of me was reaching, even when I didn't know what I was looking for."

"We're magical? No," said Robin, shaking her head. "I'd remember that."

Wren tilted her head, making a face. "Really? You barely remember me. I'm told it's like a quirk, but for the living. I was trying to find answers about what happened to you. I followed every whisper, every trace of magic that felt familiar. I found places where you'd been. Burned edges in the veil, flashes of pain and defiance that didn't belong to me. They were echoes, and they were yours. Eventually, I realized I could send one back."

Robin stepped closer. "How are you involved in all of this?"

"I started poking around when you died. You know me, I couldn't let it go. I'm still your big sister and a bit of a nerd. At first, I didn't believe any of it. I mean, come on, undead, resurrections, a mysterious Academy. It sounded insane. I know, I know," she said, holding up a hand. "And yet I buy quirks. That didn't seem as big a stretch." Wren folded her arms across her chest against the night air. "I thought maybe grief was making me see things. I wanted you to be alive, at least some version of it. But then, I found my way into a network that traces magical anomalies, rogue resurrection signatures, Academy cover-ups. I met people like Evangeline, except off the books. Then I started to believe."

Robin's eyes widened. "Evangeline has known about you. That almost feels like a betrayal. You're working with them?"

"More like I'm tolerated, and you weren't betrayed. You were protected. Look, they've helped me stay off the radar. And sometimes I help cadets escape. The ones who come back wrong or not at all."

"Escape to where?" Robin held up her arm with the brand. "The ledger can always find us. How could someone escape?"

"There are ways, but it's tricky and it doesn't always work." Wren looked off into the distance, not saying anything for a moment. Finally, she said, "We have lost some. I'm fairly new at this, but we're getting better. I can only hope that those we lost are finally at some kind of peace."

Robin leaned against the fence beside her. "What is happening to this place?"

"Too much power. Not enough truth. That's always a bad recipe."

"And you? Where do you live? What are you doing when you're not being mysterious in the dark?"

Wren gave a small, tired laugh. "A little room above a used bookstore. I fix old things. Machines, trinkets. It pays just enough to keep me off the grid. And I wait. For moments like this."

Robin stared at her sister, trying to see the girl she knew underneath the wary, sharp-eyed woman in front of her. She was there. Older. Weathered. But there.

"How could you have figured out so much in such a short amount of time?"

"I had to," said Wren, smiling, her eyes damp with tears. "I'm your big sister and once I knew there was even a chance of seeing you again..."

"I missed you," Robin whispered.

"I miss you every day."

Robin's eyes burned. "Don't disappear again. Not without warning."

"I won't. But I can't stay, not yet. There are people who'd sense me lingering too long. I've already taken a risk by meeting you like this."

Robin nodded slowly. "And the Candle Factory?"

Wren's face grew serious. "It's not sanctioned by who you think. And someone is hoping you won't come back."

Robin's stomach turned.

"I'll be near," Wren said. "When you need me. And when you're ready, I'll tell you the rest."

Then she was gone.

Robin stood there for a full minute, unmoving. Her

hands hung limp at her sides, her breath sharp in her chest. The night felt too quiet now. No wind. No sound. Like the city was waiting.

Her thoughts spun like a wheel stuck in the mud. Wren. Not a ghost. Not a glitch in memory. Real. Alive. Involved. Watching her this whole time. *Helping people escape? To a real life?*

Robin rubbed her face with both hands, trying to ground herself. Her skin was clammy. Her fingers trembled. There was too much, too much to hold at once. Her sister had called her an experiment. Said she wasn't brought back whole. *What did that even mean?*

She stared down at the Hellhound mark glowing faintly on her forearm and whispered, "Then who did they bring back?"

A branch snapped somewhere nearby, but she didn't flinch. It wasn't fear anymore, it was something deeper. A knot of certainty.

Robin turned and walked slowly, retracing her steps. Her boots barely made a sound on the wet pavement. The city felt different now. Every shadow seemed to have depth. Every flicker of streetlamp buzzed like a warning.

She couldn't shake the image of Wren's face and the worry etched into it. The way she'd said someone hoped she wouldn't come back from the Candle Factory. That meant whoever they were, they expected Robin to falter. Expected her to die again. Or worse.

As she neared the hidden maintenance entrance behind the old student greenhouse, she paused and crouched by the fence. Phoenix fluttered down onto the nearby railing, watching her.

Robin met the crow's eyes. "She knew you too, didn't she?"

Phoenix cawed softly, then nodded. Not once. Twice. Deliberate.

Robin exhaled slowly. "You were keeping tabs on both of us."

He blinked once.

Robin reached into her hoodie pocket and pulled out the chip Jude had given her. It felt heavier now. Like it carried more than coordinates.

She slid through the bypass access point and entered the tunnels again, the damp scent of stone and metal hugging her skin. She moved quietly through the back halls, her mind racing.

They had to be watching her. Not just the instructors, but someone else. Someone Wren wouldn't name. And if Wren was right, if Robin was being tested, then she had to play smarter. No more trusting the face in front of her just because they wore a badge or carried a rank.

She made it to the locker hall without incident but paused just before turning the corner. Jude's voice echoed faintly ahead.

"Suit up. No extras tonight. We keep it clean and efficient. No ghost stories."

Robin pressed her back to the wall and closed her eyes. His tone was calm. Steady. But was it sincere? How much did he know?

She straightened and stepped out.

Jude stood outside the lockers, his arms crossed. He raised a brow as she entered. "You always take the scenic route?"

Robin didn't blink. "Had to clear my head."

He studied her a little too long, then nodded. "Fair enough." He handed her a fresh data chip. "This is updated intel for the mission. Route's been confirmed. David and Ashley are nearly ready."

She took it but didn't move immediately. "How long have you known about the Candle Factory assignment?"

Jude tilted his head. "Since the note dropped. But this," he held up a second chip "this just came through channels. The Academy's claiming the mission now. Which is interesting, considering the timing."

Robin tucked the chip into her pocket. "Maybe someone's cleaning up a mess."

Jude gave her a slow nod. "Maybe. Keep your eyes open."

Ashley was seated on a bench, lacing up her boots. She looked up. "You look like hell."

Robin dropped onto the bench beside her. "Thanks. That's the look I was going for."

David was by the weapons rack, checking field gear. "Heard we're not the only ones headed for the Factory. Other squads might be circling."

"Let them," Robin said, pulling on her gloves. "We're not there to follow. We're there to see what's really going on."

Ashley paused, then squinted at her. "You sure you're good?"

Robin nodded. "Just tired. Big day, or I guess for us, night, ahead."

Phoenix fluttered down from a rafter and dropped something into Robin's lap. A thin slice of wax with a strange spiral pressed into it.

Robin stared at it. "Where'd you get this?"

The crow tilted his head.

Ashley leaned closer. "Is that about the Candle Factory?"

Robin pocketed it. "Maybe. Or maybe it's a warning."

Ashley raised an eyebrow. "You're being cryptic again."

"Just... be careful tonight, okay?" Robin said. "Both of you."

Ashley frowned but nodded. "Yeah, you too."

Robin rose and zipped up her jacket. Whatever was waiting for them at the Candle Factory, she wouldn't walk into it blind.

And this time, she wouldn't be alone. She had a sister out there. Watching. Waiting. And maybe, just maybe, ready to fight.

CHAPTER FOURTEEN

The Candle Factory loomed in the pre-dawn gloom, a hulking silhouette against the slowly fading stars. Robin crouched behind a rusted out truck bed, her knees aching from the cold and her nerves drawn tight. The waxy scent of melted candles hung faintly in the air, clinging to the building like a memory that refused to fade.

"This place gives me the creeps," Ashley muttered, peering through a crack in the sheet metal fence. "Why would anyone bring people back here?"

Robin didn't answer. The spiraled wax Phoenix had dropped was still in her pocket, heavy like a warning. She scanned the perimeter again. David was to their left, crouched behind a pile of crumbling pallets, his saber already drawn. No sign of surveillance drones. No visible security. That was the first red flag.

The second? The place wasn't dead.

Candles flickered in the windows. Dozens of them. Each one pulsing in a slow rhythm, as if synced to a single beating heart.

Jude's voice crackled in their comms. "All teams in position. Keep silent unless necessary. The internal scan is unstable. Something's interfering with our readouts. Proceed with caution."

Robin tapped twice on the transmitter clipped to her collar. She was signaling to Ashley and David. They moved like clockwork—silent, efficient. They went swiftly up the alley and over the fence. Next, through the side door Jude had marked on the schematics.

Inside, the air was humid. Oppressive. Wax coated nearly everything including the walls, ceiling, and even parts of the floor. The scent was stronger now. Robin lifted her nose in the air. *Clove. Lavender. Something bitter underneath.* A spell laid over everything like a damp cloth.

Ashley winced as her boot stuck to the floor. "Gross."

"Quiet," Robin said, leading them through the maze of shelving and overturned molds.

They reached the central atrium, where rows of tables stood, resembling an abandoned workshop. In the center of the room there was a basin. It was a deep copper bowl filled with clear water. Candles surrounded it in concentric circles, all burning, with their flames unnaturally still.

David scanned the space. "Resonance spells. But they're not Academy issue. This is something older."

Robin stepped closer to the basin. As she leaned in, the surface of the water rippled. Her reflection didn't look back. Instead, Wren's face emerged. She looked frightened. Then she mouthed one word. *Run.*

The candles all abruptly flared at once. A blast of air was strong enough to knock Robin backward into a shelf of wax forms, sending them clattering to the floor.

"Contact!" Ashley shouted, raising her saber.

Writhing shapes began to emerge from the shadows. Figures wrapped in waxed robes slithered out, with faces obscured by dripping veils. They moved in unnatural jerks, like marionettes fighting their own strings.

Robin scrambled to her feet. "Defensive arc! Fall back to the corridor!"

David covered their retreat, throwing up a kinetic pulse that shattered a line of candles. The figures hissed, recoiling.

"Not ghosts," he shouted. "They're constructs with only partial bindings. Someone's trying to form bodies with borrowed souls."

Ashley swallowed hard as she threw a stun rune that fizzled in the waxy air. "They're not holding! Something's suppressing our gear."

Robin pressed her back to the wall, breathing hard. She held out her hands and felt them tingle. The pick Wren had left her, the one she'd been using to play echoes, was still in her belt. She slipped it out and gripped it now.

"Form a circle! Tight!"

Despite the chaos, they moved like a single organism with Robin covering Ashley's left, and David sweeping the flank before she had to ask. A deep trust in every step. Practice rounds were paying off.

Phoenix dive bombed the nearest figure, tearing into the wax with his talons. The thing shrieked and staggered, leaking amber smoke.

Robin slapped the pick against the floor and sent a pulse through it.

The room shuddered and the basin cracked. Every

candle went out at once and darkness swallowed the space. Then silence.

David lit a small torch rune, just enough to illuminate their faces.

Ashley's voice was barely a whisper. "What was that?"

Before Robin could answer, one of the wax wrapped figures lunged from the shadows and tackled David. "No!" he yelled, caught off guard. They slammed into a table, the clang of metal and wood snapping the quiet like dry twigs.

"David!" Robin shouted, spinning and slicing her saber across the thing's midsection. It howled a reedy, high pitched screech like boiling steam.

David wrestled it off, boots kicking, and rolled, coming up with his saber lit, dotted with wax residue. "They're still active!"

More of the constructs emerged from the walls, peeling away from the wax coated surfaces like nightmares shaking off sleep. The veiled faces were twisted toward them.

Ashley backed into Robin, holding her saber two-handed. "I count seven—no, eight!"

"Eyes on the ground!" Robin barked. "They move faster on clear surfaces. Push them toward the wax!"

She lunged forward and struck the nearest figure low, catching its knee. The wax splintered and collapsed like shattered porcelain, but it didn't fall. It staggered and shrieked, grasping wildly.

David leapt past it and slapped a circular micro disruptor onto its chest. It was one of his custom pulse tags that buzzed faintly with built-in kinetic charge. It beeped twice, then released a focused energy burst. The construct convulsed, limbs flaring out in all directions, then collapsed into a puddle of liquefied wax. The thing pulsed once, a blue light radiating out, and then caved inward with a wet sucking sound, melting into sludge.

"That's one!" he shouted.

"We need more of those!" Ashley yelled, swinging wide and catching another across the chest. But her saber didn't cut deep enough. There was too much resistance. The construct knocked her back, sending her sprawling.

Robin grabbed its arm before it could follow and twisted hard. Wax cracked with a satisfying crunch and the joint gave way. She drove the hilt of her saber into its face. "Ashley, move!"

Ashley rolled away and came up on one knee. "Okay, they don't like heat! Concentrated bursts!"

Phoenix screeched and soared above them, unleashing a small fire burst that lit up the center of the room. Two of the figures burst into flame and staggered in opposite directions, flailing.

The wax caught quickly, but it didn't stop the filmy monsters. One of them, its veil burned away, revealed the remains of a face beneath. Robin stared into a half-formed profile with eyes like dull mirrors and lips half-shaped into a scream.

She froze for half a second. "They're... not complete."

"They're something worse," David said grimly. "They're halfway souls."

"A fresh hell, great." Robin gritted her teeth and shoved forward, driving her shoulder into one of the shambling figures. It barely budged. "Ash, cover right! David, disruptor pattern—fan out!"

Ashley slid across the floor, landing near a fallen crate of candlemaker's tools. She grabbed two and flung them like throwing knives. One hit a construct's chest, nothing. The other slammed into a candle base on the far wall, toppling it into the wax floor.

A flash of green light surged up from the spill.

Robin's eyes went wide. "They've warded the floor!"

David yanked a collapsible field projector from a thigh holster. An experimental rig he'd been tweaking all week. He twisted the core, and a trio of copper prongs sprang out, whirring with a dull red charge. "Clear center!" he barked and flung it into the basin's heart. A rune spun in the air and then slammed into the basin. With a thunderous crack, the copper shattered fully, and a pulse of light radiated outward.

All the figures stopped. For one breathless moment, they stood motionless.

"Could it be?" asked Ashley, brushing pink bangs out of her face.

Then one let out a roar and charged.

"Nope, not so lucky." Robin met it halfway. Her saber sliced through the remaining wax across its arm, revealing muscle and bone, but it didn't bleed. "What the hell?" She ducked a wild swing and shoved upward with her forearm, knocking its head back.

Ashley lunged behind it, jamming a cracked oil lantern between its ribs. She lit it with a flick of her fingers. "Booyah!" The figure howled and erupted in flame.

"Two down!" Ashley cried.

"Three," David added, finishing another with a clean strike through the torso. It burst like a rotten melon.

Robin swung wide, barely avoiding another veiled attacker. Her boot slipped in the wax but she caught herself, dropped low, and cut the thing's leg out from under it till it crumpled.

Then it began crawling.

"Come on, really? They don't stop!" she shouted.

"Until they burn or melt," David said, hurling a handful of powder from a pouch. It burst into green flame as it hit the air, lighting two more figures ablaze.

The smell was choking the air. A noxious combination of wax, smoke, and something chemical with a whiff of rotten underneath.

Robin's breath came fast, her lungs screaming. Even the undead couldn't take whatever was hanging in the air. "Push them back! Toward the corridor! Funnel them!"

They tightened their formation. Ashley flanked left, David took point, as Robin held rear guard, slashing down the slower crawlers.

Phoenix shrieked overhead, darting and clawing, raining down distractions. The bird was relentless.

A construct lunged at Ashley from behind, but Robin saw it and dove, knocking it off course. The two cadets tumbled into the shelves, scattering broken molds.

Ashley grabbed her arm. "You good?"

"Fine, keep moving!"

Only three constructs remained.

David crushed one under a toppling shelf and stomped on its head. The wax exploded with a *goosh*, covering his boot.

Ashley gutted another, fire running along her blade.

The final one charged Robin directly.

She dropped low and swung her pick in a circle, hitting it across the temple, watching it stumble. She knew better by now than to think it had given up.

She planted her boot and drove upward with her saber, straight through the chest and twisted. The wax cracked with a loud *snap*, and it fell backward, convulsing.

Then, stillness.

They stood in the ruin of the factory floor. Shelves were splintered. Molds shattered. Wax burned in small pools, casting flickering light across the soot-darkened walls.

Robin dropped to one knee, panting. Ashley leaned on her saber. David flicked his fingers, extinguishing the last flame on his coat.

"You okay?" Robin asked.

Ashley gave a shaky thumbs up. "I will be. What was that?" She kicked at the remains with the tip of her boot.

David glanced at the scorched remains of one of the wax wrapped enemies. "Constructs like those? They're stitched together from materials and magic. Not born and not fully dead either. I read about them in one of the Academy files. Someone builds them to do their dirty work, and when you see that many in one place, it means someone's practicing." He walked toward the remains of the basin. "Whatever they were doing here, we stopped it, but not for long."

Robin went and looked down into the basin. It was empty now, but something in the bottom shimmered. A ring blackened and burned. She reached for it, but Phoenix cawed sharply, making her pause.

"Jude," she whispered into her comm, "we found something. There was an active ritual here with partially constructed beings. Some kind of half soul. We disrupted it."

"Understood," Jude's voice came back, tight. "Pull out. Now."

Robin hesitated. Wren's warning rang in her head. She picked up the blackened ring anyway and tucked into a pouch and turned to the others. "We're done here. For now."

They moved fast and quiet through the ruined corridors, back into the night.

But Robin knew this wasn't over.

It had only just begun.

The rain had returned by the time they reached the perimeter wall. Thin droplets hissed as they hit the stone, and the smell of ozone layered over the lingering wax and smoke that clung to their gear. Robin's boots splashed silently through puddles as she led Ashley and David through the narrow, overgrown passage between the Candle Factory and the south end of the industrial district.

"That was not an Academy mission," David muttered. His voice was quiet, but the edge in it cut clean.

Robin glanced over. "You noticed too?"

"Constructs. Unstable bindings. Rogue resurrection threads." He counted them off on his fingers. "That wasn't cleanup. That was mid process," he said.

Ashley wiped a smear of wax from her jacket. "And it's

still fresh. I don't think we stopped anything. We just hit pause."

Robin said nothing. Her hand drifted to the pouch at her hip, where the scorched ring sat. It pulsed faintly against the fabric, too warm for comfort.

She looked at the others. "No one mentions the ring. Not to Jude. Not to anyone."

Ashley blinked. "We're hiding things now?"

"We're surviving," Robin said. "Wren warned me. This mission wasn't about reconnaissance. It was a setup. Someone wanted us out of the way, or gone."

David grunted. "Wouldn't be the first time someone inside played both sides."

Ashley frowned. "You think Jude's in on it?"

"I don't know." Robin shook her head, wanting to believe in him. "I don't think so, but until I do know for sure, we keep this between us."

They cleared the fence and dropped into the side corridor that led back toward the Academy's maintenance tunnels. As they walked, the ambient noise of the city returned. Robin listened to the faint echo of traffic in the distance, the occasional buzz of security drones high overhead. It was calming in its own way.

"We need to analyze the ring," David said after a long silence. "Off-site. We can't trust internal labs."

Robin nodded. "Evangeline. She won't ask too many questions."

Ashley glanced over her shoulder. "She better not."

By the time they reached the concealed hatch behind the old training field, the adrenaline had begun to fade. Robin could already feel the backlash. Too much exertion.

Too many spikes of emergency juice pushing her reanimated system past what it was built to handle. Evangeline had warned her that too much adrenaline in a returnee could short out memories or burn through their soul tether like dry rope. Her muscles ached, her boots squelched. The quiet between them stretched, tense and tired.

The trio slipped through the hidden door and back into the Academy's sublevels. Robin led them along a maintenance route that bypassed security checkpoints and landed them one floor above their dorm wing. She stopped just before the turn.

"Go in separately," she said. "We weren't out together. We weren't even out."

David hesitated, then nodded. "We share the risk. We always have."

Robin gave a tired smile. "Exactly. We go in together, we come out together, just maybe with more burns and weird artifacts. Not suspicious at all. Go, it's okay. We have each other's back and we know it."

Ashley nodded. "All the way. If they come for one of us, they come for all." She gave a tight nod and peeled off toward the hall.

Robin waited until the others were out of sight, then leaned against the wall and slid down until she was crouched low. Her pulse hadn't fully slowed.

She pulled the ring out of the pouch.

It was blackened metal, cracked along one side, but something shimmered within it. A hint of blue light, like frozen fire. She didn't recognize the sigils, but something about the way they circled felt intentional and ancient. Like it was designed to loop forever.

Phoenix landed beside her, his talons clicking on the floor.

"You knew this was more than a recon, didn't you?" Robin asked.

The bird tilted his head.

"Wren said someone hoped I wouldn't come back."

Phoenix cawed softly and hopped closer.

"If they wanted to kill me, why not send me somewhere obvious? Why here, now?"

She stared at the ring again, an understanding coming over her. "Because this wasn't about me. It was about what I'd find. And maybe... who I'd tell. They're trying to root out the others by using me."

Robin didn't sleep.

She lay in her bunk fully dressed, one hand on the pouch hidden beneath her pillow, her mind a swirl of fire and fog. The basin. Wren's face. The constructs. The flare of wax and soul that had rushed the room.

They hadn't defeated anything. They'd interrupted a ritual in progress, which meant someone out there was still trying to complete it. And if they were using a ring like this one, they weren't acting alone.

She sat up quietly before dawn and made her way to Evangeline's lab. The door opened before she could knock.

"You always show up before I finish my tea," Evangeline said, holding the door.

Robin stepped in, her eyes already scanning the humming equipment making her stomach churn. "Could the ring or the basin have been used on me?"

Evangeline leaned in, her expression shifting from analytical to serious. "No. Your energy doesn't match this frequency. Whoever brought you back used sanctioned tech—or at least a more refined version. This ring is cruder, more volatile. If someone had used it on you, you'd feel the instability. You wouldn't be functioning this well."

Robin nodded slowly, processing.

"But," Evangeline added, her tone sharpening, "it might've been used on someone you know. Maybe recently. Maybe more than one."

Robin's pulse picked up. Her mind darted to the wax faced constructs in the Candle Factory. She pressed the heel of her palm to her chest remembering their misshapen features, the jerky way they moved, and how one of them had almost looked like it was trying to speak. She didn't want to believe it, but a part of her already did.

"The figures in the factory," Robin murmured. "They weren't just guards. They were prototypes."

Evangeline gave a grim nod. "Good for you. Yes, they were failed bindings. Whoever made them was trying to do what the Academy does, only without the safeguards. They probably used partial soul anchors. That's dangerous, sloppy work. And incredibly painful for the fragments trapped inside."

Robin sat back, unsettled. "So they weren't fully... people."

"They were pieces of people," Evangeline said. "Ripped from somewhere, or someone, and shoved into a wax shell designed to hold them just long enough to act. They're constructs, Robin. The magical equivalent of test dummies, but built to fight. Not to live."

Robin ran a hand over her face. "David said something like that."

Evangeline raised an eyebrow. "Smart guy and very resourceful."

"He called them halfway souls," Robin said. "Like they were never meant to be whole."

Evangeline nodded again, more slowly. "That's a fair way to put it. It's dark work, what you found. And deliberate. Someone wanted to test the process before scaling it up."

Robin's stomach turned again. "That means this wasn't a one off. They're planning more."

"Almost definitely."

She stood and started pacing. "Wren warned me. She said someone was hoping I wouldn't come back from that mission. They knew we'd run into those things. Knew we'd either be wiped out, or bring back a piece of their puzzle for them."

Evangeline tilted her head. "She told you that?"

"Sort of," Robin said. "And she was scared. Not just for me, for everyone."

Evangeline stepped closer. "Then we have to assume this ring wasn't just left behind. It was planted."

Robin looked up. "It's bait."

"Or a beacon," Evangeline said. "They might be tracking the energy signature even now. I'll cloak it, but don't keep it on you. It's too risky."

"I didn't think of that." Robin hesitated, then handed the

ring over. Evangeline wrapped it in a length of copper mesh and placed it into a locked box that disappeared behind a panel in the wall.

"Whoever made this," Robin said, "they're experimenting on the dead. Twisting them into weapons, and the Academy has to know something. Jude said the mission came from 'outside,' but they accepted it after the fact. Why?"

Evangeline folded her arms. "Because they're scared, or compromised, or both. I've worked here long enough to know the signs. Someone high up is playing a long game but not by choice."

She adjusted something on her screen. "It's not just hesitation," she said, her voice low. "It's strategy. The Academy isn't reacting because it's already accounted for these risks. They knew this kind of experimentation might happen, and they didn't shut it down. Plus, they've allowed just enough distance to deny involvement if it comes to light."

Robin frowned. "They're playing both sides."

"It looks that way and letting someone else do the dirty work. They're standing back and letting someone build an army in secret. Then they can swoop in and 'solve' it when things fall apart. It's textbook power consolidation."

Robin crossed her arms. "And we're the test group."

Evangeline tapped a finger against her cheek. "You and your team aren't just cadets anymore. You're pressure valves. Sent in to see how much the system can hold before it blows."

Robin put her hands on her hips, her courage growing. "Then we need to play a game of our own."

Evangeline gave her a small, crooked smile. "That's what I like about you, Sullivan. You don't back down when the story turns dark, you sharpen your blade. I noticed the same quality in your sister."

"Thank you for helping her." Robin started to ask a question, but Evangeline stopped her.

"I know you want details," said the Archivist, "but not now, not yet. It will only distract you and if you don't focus, whoever is doing this may win. I don't even want to think about what losing would look like."

Robin sighed. "I just want to make sure the next cadet who walks into something like that doesn't die for it."

"Then we start small," Evangeline said. "We map every signature tied to that ring. We watch for overlap in the cadet database. We look for missing records, altered files, reassignments that don't make sense."

"And if we find a link?"

"Then we follow it," she said. "All the way to the source."

Robin stood, steadied by resolve. Her body ached and her mind was fraying at the edges from too little rest and too many shocks, but she was focused now. The kind of sharp attention that only came from a clarity of purpose.

"I should get back," she said.

Evangeline nodded. "Go. But don't tell anyone else yet. Not even your team. Not until we know more."

Robin's jaw tightened. "They'll ask questions. They already have."

"Then buy time," Evangeline said. "And when it's safe, you loop them in. But not before."

Robin paused at the door. "If they come for me..."

"They'll come for me first," Evangeline said.

Robin didn't smile, but her voice steadied. "Thanks." She slipped out into the hall and didn't look back.

CHAPTER FIFTEEN

Robin stepped into the cramped briefing hall and felt a heaviness claw at her undead gut. The overhead lights pulsed every few seconds, casting odd shadows across the concrete walls.

She noticed half a row of empty chairs up front. "That's not normal. Have more been recalled?" she muttered. Phoenix, perched on her shoulder, made a low croak, confirming that a few more cadets had been forced back. The possibility of disappearing like that, with no explanation, simply gone, sent a jolt of dread through her. She refused to show it and let out a slow breath she didn't need.

An instructor in a black and green Austin FC soccer shirt paced near a digital display that glimmered with an eerie swirl each time he tapped the surface. He looked young enough to pass as a college student, except for the lines around his eyes that said he had seen far more than any typical observer. She recognized him from a distance. He was short with clipped hair, a wiry build, and an almost feverish intensity in his dark eyes. He set his phone-like device against the display and nodded for everyone to pay attention.

"Over the past few nights, we've picked up traces of unauthorized undead running through downtown," he said. "These are unregistered, with no marks on their arms, and no official entries. You know what that suggests."

Robin leaned against the chipped chair, her arms crossed. "Real zombies, great," she muttered. She spotted Ashley two seats away, her hair dyed a riotous pink, trying to appear calm. However, Ashley's sneakers tapped the floor enough to betray her nerves.

Phoenix stretched his wings and settled them again as if he agreed with Robin's comment. The instructor's phone stuttered with a glow. "We have reason to suspect an illicit resurrection ring. They're peddling second chances to anyone who can pay," he continued. "These are not Academy approved revivals."

Robin tensed. She turned toward Ashley and noticed the slight tremble in the other girl's fingers. That was saying something. It took a lot to rattle Ashley. David stood behind them, quiet and focused, his arms locked across his chest. His posture hinted at a hundred questions beneath his calm exterior. The same tension vibrated in Robin's chest. Until now, she had thought only the Academy could bring someone back, but that was not the case. Her whole reason for walking around in undead form might be tangled in a black market scheme.

She studied David's profile. He wore a serious expression that made her wonder what he had uncovered in the Academy records. He had hinted before that unauthorized methods existed and were rumored but never confirmed.

This could be the missing piece of her puzzle. If someone was offering twisted deals, then they might have interfered with her fate. *Did they give me the infection?* A flicker of memory teased the back of her mind. Something was trying to bloom. She pressed her eyes closed briefly and saw hooded shapes along with the sensation of being restrained, but it vanished before she could grasp it. She opened her eyes and let out a frustrated sigh.

The instructor lifted a hand. "We've identified one lead. It's a fight club operating somewhere off Airport Boulevard. It's likely an underground space catering to living thrill seekers and newly resurrected participants." He looked out over the group. "We want infiltration. We want you to observe, confirm, and then exit. No showboating. Do I make myself clear?"

Robin exhaled. She felt Jude's arrival more than she saw it. He moved from the far side of the hall and stopped a few rows behind her. She took a look back at the tall, lean man with his hair slicked back. He was wearing worn jeans and a t-shirt snug enough to reveal the tight lines of muscle in his arms. She noticed how he kept one hand near his holstered weapon. He and the instructor exchanged a curt nod, some silent arrangement passing between them.

Robin hesitated. Just for a breath. Wren's face flickered behind her eyes along with the memory flash, the warning, and the missing pieces that never settled. She hadn't said it out loud yet, not even to Ashley, but she knew this ring wasn't just another job, either. It was tied to her.

Maybe even to how she died.

"I'll take point," Robin said, locking eyes with Jude. "We need to do this clean."

Ashley came closer, her voice low. "I don't like this, and I'm not letting you walk in there alone. If something happened to me, if I came back wrong, I'd want someone asking the hard questions too."

Robin glanced at her, surprised. Ashley gave her a half shrug. "Don't look so surprised. Besides, you're the only one who'd probably drag my half dead body back out again."

"You know I would," Robin said.

Ashley nodded. "Then let's go make a mess."

Robin stood, ignoring the sting of Jude's narrowed eyes. "We can't wait around while some group out there hands out shady resurrections."

She waited for him to push back. To say she wasn't ready, or worse, that she was letting memories cloud her judgment. But instead, Jude gave the slightest nod, barely more than a breath.

"Watch your corners," he said. "And don't assume the dead stay put."

It wasn't praise. But it wasn't a warning, either. It was as close to trust as he ever gave.

The instructor's focus landed on her Hellhound mark. "You sure you're up for it?"

She forced a confident shrug. "I'm already dead. Might as well do something with it." A couple of cadets fixed her with uneasy stares. A spike of adrenaline hit as she imagined creeping through some illicit den. She couldn't shake the feeling that this place with the whispers, the energy, and the pulsing hum of something wrong, was familiar. Not in a literal sense, but the way a half dream clings to the corners of your mind when you first wake up. Faces in the crowd around her blurred at the edges. One of them turned, just slightly, and for a heartbeat, she thought it was Wren watching from the back row. It wasn't, but the idea rooted in her. She remembered Wren's voice. *Don't trust everyone giving you orders.*

That warning wasn't theoretical anymore. Not here. If this ring had anything to do with her murder, she needed to find the connection. And if someone else had already used it? If another cadet had been pulled back—without consent, without their memory? That was more than reckless. It was playing God with broken pieces.

Robin felt the pick Wren gave her shift slightly at her hip, a reminder of what she'd lost, and who might still be watching. She wasn't just chasing shadows. She was chasing a blueprint someone else had already followed.

David shifted closer. "I'll help. I've got methods for analyzing data on site." His voice carried a soft, thoughtful quality. She remembered how he could slip into locked Academy systems. He'd probably crack that fight club's network wide open if given half a chance.

Ashley wore a conflicted expression. She walked over and tapped Robin's arm. "I'm all in, but we're not doing anything reckless," she whispered. "If this ring is serious, they're not amateurs. We don't know how strong they are."

Robin offered a rueful grin. "Might be dangerous, but we're short on answers. We saw how weird it's getting out there." She wasn't eager to drag Ashley into more trouble, but it felt good to have at least one friend who worried for her undead skin.

"I tapped into the comms while you were talking,"

Ashley murmured. "There's interference bouncing around the site. Not ours. Somebody's hiding a signal."

Robin glanced at her. "Academy?"

Ashley shook her head. "No tags. Could be rogue. Or bait."

Robin didn't reply, but Ashley's voice dropped even lower. "I don't scare easy, Robin. But this one? It feels like we're walking into someone else's memory."

Robin nodded once. "Then let's make sure we walk out with proof."

Jude cleared his throat. "Count me in on the mission," he said, dipping his chin at the instructor, then his cool stare landed on Robin. "I'm not letting this turn into a circus."

She rolled her eyes. "Yes, because you're all about subtlety, aren't you?" Her voice had an edge, but it didn't hide the undercurrent of curiosity. She didn't trust him, not yet, but she didn't hate having him on the team either. The tension between them was shifting. Still risky. Still uncertain. But maybe… useful.

Jude didn't say anything, but his eyes lingered on her a moment too long like he wanted to warn her and couldn't. Or wouldn't.

She caught the hesitation. It was gone fast, replaced with his usual unimpressed stare, but it was there. He knew something, she was sure of it. And he wasn't ready to share.

That made him dangerous. But maybe not in the way she'd first assumed. Dangerous to somebody else.

A short chuckle escaped the instructor. "Glad we have volunteers, because the rest of you are needed for other tasks. Stealth is essential. Do not blow the operation for cheap heroics." He fiddled with the toggles on his phone, and the swirling shapes vanished. "We traced a lead to a rundown building near a row of trailers. Rumor says that's the place. If you confirm illegal activity, step back. Don't engage unless you have no choice."

Robin's hand curled into a fist. She didn't like the idea of tiptoeing, though it was smarter. The instructor gave them a few instructions on covering their Hellhound marks. They had to keep them hidden or risk tipping off the ring. She frowned at hers, feeling the icy press beneath her skin. It had become as much a part of her as her heartbeat used to be.

When the briefing ended, the instructor marched out, leaving the group in a hush. Ashley lingered, biting her lip, while David studied something on his portable device. Jude stood at the back, no doubt waiting for an excuse to scold Robin. She decided to confront that tension head-on.

She made her way over to him, falling into step beside him as they moved down the hall. "Looks like we're doing this together," she said.

Jude nodded, still moving down the hall. "Underground fights are messy. The ring's signature could be buried under layers of interference."

Robin kept her tone steady. "Then we don't miss anything."

"You lead," he said. "But if it goes sideways, I step in. No hesitation."

She didn't argue. "Understood."

Their rhythm wasn't easy, but it was aligned, for now. The mission came first.

"The target is a resurrection leakage," Jude added. "Fighters showing signs of alteration. If you sense anything like energy spikes, or memory distortion, you say something."

She stepped away, Phoenix coming to rest on her shoulder, and joined Ashley and David in the corner. Ashley stood relaxed but ready, watching the corridor without fuss. "I've got the comms prepped to flag anything off pattern," she said. "If the resurrection ring's signal is down there, we'll catch it."

Robin gave her a nod. Ashley didn't need a pep talk. She was ready and already thinking ahead.

"Hey, I've been looking at the city's public records," said David. "There are areas that never show up properly on the Academy's grid." He lowered his voice. "Some might be unlisted zones, exactly where a ring could operate."

She peered at his screen and saw a pattern of connected blocks, each highlighting a potential blind spot. "You're saying they hide right in the city, but the Academy never flags it."

He nodded. "Or the Academy chooses not to flag it." His voice sounded troubled. "I don't want to accuse anyone without proof, but if someone on the inside ignored certain signals, we'd never know. These resurrection rings must have help."

Ashley folded her arms. "If that ring's got ties inside the Academy, this isn't just about some fight club. It's bigger. But we need to be smart. We're not exactly on Command's favorites list."

Robin gave a small nod and touched her shoulder. "We're not going in swinging. Just gathering intel and getting a better picture of what we're up against." She hesitated. "It might be the closest we get to the truth about what happened to me, maybe to you."

Ashley held her gaze. "Then let's get to it. Better than sitting around wondering who's pulling the strings."

"Thanks," Robin said, meaning it.

Jude intercepted them on the way out, stepping into their path. "We leave in two hours. Minimal gear. No point hauling around a bunch of equipment if we aren't there to fight. Wear something that covers the brand. And keep your mouth in check."

She forced her lips into a smirk. "No promises."

Jude stared at her a moment too long, taking a look at the crow.

The overhead lights hummed in the corridor. The entire place seemed to hold its breath as people dispersed, leaving behind tension that coiled in the stale air as if alive.

Robin turned to David. "Thanks for offering to help. I know this is risky."

"You're not alone in this," he replied, his voice subdued but determined. He glanced at Phoenix, who bobbed his head as if ready for some midnight infiltration. "If that ring is tied to your...well, your rebirth, we need the truth. For all our sakes."

She exhaled. "Ready or not, we suit up in two hours." With a shaky laugh, she added, "I've never been a big fan of cage fights, but hey, guess that's the new normal."

Jude frowned at them both, then turned and headed for the exit without a word. Robin watched him go, unsure what to make of him.

He was frustrating, sure, always five steps ahead and

acting like he didn't trust her to keep up. But she'd seen something else tonight. A flash of concern he hadn't meant to show. And he'd shown up, again. He always did, even if he never explained why.

Maybe he isn't trying to undermine me. Maybe he is trying to protect something or someone, and didn't know how to include me in that plan.

Either way, she wasn't waiting for permission. There was a job to do. If chasing down resurrection tech meant brushing past rules or raising eyebrows, she'd deal with it. She wasn't here to win anyone over. She was here to get answers.

The hallway emptied, and the display glowing on the wall faded. Robin spotted Jude speaking with another instructor near the stairwell. They stood close, voices low, but the body language told her everything. Tension. Disagreement. Jude glanced her way and didn't nod, didn't speak. He just turned back to the conversation, his hands tightening behind his back.

Fine. Let him watch, she thought, surprised she cared that much. "It doesn't matter," she muttered, shaking her head. She had work to do.

She moved quickly through the quiet corridors and into her dorm room. *Time to get ready*. She mentally ran through the list. Tactical gear—nothing flashy. *Got it.* Black cargo pants, a long sleeved compression shirt, boots with reinforced soles. *Check.* Lightweight armor over her chest and spine. Her hair pulled back, efficient. The mark on her arm covered. Not for shame but for strategy. She didn't need questions tonight.

Check, check and check.

The room's night orb hovered in the upper corner, casting its usual soft glow. It would dim when she left, same as it always did, but its quiet presence reminded her she was still here. Still functioning, still in control.

She double checked her gear, then stepped out into the corridor without hesitation. No final glance and no pause.

Sublevel C was colder. It always was. She moved down the stairwell, the air sharpening as she descended. These corridors hadn't been properly maintained in years. Dust clung to the edges, and the hum of outdated lighting buzzed low overhead.

At the gear lockers, she keyed in Ashley's override with six digits that no one else would think to try and the door clicked open. Inside were a compact sidearm, two low energy disruptor discs, and a comm patch with scrambler overlay. Nothing heavy. Just enough to get in, make contact, and get back out if it all went wrong.

She clipped the sidearm to her thigh, slid the discs into her belt pouch, and secured the patch inside her collar. The locker door whispered shut behind her.

On the far end of the hallway, the tunnel access stood open. She'd expected to meet the others here, but they weren't early. That tracked. Robin preferred a head start anyway.

She stepped through the threshold and into the first tunnel. The temperature dropped again, this time with a sharp bite that settled at the base of her skull. Her boots scraped softly against the stone floor. Every sound echoed twice.

This path led under the Academy's southern perimeter wall, toward the city's buried utility corridors. Most cadets didn't know these existed. Even fewer knew how to navigate them.

Robin did. She'd memorized the maps David had decrypted, noted every blind spot and crawlspace. She passed a rusted grate on her right and ducked under a hanging pipe that leaked slow drops of condensation. If someone was watching, they hadn't made a move yet.

The mission brief had come in two lines and a location code.

The first line said, surveillance only. Second one, observe the fight club. Identify any resurrection linked activity. Do not engage.

Which meant they'd almost certainly be engaging.

She paused at a junction where the tunnel split and checked the wall for the marking Jude had described. She was looking for a smudge of black paint shaped like a sideways crescent. She smiled, her shoulders relaxing just a little. It was there, half faded but readable under the beam of her pocket torch. She turned right.

The further she moved, the less the tunnels felt like city infrastructure and more like someone else's domain. Old metal signage in languages she didn't recognize. Burned-out sconces that hadn't held torches in decades. She noted the waxy residue on one wall; just a streak, but enough to raise the hair on her arms.

It was becoming obvious. The ring wasn't some artifact anymore. It was part of a network.

Someone was using it, or versions of it, to experiment. To test, maybe even build. The wax based constructs they fought at the Candle Factory weren't the end of the line. They were prototypes. Disposable half souls that were made up of parts of living beings. A shiver went down her spine.

Robin reached the staging corridor near the old lift shaft. The air shifted, cooler again, and damp. The metal gate stood half open, rusted at the corners, a remnant from when this level had served as part of the city's freight system.

She checked the timer on her band. Four minutes early. Footsteps approached behind her. Just one pair. She didn't turn. "You're not late."

Ashley's voice came steady and low. "Didn't want you making friends down here without backup."

Robin allowed herself a small smile. "Appreciate it."

Ashley stepped up beside her. Tactical gear on, comm earpiece already lit. "David's patching in remotely. He's running a scan sweep for resurrection frequencies and local energy signatures. He said to tell you he'll ping if something spikes."

Robin nodded. "Good."

They stood in silence for another minute. Robin studied the grated floor and the faint shimmer of condensation catching the light from Ashley's visor.

She didn't say it out loud, but she knew they weren't alone. Not yet seen, but noticed and watched.

Which meant they were close.

She touched her collar mic. "Team Two is in position."

Static. Then a reply. Jude's voice, quiet and dry. "Copy. Fight club entrance is two levels down. Watch for runners."

Robin acknowledged and turned to the narrow stairwell that wound down beside the shaft.

They moved without talking. No posturing. No jokes. That part had passed.

When they reached the second sublevel landing, Robin crouched and scanned the corridor ahead. A metal door stood flush with the wall, unmarked except for a sticker peeling in the corner. Some kind of fire code label. Useless now.

Robin gestured. Ashley moved to the panel. She pulled a slim scanner from her belt and ran it across the door frame. Lights blinked green.

"No alarm triggers. Manual latch. Probably a secondary access."

Robin tried the handle. It opened on the first pull.

She slipped inside and found herself in a narrow hallway that smelled of sweat, smoke, and more old wax. Voices echoed somewhere ahead low, and excited. A beat of music pounded faintly through the walls.

Ashley stepped in behind her, shutting the door quietly. Robin exhaled, slow and steady. It had begun.

CHAPTER SIXTEEN

The hallway opened into a wide space with a low ceiling, lit by flickering neon panels and streaks of rune glow carved into the support beams. Robin stepped carefully, staying in the shadows near the wall, her eyes adjusting to the chaos unfolding ahead.

Rows of makeshift benches ringed a sunken pit at the center, where two fighters were circling each other under harsh white lights. The crowd roared as one of them landed a heavy blow.

Near the far wall, a hairy, fat bouncer leaned against a stool that looked like it had given up holding his weight an hour ago. His arms were crossed over a barrel chest, eyes half lidded like he'd seen it all and cared about none of it. But his gaze still tracked movement, especially the kind that didn't come through the front door.

Robin motioned for Ashley to hold back as she scanned the crowd. Most faces were human, but a few glowed faintly with undead signatures just beneath the surface.

Something was off. She could feel it in the way the air buzzed against her skin.

Jude was already somewhere inside. Probably watching, probably two steps ahead.

Robin leaned close to Ashley. "Let's stay high until we're sure what we're looking at."

Ashley nodded. "We've got partial echoes coming through. Residuals from resurrection markers. Not a lot, but definitely present."

Robin didn't respond. She just kept moving.

Jude peeled away from the far side of the corridor. She clocked his tall frame in a faded jacket, hair pushed back like he took pains to look scruffy. He sent them a curt nod that could have been acknowledgment or a warning. Earlier, he had said he would pose as a gambler spoiling for a fight, so his presence would raise fewer questions. The last thing Robin wanted was Jude's brand of glowering, but here they were.

He tilted his chin toward a larger subterranean chamber, then turned and vanished into the crowd without a farewell. She swallowed a retort and focused on what lay ahead.

A wide basement opened before them. The space was packed with spectators pressed around a makeshift cage at its center. Two men swung at each other inside the cage, blood and spit flying across the metal mesh. They looked supercharged, faster and stronger than any living fighters ought to be. Robin spotted bare wrists, fresh marks she did not recognize, and eyes that glowed with a sunken energy. Undead or near enough.

Ashley edged closer to Robin, her eyes scanning the

crowd with quiet focus. Despite the tactical gear under their jackets, they kept their movements casual, their shoulders loose, and eyes curious like they were just another pair of locals watching a fight.

"We've got more than echoes," she said under her breath. "I'm picking up three concentrated heat signatures—back row, left side. Could be shielding something."

She tapped her comm once. "I'll loop through the signal feeds, see if I can isolate anything. Cover me."

"Yeah," Robin said. "This crowd might be nastier than the illusions the Academy trains us to chase."

An abrupt hush fell near a corner table. A sleek figure stepped into view. Robin's pulse spiked with a familiar, futile burst of adrenaline. The ringmaster. He wore a tailored coat with satin lapels, the metal studs on his belt reflecting the dim overhead light. His face looked too pale, as if he toyed with death so often it had stained his expression. She felt an odd tug of memory. This room reeked of second chances sold at a discount, reanimation off the books. Her own resurrected existence gave her a twisted sense of kinship with these half humans, but it also fueled her anger.

He prowled around the cage, spouting promises that made Robin's nails dig into her palms. She caught phrases like "fresh start," "upgrade your body," and "limited re-entry," though the roar of the crowd swallowed the rest. A wave of revulsion roiled her gut. She half wondered if her murder had lined someone else's pockets. That question kept her awake each night when she rested like the undead in the Academy's cramped dorm.

Ashley nudged Robin's arm. "Look at their tattoos," she

said under her breath. "They resemble the shapes that Phoenix delivered to you in that envelope."

Robin's eyes narrowed. She saw the lines curling over the skin of certain bystanders, swirling in ways that mirrored the images from the cryptic slip of paper. A low heat of fury rose in her. "Then we're definitely in the right place." She forced a thin smile. "Let's find a ledger or some digital proof of these deals. We need more than rumors."

Ashley inhaled with tense resolve. "I'll scout the perimeter." Her voice carried a shaky confidence that Robin found oddly reassuring.

"Sure," Robin said quietly. "I'll keep watch."

She felt Phoenix's presence before spotting him. The crow roosted atop a crossbeam overhead, silent and watchful, black feathers gleaming. Another hush spread at the sight of the bird, as though some primal instinct told everyone that a crow from the underworld was no random decoration.

Ashley disappeared into the throng. Robin edged toward the cage, pretending to cheer with the rest as the two supercharged fighters slammed each other into the chain links. One man roared, exposing sharpened teeth, while the other spat an inhuman hiss, while spectators egged them on. The ringmaster circled closer, directing attention to the brutality, his voice smooth as oil. "Pain is the currency, but purpose is the prize. Every blow in this cage buys a step closer to a second chance—if they survive the tab."

A slender guard loomed behind the ringmaster, scanning for threats. His shaved head and sleeveless vest showcased muscular arms inked with swirling shapes that once again matched those on some of the fighters. His gaze jumped across the crowd, never resting long, but when they swept past Robin, she was sure she saw him hesitate and she felt it like a warning.

She kept her posture relaxed, forcing a laugh as one fighter took a brutal jab to the ribs. The sound didn't feel real coming from her, but it served its purpose. Robin knew how to play a role when needed. She nudged Ashley with her elbow. "Time to do your thing."

Ashley nodded once and veered toward a cluttered table stacked with betting slips and a battered tablet. Robin scanned the crowd for Jude and David. Jude prowled near the edge of the cage, scanning exits. David leaned against a rusting support beam, playing casual but alert. A team, all in place.

Ashley moved gracefully, slipping between loud spectators. The guard's gaze tracked her movement, but Robin stepped into his line of sight, clapping and hollering like a true fight fan. "Yeah, tear him up!" she shouted. A couple of nearby watchers cheered with her. She gave them a crooked grin.

The guard took the bait, shifting focus to her. Ashley slid the tablet off the table and tucked it under her arm with a quick glance back. Robin gave a slight nod.

"Hey," a voice boomed. The ringmaster had turned. His pale gaze met hers across the crowd. "We're all here for fun. Let's keep it friendly."

Robin lifted her chin. "Just hyping the crowd." She exaggerated a tipsy sway. "Didn't know you were so sensitive."

The ringmaster's lips curled into a polished sneer. "Be

careful with the insults. Sensitivity can save lives in a place like this."

Ashley stepped beside her, tablet secure. "Got it," she whispered.

Robin gave her a nod. "Jude," she said into the comm bead tucked behind her ear. "You good?"

"Two exits, one guard each. No extra muscle yet. You got what you need?"

Ashley answered. "Logs, bets, client codes. And something weird. A schematic, maybe. Looks medical."

"Copy that," Jude replied. "David's got your six."

Robin glanced at David, who gave her a small nod. He moved to cover their flank.

The ringmaster clapped his hands. "And now, for our next contender... a true original. Self-taught, my friends. Rebuilt, not reborn."

A figure stepped into the ring, his movements jerky but fast. His eyes glowed faintly yellow. Robin tensed. That glow was unnatural, wrong. It made her skin crawl with a memory she couldn't quite access. Whatever had been done to her... this felt close. Too close.

Ashley muttered, "No Academy signature. That's black market stitching."

David joined them, keeping his voice low. "I've seen something like that before down near the Austin rail yards. Same glow."

Robin drew a breath. "Let's keep watching. We need to link this to the resurrection ring rumors. Ashley, record everything you can."

The ringmaster paced the cage's edge, his voice oily.

"What about infections?" Robin asked suddenly. "The kind that linger even after resurrection. You seen those?"

The ringmaster's smile thinned. "Some souls come back... changed. It's not always the stitching." He turned away from her to face the crowd, his arms spread. "This, my friends, is evolution by necessity. We don't wait for permission. We create opportunity."

Jude's voice crackled again. "Movement near the left stairwell. Might be a delivery or more guards."

Robin motioned to David. "Cover Ashley." Then she moved forward.

The ringmaster saw her approach and smiled wide. "Decided to take me up on my offer?"

"Not tonight," she said coolly. "But I'm curious. Where do you find your fighters?"

He raised an eyebrow. "Here and there. The city is full of desperate souls. Some want a second chance," he said, grabbing his lapels. "Others, a stage."

"And the stitching?" Robin pressed. "Looks expensive."

He chuckled. "Some donors are very generous."

Robin felt Ashley step behind her again. "He's dodging," Ashley murmured.

"Of course he is." Robin stepped closer. "Let's stop dancing. You're connected to the reanimation ring. I want names."

The ringmaster's smile never wavered. "Brave words. But I think you know how this works. Information comes at a price."

From the edge of the crowd, a commotion broke out. Jude had started a scuffle with a pair of gamblers, drawing several eyes, including the guard's.

Robin seized the moment. "Then let's deal." She grabbed the tablet from Ashley and shoved it at the ringmaster's chest. "We have logs, names, and procedures. You give me the truth, or this goes to the Academy. All of it."

The ringmaster's hand hovered over the device, his expression darkening.

David stepped forward, hand near his disruptor. "Don't test us."

A long pause stretched between them. Finally, the ringmaster took the tablet and handed it to his guard. His mouth was tight, but not with anger—something sharper flickered behind his eyes. Fear, maybe, but not of them.

"Fine. Follow me."

He led them behind the cage, and past a steel door. Inside was a room lined with filing cabinets and old servers. A projector glowed faintly, displaying a diagram of a resurrection pod with unlicensed notes.

"This is just a slice," he said. "The real operations are deeper. You want the ones pulling strings? Look for the shadow contracts tied to the Cedarshell Clinic. That's where the premium bodies go."

Robin's breath caught. "You're admitting you supplied victims?"

"I'm saying I run a service," he replied. "The Academy turns away a lot of people. Some find their way to me."

Ashley's voice was hard. "And you profit off their bodies."

The ringmaster shrugged. "I get paid for my time and connections. Better than rotting."

Robin narrowed her eyes. "You mentioned donors. Who pays for this?"

His smile returned, tighter this time. "You've heard of the Masked Circle?"

Ashley glanced at Robin. "That's the first time we've heard that name."

The ringmaster gave a short nod. "Then let me give you a primer. They're an old network, think secret society meets biotech investors. They want to rewire how resurrection works. And they don't mind funding small operations to test the edges of what's possible. Some Academy alumni have found new homes in their ranks, if you catch my meaning. Connections run deeper than most want to admit."

Jude stepped inside. "I've heard of them."

The ringmaster's voice dropped. "Then you know they don't tolerate betrayal."

A muscle twitched in the ringmaster's jaw. "But they never expected me to improve the formula." He offered a tight smile, but it didn't reach his eyes. "They built the cage. I just made it profitable."

Robin saw her opportunity. The ringmaster knew he was playing with fire. She squared her shoulders. "We're not leaving empty handed. Give us enough to take this to Command."

He leaned closer. "They used your name. That night, you know, that you died. Said your soul had... potential."

Robin's vision swam. "That's enough."

David touched her arm. "We need to go. Now."

Ashley snapped photos of the display and files. Her brow furrowed as she scrolled through one of the file headers. "Robin," she said, "one of these donor codes is tagged with an Academy clearance level. High access.

Someone on the inside is helping them." Jude opened the door. "Cadet backup's two minutes out."

Robin turned to the ringmaster. "You'll answer to more than just us."

"Maybe," he said, tapping his chest. "But I never die easy."

They backed out of the server room in silence, the heavy door easing shut behind them.

Robin didn't speak. The team slipped through a side corridor, bypassing the main floor of the club. The fight sounds still thundered through the walls, oblivious to what had just unraveled behind the scenes.

Ashley was already scanning for a quiet spot. "There's a side room under the maintenance stairwell that's out of the cam grid."

Robin gave a short nod. "We hold there. Ten minutes max. Then we plan our next move."

Behind them, the noise of fists and cheering swallowed their footsteps.

The Masked Circle, whoever they were, had just lost control of a secret, and Robin intended to use it. Not the fighters, not even the reanimation rituals, but the volatile echoes they'd stirred up and failed to contain. The kind that could think for themselves, bleed into the living, and rewrite what death meant. Robin had seen the signs with Malachi's haunted music warped by a spectral grip, or the banshee's scream delivering more than sound, and now the cage fighters twitching with memories that weren't entirely their own. These weren't accidents. They were echoes that refused to stay buried.

CHAPTER SEVENTEEN

They didn't speak as they left the back room, the heavy door clanking shut behind them. The roar of the crowd echoed off the concrete, sounding distant but ever-present. Robin led them into a narrow side corridor that veered away from the ring, the walls sweating with condensation and neglect.

Ashley spotted a cracked utility door and pushed it open. "I think we found it." Inside was a half gutted maintenance room with stripped wires curling from the ceiling and broken shelves littering the floor. A single emergency bulb buzzed overhead, casting a sickly yellow light.

They filed in quietly and shut the door.

Robin leaned against a wall, letting her breath slow. The others gathered around a low crate. Ashley was already unzipping her satchel.

She booted up the stolen tablet and linked it to her sim band. "We've got donor IDs, blacked out transfer destinations, and fragments of a program called Recovery Cycle V2. It's biotech. A reanimation tied to neural adaptation."

Robin raised an eyebrow. "Meaning?"

Ashley's voice was steadier. "They're modifying people, not just bringing them back. They're tethering resurrection to programming. It could explain what happened to you."

Robin bit her bottom lip as the pieces fell into place. "I get it. The modification caused the virus. But how did the Academy get a hold of the modified bodies?"

Jude stopped pacing. "They didn't. Not knowingly. If this place is feeding candidates back into Academy intake, someone's rigging the resurrection chain upstream. Filtering infected subjects into training under false pretenses."

David stepped forward. "This one has a live ID," he said, pointing to a name on the screen. "Timestamp is only four days ago. Says 'observed phase compliant.'"

Robin stared. "That's a tracking log. Someone came through here and passed their test."

Jude paced near the door. "This place is more than a ring. It's a proving ground."

He glanced back at them, jaw tight. "If they can slip their modified candidates into Academy training, they get access to combat data, magical response metrics, maybe even see how far the infection can go without detection. The Academy tests their limits for them, for free."

David's expression darkened. "And the ones who pass? What are they being groomed for?"

Jude didn't answer right away. Then, he said quietly, "Deployment. Control. Maybe even replacement. If the Masked Circle can prove stability, they can embed these modified cadets anywhere. Think governments, magical guilds, or even inside the Academy leadership."

He looked at Robin. "And my guess is you're still being tested. The infection didn't end with your resurrection; it started something they're still watching." His voice dropped a note lower. "And if they decide the results are promising enough… they'll come for you. One way or another."

Ashley clicked her tongue. "We've got a lot, but it's all fragments. The list of recipients is cut off."

Robin stepped back from the screen, her stomach tight. "This is real life Body Snatchers," she muttered. "Only I'm not the one getting replaced, I'm the prototype." She crossed her arms, hugging her body. "So, we don't know where they're sending the bodies."

"Or which ones are being modified," Ashley added. "But if I can get a clean shot of the guy in the red hoodie, I might be able to run a facial ID match. I saw him enter from the back hallway, near the admin office."

David nodded. "Still in the stands. I clocked him during the last match."

Robin paused. Her eyes scanned the narrow room, her mind already shifting gears. "Then we go back, just long enough. Get the ID and drop a tracker if we can. Then we vanish."

Jude looked up. "That's a risk."

"Everything is a risk," Robin replied. "But if we leave now, we leave with questions. And I'm done with questions."

No one argued. They geared back up.

Minutes later, they slipped out of the maintenance room and retraced their steps through the damp corridor, the muffled roar of the crowd growing louder with every turn. The stairwell creaked beneath their boots as they climbed back toward the main floor. By the time they reached the edge of the arena, the noise had swallowed them whole once again with the pulsing lights, a fresh match underway, and the chaos of the crowd pressing in from all sides. They weren't done yet. This was just recon. They were there to get the ID, drop the tracker, and disappear into the annex before anyone noticed they'd been hunting for more than bloodsport.

Shouts rang out around the cage, echoing off the bare walls. Sweat and adrenaline mingled in the air, and the back of Robin's neck prickled with tension she didn't realize she was holding.

She hovered at the edge of the throng, breathing steady and chest tight. Ashley stood close, pink hair twisted into a practical knot, eyes scanning the ring with practiced focus. Her gaze moved with purpose. She was watching fighters, memorizing faces, and tracking patterns in the betting slips changing hands. Around them, gamblers shoved forward, barking odds on undead brawlers trading heavy, deliberate blows beneath bare overhead lights. Each hit landed like a countdown. Robin's stomach clenched, but she didn't look away. This wasn't just a spectacle. Somewhere in the chaos, someone had left a clue about who had stolen her life, and why.

A few ragtag enforcers loomed near a makeshift barrier, guarding the ringmaster's transaction booth. Robin considered slipping behind them while Ashley created a distraction, already pulling a compact sensor jammer from her belt pouch.

A surge of excited chatter at the entrance snagged her attention.

She spotted movement near the edge of the stands. Someone was cutting through the crowd with precision, hood up, and a familiar gait. It was David. She hadn't seen him break off, but of course he had. Recon was one of his specialties.

He drifted closer as the crowd roared over a fresh knockout. When his eyes found hers, she saw the flicker of relief behind them. She gave him the briefest of nods.

"Slipped into a security hub near the betting corridor," he murmured, voice low as he joined her near the back railing. "Found overwritten resurrection entries. They looked scrubbed, but not clean. Your name showed up, once. Flagged, then erased."

Robin's pulse kicked. "Erased how?"

"Replaced with generic entries. No death timestamp. No Academy cross reference. If they logged it, it never went public."

Her hand moved instinctively to the inside of her forearm, covering the Hellhound mark. "You find anything else?"

David pulled a folded slip from his coat. "Reroute logs. And an address. It was tagged as a holding site. No staff signatures. That's where you were taken."

Robin took the slip and slid it into her sleeve. "We hit it after this."

David nodded, eyes scanning the floor. "Whoever set

this up didn't expect anyone to look twice. They should've known better."

Robin exhaled slowly, her voice steady. "Yeah. They should've."

A hush rippled through the basement as the ringmaster announced the next match, his voice crackling through a microphone that had seen better days. The crowd pressed forward, a volatile mix of locals, thrill seekers, and the kind of people who stayed off official records. Faces were half hidden by hoodies or streaked in neon tattoos, they shouted and shoved, their breath steaming in the dank underground air. The stench of sweat, blood, and PBR clung to everything. Bits of old signage and mismatched wiring flickered overhead, casting the room in a grim, pulsing glow. The crowd shifted, and on the far side of the cage Robin spotted Jude.

He didn't look angry, just focused. The set of his jaw was as severe as ever, but his stance was more protective than punitive. Not the man who had once threatened to haul them in, but someone who understood just how deep this mess ran and wanted the same answers.

Robin straightened instinctively, tension flickering in her chest. She still didn't trust him completely, but something about the way he scanned the crowd, not just for threats, but for exits, made her wonder if he wasn't just following orders. Maybe he was stuck in the system, same as them. "Who are you, really?" she muttered.

David edged closer, his voice low. "I hit the archives. Found an entry from the night you died. Your name was in it," he said, keeping the words to a minimum, just like their training. "Buried in the routing logs, tied to a shell group connected to these fights."

Robin's eyes narrowed. "The ringmaster?"

David nodded. "Not just him. It's a network. This isn't some street level resurrection hustle. It's structured. Funded."

Her hands balled into fists. "Then we need a link. Something traceable."

Before David could respond, a startled murmur rose from a nearby row of gamblers, heads turning like a ripple on water. Robin followed their gaze, and there she was again.

Wren had found her way to the fight club. Her sister stood there in the same combat boots and flannel from their last meeting in the alley near the Sixth Street clubs.

She was pushing through the crowd, her expression resolute. "You left without saying when you'd see me again," she said when she got close enough, her voice low but firm. "I waited, but you never showed. So, I started following the trail myself."

"You are really good at this. A little too good." Robin stepped forward automatically, aware of the shifting attention from the crowd. "You warned me this was bigger than I realized. You were right."

Wren's eyes softened. "I knew you needed me. Not just hoped, I knew. The pull, the one Mom used to talk about... it flared up stronger than ever. I felt something shift, like a thread inside me tightening. That's how I found you. You didn't know I'd already started asking questions before you found me, did you?"

Robin blinked. "What kind of questions? Are you safe?"

"You remember what I said about Evangeline?" Wren asked, stepping closer. "About how she helped me after your funeral? Turns out, she knew a lot more than she said. She told me to disappear, to stay off the grid, but she never mentioned you might come back. When I saw you that night in the alley and told her... she didn't even blink. Like she'd been waiting for it. Evangeline never told me you might be alive."

"Kind of alive." Robin stared at her. "You think she was part of it?"

"I don't know if she was in on it. But she's always been three steps ahead. And she definitely didn't seem surprised."

Robin's jaw tightened. "Why would she keep that from me?"

"Because she doesn't seem to trust anyone. And maybe because she thought I'd get in the way."

David reappeared at Robin's side, glancing warily around them. "We've got company watching us. If she's going to be here, she needs to move now."

Robin glanced at Wren. "You shouldn't have come."

"I had to," Wren said. "You're into something deep. I could feel it, even before we talked last time. After you left, I couldn't stop thinking about that glow in your eyes and the way you hesitated when I asked what they did to you. You're not just some ghost wandering a second life, Robin. You're my sister. You think I was going to sit in my apartment and hope you didn't get erased again?"

Ashley joined them, voice taut. "Fight's ending. If the ringmaster notices her, it's over."

Jude approached, keeping a close eye on the crowd

surrounding them. "She's got guts, I'll give her that. But guts won't keep her alive down here."

Wren's chin lifted. "You're the one who told her not to get too close to the living, right? Well, too late. I'm here, I saw her. I'm not going anywhere until I know she's safe."

Robin pulled Wren aside by the elbow. "Listen to me. You showing up here, this isn't just risky. It's bait. The wrong people see us talking, and you're a target. I need to finish this, and you need to walk out of here. Now."

Wren searched Robin's face, her jaw tight. "You remember anything else? What happened to you? Why they brought you back?" She hesitated, then added, "And don't forget the pull. You can reach out with it, too. Not just feel me but call me back. We could always feel each other. That hasn't changed."

"Not all of it," Robin said. "But I'm starting to remember what matters, and that includes you. Right now, I have to finish this. But after that, we talk. Everything."

The words must have landed because Wren gave the smallest nod. "Then finish it. And come find me."

"I will," Robin whispered.

Jude glanced behind them. "Time's up. Bouncers are spreading out."

Wren's hand squeezed Robin's one last time. "I'll go. But I'm not disappearing either, just so you know."

Robin held her gaze. "I wouldn't expect anything less."

Wren hesitated before turning. "You remember the lake? That last trip we took before everything fell apart? You were quiet the whole time. I thought it was about school... but I think it was already starting."

Robin's breath caught. The lake. Bits of memory

sparked of birdsong, and wet earth, Wren handing her a cup of coffee and asking if she was okay.

"I wasn't okay," Robin said softly. "And I didn't know how to say it. I still don't know what it was, though."

"You didn't have to," Wren replied. "But next time, you will."

She touched Robin's hand once more but paused. Her fingers skimmed the surface, and her brow furrowed.

"Your hand feels off," Wren said, her brow tightening as she held it a moment longer. "Not cold, exactly... just not warm either. And the texture, it's like your skin isn't yours anymore. Like it doesn't remember being alive."

Robin glanced down. "They didn't fix anything. They just hit restart and dropped me back in like I hadn't been gone. Whatever death did to me, I'm still carrying it."

"You always tried to carry it all yourself," Wren said quietly. "Just remember, I've been carrying the weight too. We're connected, forever. This side or another. You're not alone, even if you come back broken."

Wren's hand squeezed Robin's one last time, but her eyes drifted past her sister's shoulder. She stiffened.

"There's a man near the north exit," she murmured. "He's been trailing me since I got down here. I thought I lost him in the service corridor."

Robin didn't turn. "Security?"

"Maybe. But he's not watching the fights, he's watching people. Faces. He clocked me when I walked in and hasn't looked away."

Robin clenched her jaw. "Why would anyone be following you?"

"I don't know. Maybe it's someone from the Academy

who caught wind of my digging. Or maybe Evangeline's silence wasn't just caution, it was cover."

Robin exhaled. "Then disappear. Lay low."

"I will," Wren said. But not for good. You'll find me at the place by the lake. The one with the fire pit."

Robin met her eyes. "I'll be there."

Wren gave a final nod, then turned and vanished into the crowd with practiced ease, like someone who had already mapped her escape.

David leaned in. "You okay?"

Robin didn't answer right away. Her heart wasn't pounding, technically it couldn't, but the ache was just as loud.

Jude looked between them. "We move now. The ringmaster's shifting his focus."

Robin nodded once. "Let's finish what we started."

The ringmaster's voice cracked through the last murmurs of the crowd like static peeling off an old wire. He flipped off the mic, and the hush that followed sank into Robin's bones. It wasn't silence. It was expectation, raw, and electric. Heads turned in their direction, suspicion blooming in the space where spectacle had lived just moments before.

Robin took a breath, deep and steady, brushing away the sting Wren's departure had left behind. She squared her shoulders. "Let's move. And Jude, try not to slow us down."

They had drifted toward the upper stands again, letting the press of bodies and the noise of the next fight swallow them whole. Most eyes were fixed on the cage, making it easier to blend in.

Robin kept scanning the edges. Her voice was low, almost a murmur. "We're too exposed here."

Jude nodded subtly. "There. Behind the crates near that old cart."

Robin followed his gaze and caught it. It was a narrow stairwell that was tucked behind a rusted service shelf, half obscured by shadows and motion. She leaned back slightly, enough for David and Ashley to clock the location.

David moved up beside her, voice barely audible. "That's our way in?"

Jude's reply was a grunt. "Yeah. Annex corridor. Control room's down there."

Robin gave a tight nod. "Then we finish this."

Jude gave her a sidelong glance, mouth twitching like he wanted to say something, but he only muttered, "Don't do anything dumb," and took point.

They slipped into the current of bodies. The crowd hadn't thinned, but its attention had. People pressed closer to the cage again, riding the high of blood and spectacle. Robin kept her steps light, calculated. The press of bodies made her skin crawl.

David moved up beside her, his face drawn and alert, scanning sightlines, exits, every twitch of movement. Ashley fell in behind them, her movements sharp and deliberate. Her usual habit, chewing the inside of her lip when plotting, was gone, replaced by a stillness that looked more like readiness than fear. Her jaw was locked, eyes tracking every shadow. The stolen tablet was pressed flat under her jacket, shielded like a live wire. Without breaking stride, she brushed her thumb twice against her thigh. It was a silent signal Robin would recognize from training. Eyes up, danger close.

Overhead, Phoenix cawed once from a rusted beam, a flurry of feathers and irritation. Robin tilted her chin just enough to catch him in her peripheral. "Yeah, yeah," she whispered. "We're going."

Jude muscled through a knot of spectators with a firm elbow and a murmured warning. David mirrored him on the other side. Robin stayed fluid, pulse thumping not from fear, but drive. She felt the throb of unfinished business deep in her chest, dull and constant. Wren's voice still echoed, fierce and clear. Her face, determined, too brave for her own good, wouldn't leave Robin's mind.

Every part of her wanted to run after Wren, pull her out of the building, get her somewhere safe. But that wasn't the mission. Not now. Besides, Wren wouldn't have let her do it.

Robin gritted her teeth. *Focus. Get the evidence. Shut it all down.*

They were nearing the far side of the club, where fighters disappeared between matches and the real deals got made. The shadows were thicker there, layered with smoke and stale sweat. Bouncers drifted through, eyes sharp, hands never far from the weapons strapped to their thighs.

She kept her voice low as they passed another knot of gamblers. "Stick to the plan. Ashley, how's the signal?"

Ashley didn't slow. "Holding. I spoofed our trail three exits back. If they're tracking, they're chasing ghosts."

David gave a small nod. "Smart. We keep tight and finish this. Then we find that address."

Robin glanced sideways. "You still have it?"

He tapped his jacket. "Safe."

Jude's voice cut in from the front. "Stairwell coming up. Looks like the corridor to the control annex."

Robin took the lead beside him. "That's where we dig."

Behind her, the crowd surged with renewed interest. A new match was firing up with more noise, more distraction. But Robin felt the attention brushing their backs like a loaded trigger. There were too many eyes. Too much interest.

She looked back, scanning for any sign of Wren.

Gone. Smart. Fast. Just like Robin remembered.

She swept the stands again, searching for the man in the red hoodie. Nothing. Either he'd already vanished, or he'd made them first. So much for planting a tracker.

David leaned in slightly. "You good?"

Robin exhaled through her nose. "Not even close."

He didn't smile, but his voice held something close to reassurance. "Doesn't matter. You're leading us anyway."

They turned down the stairwell. The noise above dimmed, but not completely. Boots hit metal, then concrete. Robin's fingers brushed the hilt of her knife. She didn't expect to use it. But she'd be damned if she hesitated again.

Every instinct screamed that they were walking into the belly of the machine. But if this was the heart of the ring, it was where she'd tear it out.

And this time, no one, especially not Wren, was going to pay the price for her unfinished past.

They reached the far side of the arena just as the ring

lights flared to life. A new match was being set up, but this time the spectacle wasn't just inside the cage, it was her.

Robin stepped forward, feeling the others pull back, fading into the crowd for cover. Jude flanked her right but stayed just out of reach. Ashley hovered near the corner with the tablet hugged to her chest. David melted into the shadows across from her, eyes sharp and ready.

Robin planted her boots near the cage's edge, the heat from overhead bulbs baking into her jacket. The floor was tacky underfoot, and the scent of blood, sweat, Axe body spray and cheap liquor thick in her nose. Around her, the noise shifted to curious, and hushed, like prey sensing the arrival of a new predator.

The ringmaster was already moving toward the cage, a silhouette of sleek menace in a shimmering coat.

Robin didn't flinch. She locked eyes with him. "I'm done hiding," she muttered to herself.

A hush swept through the pit. Let them watch.

CHAPTER EIGHTEEN

A jolt of tension shot through Robin as she stood at the edge of the makeshift cage. The stank of the crowd was mingling with something indefinably darker. Seeing Wren vanish in the sea of bodies was harder than she had expected. Even though Robin didn't remember everything about her, she still felt a pull toward her.

She had thought the place was seedy before, but watching the ringmaster step inside the chainlink enclosure made everything feel far worse. He was tall enough to look over most heads, dressed in that sleek coat that shimmered beneath erratic lights. His pale skin and glossy black hair gave him the eerie look of a human mannequin. Then his lips curled into a vicious grin aimed straight at her.

Robin forced her shoulders back. She hated feeling cornered, but this was his territory. She knew she had to stand her ground. Any sign of weakness would be blood in the water, and the watchers around the cage seemed to savor the smell of even undead fear. Her sleeve had gotten hitched, exposing part of her tattoo. Some noticed the

Hellhound mark, pointing and muttering "Academy rat" or "Hellhound" as if spitting curses.

She searched the crowd for Ashley first. A flash of pink hair popped into view near a cracked support column, then disappeared again behind the bulk of a roaring spectator. Ashley was still clutching the stolen tablet close, her gaze darting—not panicked, but calculating. She was already scanning escape paths, mapping angles like she was still running simulations back in the Academy lab. Robin exhaled. Ashley wasn't frozen, she was preparing.

David hovered nearby, partially concealed by the crowd, his hood low but his posture rigid. That tight jaw said everything. He was ready for things to go sideways.

Jude prowled the edge of the ring with his disruptor drawn but low, the look in his eyes sharp and grounded. Focused. He wasn't here to pull rank; he was here to keep them alive. Robin finally got it. He was on their side, her side. *Maybe.*

The ringmaster pressed elegant fingers against the cage's metal links. He smiled, a gold crown displayed prominently in the front. Then he spoke, his voice surprisingly smooth. "I've been expecting a nosy Hellhound," he said, his gaze locked on Robin. "I never guessed it would be you again." He flicked an imaginary speck of dirt from his sleeve. "You look a bit worn around the edges."

Robin swallowed. Her pulse thundered in her ears, and the Hellhound mark on her forearm flared cold. The ringmaster had seen her here before. She longed to snap back, but instead she drew a slow breath. "You should change your décor," she said at last. "Screams health code violation."

Weapons and fists sprouted among the audience behind her. Men and women with vacant stares stepped away from the ring and formed a loose circle around the cage. The ringmaster gave a theatrical wave to his thralls. "These are just some of my customers," he announced. "Those who didn't choose the Academy path have other options here. And people say capitalism is dead."

He laughed at his own joke. Robin listened to the hollow note of it and felt revulsion stir in her gut. This clown carried a brand of arrogance even the Academy higher-ups lacked. Worse, the thralls in front of him moved with no natural rhythm. Their chests rose and fell in short, unnatural gasps, and their eyes were distant. Whatever had dragged them back from the underworld clearly lacked the Academy's playbook of reanimation.

David sidled next to Robin. His dark brown hair was damp with sweat, and he looked between the ringmaster and the growing circle of onlookers. "Where's Jude?" he asked, his voice low. He kept his back close to Robin's in a show of solidarity, and she could almost feel the tension in his muscles, ready to defend.

"Stalking the outer ring, presumably," she answered. She soon spotted Jude's silhouette weaving through the haze. He looked coiled for violence, and a dark part of her appreciated that. Common ground sometimes showed up in strange places.

She noticed the ringmaster's attention drift. He gestured toward the raised platform at the center. "I believe you're interrupting my show. But I'll indulge you, since you're so very intrigued by my operation. Unchecked resurrections, scandalous, yes?" He laughed again, the sound scraping along Robin's nerves.

Before she could reply, the ringmaster signaled to one of his underlings, and lights glimmered erratically across the old basement. The air in front of Robin shivered, revealing faint outlines. They were specters, half there and half not, lurking among the living watchers. The illusions made the place look even more like a carnival of horrors.

A wave of panic rippled through the crowd, though some onlookers roared with excitement. Robin felt David tense at her side. She wondered if she should have grabbed a baseball bat on her way in. Instead, she balled her fists. "Stop messing around," she said, her voice pitched low so only David heard. "We're not leaving without shutting this place down."

A crash erupted from the far side of the ring. Several thralls stumbled forward, swiping at Jude, who moved like a knife in the dark. His disruptor flared, and he unleashed arcs of punishing energy into the nearest thrall's torso. The creature dropped to its knees, but more advanced on Jude with slack-jawed persistence.

Robin caught sight of Ashley near a cluster of crates. She looked small and pale, but her eyes shone with determination, and the bright pink hair was the only cheerful color in this misery pit. She raised a strange remote, presumably the one she had snagged from a table earlier, and pressed a button.

A pulse stuttered through the basement, a strobing wave that warped the air. Several spectators shimmered, revealing wraithlike forms that had been possessing them. The illusions wavered. One ghostly shape turned in

Robin's direction, confusion and a raw hunger twisting its expression.

The ringmaster moved faster than she expected. He grabbed a chain from the cage wall and snapped it toward the wraith. Sparks briefly danced across the ghost, driving it back. He grinned at Robin. "Neat trick, right? My illusions keep the party interesting, but I do hate a messy scene." Then he glanced at Ashley with a sneer. "You and your friends meddle where you don't belong. Some of us provide valuable services. If the Academy doesn't want to resurrect them, I certainly will."

Robin felt a surge of anger at the dismissive way he referred to "services." She remembered her own forcibly revived state. If this man had anything to do with her death or the ritual that put her in the Academy's crosshairs, she wanted answers. She lunged forward, ignoring David's cautioning gesture.

Thralls lunged as well. One, a stocky figure with glazed eyes, caught Robin's arm. She pivoted and hooked her leg around his knee. With a sharp twist, she took him down onto the pitted concrete and hissed through her teeth. He fell, but he didn't make a sound. The emptiness was worse than any moan of pain could have been.

Ashley's frantic but measured voice echoed from somewhere behind a cluster of watchers. "Robin, there are more of them popping out of the crowd. This is insane."

Robin ducked as another thrall swung a metal pipe at her head. She lunged again and drove an elbow into the creature's ribs. "We've got to end this now," she cried back.

Snarls and wordless groans filled the air. Jude had fought his way to the corner of the cage's platform and was systematically taking down thrall after thrall with energized shots from his disruptor. David leaped to block a pair of thralls from flanking Robin and jammed a heavy wooden stick into one's shoulder. The stick cracked with the impact, but he followed through and hooked a swift kick that shoved the thrall back.

The ringmaster strolled around the perimeter as though he were watching a casual sporting event. His eyes glinted with malice. "You Hellhound brats think you're so righteous," he taunted, his voice carrying over the din. "Tell me something. Shouldn't every soul have a chance to return?" He swept his hand toward the cage door.

Robin clenched her fists. "Don't preach at me. You're making a profit off the desperate."

He gave a false, theatrical bow. "Believe what you want, but your beloved Academy has no monopoly on second chances. Someone had to fill that void." He pressed a fingertip to his lips, his gaze sliding to her forearm. "That mark you wear? It's more of a brand than you realize. Even your instructors know it."

Her body trembled with anger she struggled to contain. "Tell me what you know about my murder," she demanded, her voice tight. "Is your operation linked to that ritual?"

He offered a lazy blink. "I've got a list of potential recruits that covers half of Austin, but I wouldn't mind taking a peek at your name next. Plenty of old clients prefer anonymity, of course, and that keeps business interesting. Maybe you were a special arrangement."

Robin's stomach twisted. Something in the ringmaster's words suggested deeper entanglements. She thought of the suspicious files David had seen in the Academy's database and the incomplete logs about her untimely death. It all pointed to something bigger and more twisted than one scumbag selling reanimations in a grimy basement.

If she was already at the Academy, what list could he possibly mean? Unless… she hadn't been meant for the Academy at all. Someone had tagged her for something else—another resurrection track, another purpose. And somewhere between the river and waking up underground, she'd been rerouted.

Not rescued. Claimed.

She didn't escape the system. She just landed in a different one. She looked around, searching for Wren. Her sister had been here earlier, right by the cage's edge, looking horrified. Now she was nowhere to be seen. Relief flooded her that Wren had vanished, but a part of her hurt at the distance. She still had countless questions for her sister.

A wet gurgle shattered her thoughts. One of the thralls had cornered Ashley near a tall stack of crates. Ashley fumbled with the stolen remote and pressed buttons that sent sporadic waves of distortion racing through the illusions. The thrall managed to pin her arm for a moment. Robin kicked off the side of the ring, crossed the space in a heartbeat, and slammed her shoulder into the creature's midsection, sending it sprawling. She helped Ashley to her feet.

Ashley's breath rushed out fast. Whatever fear she felt hadn't frozen her, though. She squeezed Robin's hand in thanks and brandished the remote again. "I messed with some settings on this. It's shorting out the illusions, but there are too many thralls."

David approached, stepping over unconscious bodies. One of them kept a cramped grip on his pant leg, and he had to pry the hand off before he reached them, his face grim. "We need a plan," he said. "If the ringmaster gets out of here, we lose our chance to interrogate him."

Robin's eyes snapped to the cage, where the ringmaster had turned, ready to vanish through a narrow opening in the chain link. Jude saw him, too. He fired a beam of disruptor energy, but a thrall lunged into the path and dropped in a lifeless heap. The ringmaster smirked, stepped through the gap, and nodded to unseen allies along the side.

"All right, asshole," Robin growled, pushing her way to intercept him. Specters glimmered in the air, half formed echoes of lost souls forced into a warped half-life. She ignored the jabs of fear and focused on the ringmaster's smug expression. "This place is its own version of hell."

She cornered him near the far edge of the cage, blocking his path to the exit. He looked almost amused. "That's enough," she said, her pulse thundering in her ears. "You're going to tell me who's funding this operation and how you got your hands on my name."

He lifted his chin. "I can't give you all my secrets on a silver platter. The web behind this place is bigger than you and me. Good luck unraveling it."

Movement from the crowd told Robin they were about to be interrupted again. Something about the ringmaster told her he counted on that disruption.

A fresh wave of thralls pushed inward, forcing Robin to back up. Jude crashed across the makeshift platform, firing scathing bursts of disruptor energy at the mindless horde.

He yelled, "Academy cleanup crews are on their way. Get ready to bail."

David shouted, "We still need the ringmaster or a lead. We can't walk out empty handed."

Robin whirled in time to see the ringmaster slip away, sliding around the corner of the cage. She thumped a thrall aside in frustration, sending it spinning. She caught a glimpse of the ringmaster's shiny dark coat vanishing into the swirling mass of bodies and tangle of illusions.

Ashley's remote kicked out another burst, sending more specters reeling. Some in the crowd shrieked, and a few toppled over in confusion. The illusions around them sputtered and revealed half the watchers as possessed or enthralled. It was a grotesque scene of people with mouths parted in silent screams, and phantoms gliding in and out of bodies like discarded shells.

Jude smashed his gunstock into a thrall's face, then yelled in Robin's direction, "We have to contain this before your backup from the Academy storms in. If they see you this deep in ring operations, it's not going to look good."

Robin knew he was right. While Jude nominally had official standing to be in the field, she was supposed to be under tight Academy watch. This was not exactly an approved mission, but she refused to leave these thralls to keep prowling. Her conscience snarled.

David pointed at one of the side exits. "We can corner the stragglers in that corridor, trap them until the Academy shows up, or at least keep them from running off into the streets."

Ashley's face shone with sweat, pink hair matted to her forehead. "I'll do the same if they try to slip away. It's messing up the illusions. Maybe it will keep them from scattering too fast."

"Thank you, Ashley. Jude, can you handle the ones out here? I'll help David block the exit. Maybe that'll keep the ringmaster from doubling back."

Jude nodded and fired two more disruptor shots, dropping a pair of thralls that had advanced on him. "Make it fast."

As Robin sprinted across the open floor, several watchers who had been possessed collapsed, their phantom riders forced out by Ashley's glitching remote. Wails rang out from half formed ghosts twisting in the air. Over it all came the scuffle of thralls, pinned or cornered, some moaning, some snarling in unusual tones.

Robin's breath came in harsh bursts she didn't need. Adrenaline still coursed through her undead veins, getting perilously close to her limits. She slid next to David and braced herself at the corridor entrance. He placed a hand on her shoulder, his expression anxious. "You all right?"

She nodded, scanning the swirling chaos behind them. "I'll survive," she muttered with a grim attempt at humor. Her chest tightened with frustration. The ringmaster had answers, and now he was gone.

Thralls rushed the corridor, forcing them to redouble their defense. Robin slammed her fist into the first one's temple, sending him staggering into another thrall. David kicked out, hooked a leg behind the second thrall's knees, and dropped her in a heap. They pressed forward, bodies piling around them in a gruesome cluster.

For a scorching moment, Robin caught a flash of memory. Panic surged as she thought it might be a clue, then it vanished too quickly to grasp. There was no time to ponder before another thrall lunged, teeth bared, and she rammed a forearm across its throat, driving it back.

A faint roar outside the corridor told her Jude was still battling the remaining illusions and thralls. In her peripheral vision she could see Ashley's bright hair wove among the last scattered foes, the remote in her hand. Sparks darted across the concrete floor, revealing more half formed shapes. The moans rose in a mournful chorus, and a chill crawled up Robin's spine.

When the final thrall collapsed, she and David looked around, panting out of excitement more than need. A handful of watchers lay strewn on the floor, some groaning, others still. The illusions seemed to be fading. Ashley studied the device in her grip and let out a shaky laugh. "I have no idea how this thing works, but at least it's messing up their illusions."

Jude fought his way to them. His hair was a sweaty tangle, and the front of his jacket was torn. He surveyed the thralls, the stunned watchers, and the swirling remnants of specters with a grim scowl. "Academy forces will be here any minute," he said. "We need to clear the path for them, or they'll blast the place to rubble."

Robin lifted her chin. Anger coiled inside her, fed by the ringmaster's parting words. She took in what remained of the fight club. The dark corners pulsing with leftover illusions, thralls sprawled on the ground, and the hush of people who had either fled or passed out.

Fortunately, Wren had vanished. But the ringmaster had vanished too. A creeping realization remained that something bigger lay behind all this. The ringmaster's cryptic hints about her death rattled in her mind like a warning bell.

She set her jaw and exchanged a look with David and Ashley. Jude watched her intently, the glow of his disruptor reflecting off his face. She felt the weight of her next decision. Despite the adrenaline raging inside her, she knew they had reached the moment of no return. If the Academy found them in the middle of this ring, it would lead to questions, but she wasn't about to walk away silently.

Behind them, the illusions sputtered out. A few thralls stumbled in confusion, collapsing next to battered seats and trashed crates. Sirens wailed from above the basement, though they sounded faint. The cavalry was coming, promised or not.

Robin squared her shoulders. She spotted the ringmaster's exit route, still open. The man had melted into the night. Fury, sadness, and a gnawing sense of unfinished business twisted in her chest. She clenched her fists, glancing at Ashley and David one last time before turning back toward Jude. "We end this fight club right now," she said. "But we're not done hunting that bastard or figuring out who paid for my death."

A tense hush followed her words, broken only by uneven footsteps from thralls struggling to stand. "Let's do it." Jude gestured for David and Ashley to join him. Together, they pushed through the final scattering of enthralled watchers, checking to ensure no stragglers escaped. Robin could taste her anger, raw and bitter.

A final wave of thralls stumbled forward, and she extended her arm, just as David stepped in to help. Ashley toggled the remote, sending a disorienting burst into the air. The thralls faltered. Jude aimed his disruptor. Robin felt her breath catch as the last group came crashing in, bodies colliding with battered aluminum chairs and the chainlink fence.

The basement trembled with harsh energy, and she braced herself for the incoming onslaught, resolved to break the ringmaster's stranglehold on second chances. Her murder might be tangled in all this, and she would not let the truth slip away again. "We have to find him."

CHAPTER NINETEEN

They quickly made their way outside. "Where did he go?" Robin spun in a circle, trying to catch a glimpse or some clue that would tell her where to go next to find the Ringmaster. But there was nothing.

Ashley scanned the alley's edge. "That fast? Someone must've helped him."

Phoenix gave a sharp chirp and circled once, talons twitching. He landed beside a discarded earpiece, its outer ring still faintly glowing.

"That's Academy issue," David muttered, frowning. "He didn't just run—he got tipped off."

The alley stank of piss and fried oil, but the group was only pausing long enough to check the street. Robin pressed herself to the graffiti tagged wall, her tattoo a metronome of rage and instinct. The night's failed confrontation still clung to her skin like smoke, but she couldn't let it distract her. The ringmaster had slipped their grasp, but David's hand was already reaching into his jacket.

He held up the folded slip of paper between two fingers, his forehead wrinkled.

Robin stared at it like it was cursed.

David's voice was low. "We don't get another window like this."

Ashley shifted beside her, pink hair damp with sweat, the stolen tablet still clutched against her ribs. "Academy enforcers are swarming the club. If we cut through the warehouse blocks, we can hit the address before they finish their sweep."

Jude narrowed his eyes. "It's a risk."

"Everything's a risk," Robin snapped. "I've been dead once already. Let's see what's worth dying for again."

Jude didn't argue. That alone told her how serious things had gotten.

They moved fast.

Fifteen minutes later, the city seemed to fold in on itself with strip malls giving way to crumbling warehouses, dead end alleys, and long forgotten streets that never made it into tourist maps. Robin had no memory of this area, but something in her body tensed with recognition. A bone deep thrum. The kind of dread you didn't inherit—you earned.

David came to a halt at the corner of a weed choked lot. "There," he said, pointing to a squat building flanked by rusted fencing and an overturned food cart.

The address wasn't marked. There was just a steel, windowless door bolted twice over.

Ashley frowned. "No lights. No alarms."

"That's worse," Jude muttered. "It's supposed to look abandoned."

Robin stepped closer. Her Hellhound mark burned faintly, a whisper of heat against her skin. She touched the wall with two fingers. Cold. Gritty. Real.

But it didn't feel empty.

"Let's go," she said.

David unshouldered his baton, flipping a switch that sent a faint shimmer down the shaft. Ashley activated a low frequency scan on her tablet, and Jude produced a flat bladed override tool from inside his jacket. In ten seconds, the outer lock clicked.

The inside smelled of formaldehyde and rot.

The entryway was small and suffocating, a narrow corridor choked with stacked crates and plastic sheeting. Ashley swept her tablet's light in a slow arc, scanning for movement.

"No heat signatures," she whispered. "But this place is... layered. Like someone's trying to mask what really happened here."

David stepped past her, sweeping the space with careful eyes. "Whoever used this last didn't leave in a hurry. They covered their tracks."

"Or cleaned up a mess," Jude said.

Robin's hands curled into fists. Every cell in her reanimated body wanted to turn around and leave. But her mind wouldn't let her.

She pushed deeper.

At the back of the hallway was a second door, this one splintered from the inside, as if something had broken out.

Robin crouched to inspect the shards. Her vision sharpened in the low light. There were faint boot scuffs... and drag marks.

"Someone was held here," she said. "Or worse."

David lifted a small object from the floor. It was a half melted silver coin, crusted with soot and etched with a symbol Robin didn't recognize.

Jude hissed. "That's Masked Circle currency. High tier. Used to buy favors, rituals, even souls."

Robin's stomach turned.

They pushed into the next room.

It wasn't large, but the layout was deliberate. A wide, open concrete space circled with scorched marks and embedded drain lines. Robin's boots crunched over shattered glass and blackened residue. The smell hit her next of a chemical burn mixed with something organic, like spoiled copper.

In the center, a low slab of concrete jutted from the floor. It was a platform streaked with old fluids, and rust around the edges. "Looks like something medical," whispered Ashley. "It looks like a place where things were tested."

David halted behind her. "This wasn't a lab," he said, his voice tight. "It was a staging site."

Robin stepped closer, her chest going tight. The air shimmered in front of her. There was something about the space that held memory like a static charge.

She reached out and touched the slab.

The room dropped away and her eyes rolled into the back of her head.

She was back in a haze of noise and cold. Not water, something thicker. Something like smoke with weight. Her limbs were heavy. Her mind buzzed and flickered. Figures moved around her in blurred motion, faces half lit by flickering overhead bulbs.

Hands strapped her down. A voice murmured something clinical. Not a language she didn't understand. Instead, *terms* she didn't remember agreeing to. She felt pressure in her chest, behind her eyes. And then a sting in her neck.

Then her name.

Robin Sullivan.

Not shouted. Not called. *Logged.*

As if someone was confirming: *Subject identified. Begin process.*

Her vision went white.

Robin stumbled back from the platform, nearly falling, blinking rapidly.

David caught her by the elbow. "You okay?"

She didn't answer right away. Her eyes were wide, breath shallow, hands trembling.

"They processed me here," she said at last. "I was being... examined. Tagged. Like an asset."

Ashley's face paled. "Then this was the first step."

Robin nodded. "And someone made sure I walked out alive. Did I agree to this? They knew who I was. It wasn't random."

Ashley's voice cracked. "This was the site where you were infected."

Robin nodded, jaw tight. "And maybe not just me."

Jude moved around the platform's edge, inspecting the walls.

"Found something," he said, prying loose a panel behind a rusted cabinet.

Inside was a hidden alcove lined with scorched folders and three glass vials filled with dark red fluid. Ashley scanned them.

"Blood samples. Active resonance markers. If these are linked to past infections, we can match them to cadets."

David pulled a folder from the top of the pile. It was partially burned, but Robin's eyes caught the remnants of a typed heading:

SUBJECT: SULLIVAN, R. — DESIGNATION: ECHO FLARE INITIATIVE

Robin froze as Ashley grabbed a second folder. "Another subject. This one... Wren."

"They planned to take both of us," Robin said softly.

Jude looked grim. "And someone changed the plan. They rerouted you. Maybe saved you. Or maybe... delayed whatever was supposed to happen."

Robin burned with sudden clarity. "They didn't just kill me. They tested me. They were waiting to see what I became."

She grabbed the Sullivan file and tucked it into her jacket. "No more waiting."

Sudden static crackled from Ashley's tablet.

"Movement—outside. Two, maybe three figures. Human."

Jude took point, voice flat. "Time's up."

Robin grabbed the second file, the one marked Wren, and bolted after him. They exited through a side hallway that led to a half collapsed garage. Lights flickered behind them.

David slammed the exit door shut just as the lock panel shorted. "That won't hold long."

They darted down an overgrown service road as footsteps pounded behind them. Robin glanced back just long enough to see two masked figures step into the light, one holding a black sheathed dagger etched with silver runes.

"Those are Circle operatives," whispered Jude. "Come on."

Ashley pulled Robin into a side passage just as a disruptor blast sizzled over their heads and concrete exploded behind them.

They didn't look back again.

They regrouped several blocks away in the skeleton of a half demolished warehouse. Everyone was panting, sweat and soot streaking their faces.

Robin opened the folder marked "SULLIVAN, R." again. The interior pages were mostly ruined but the last sheet was still legible.

At the bottom, handwritten in ink:

"Subject rerouted under failed containment. Resurrection permitted under Black Protocol. Outcome: unknown."

She turned to the group.

"They never meant for me to make it to the Academy."

David's expression was unreadable. "Then who pulled you in?"

Robin looked down at the folder, then out at the Austin skyline beyond the broken wall.

"That's what I plan to find out."

CHAPTER TWENTY

Robin leaned against the warehouse wall, drawing a long breath of night air. It was cleaner than the scorched, musty air in the bunker they'd just come from, but her chest still felt tight. Her forearm buzzed faintly with the Hellhound mark. A brand no one had asked if she wanted.

The address David had been carrying hadn't been empty, it had been staged. But they'd found enough. A hidden file. A name. A protocol buried under false headers.

Ashley's tablet now held a breadcrumb the Academy had tried to erase.

"They wanted it scrubbed," Robin said. "Which means it mattered."

David paced nearby, lips moving without sound, frustration written in every step. Ashley stood watch at the edge of the alley, her tablet under one arm and a tired set to her shoulders. Jude hung back, arms crossed, gaze sweeping the shadows like he expected another ambush.

Robin turned, watching the dark shift and settle. "The

place was scrubbed, but not clean," she said. "They didn't expect anyone to come looking."

David stopped pacing. "And if we hadn't? That file fragment would still be stuck in a wall."

"They wanted it erased," Ashley added. "Which means it mattered."

Jude finally spoke, voice low. "It still might."

Phoenix let out a sharp cry overhead. A reminder. Watchers still moved in the city's underbelly.

Ashley tugged at Robin's sleeve. "We should move."

Robin nodded. "Back to the fallback point. Quietly."

They moved. Single file. Fast.

By the time they reached a small warehouse courtyard, the adrenaline had thinned, leaving exhaustion and open-ended questions. Robin leaned against a crate and scanned the others.

David was the first to speak. "There's a pattern."

Robin arched a brow. "To what?"

He hesitated, then dropped his voice. "Resurrections. Some don't follow protocol. They get pushed through off the books. Someone's bypassing checks, and someone else is funding it."

Ashley didn't blink. "You're saying what happened to Robin wasn't random."

"I'm saying there's money moving through ghost channels. Fake projects. Fabricated cadet IDs. Enough to bury a dozen mistakes and start again. Someone's testing things. Quietly."

Robin folded her arms. "And the Academy?"

David gave her a look. "At best, they don't know. At worst…"

"They're in on it," Ashley finished, flat and low.

Jude's posture didn't shift, but something cold settled behind his eyes. "This isn't about one corrupt instructor."

"No," Robin agreed. "It's bigger."

David glanced at her. "And you're the only proof it worked."

Robin's voice stayed even, but her fingers twitched. "That's why they're watching me. Why they didn't wipe everything."

Ashley shook her head, pulling out the tablet. "We've got logs. Not full access, but enough to show something's wrong. Resurrections with missing entries. Time gaps. Redacted names." She tapped a corner of the screen. "One of the corrupted logs is tagged with a project name. It says *Echo Gate*. No matching record in the Academy systems. It could be a false header, or something they buried deep."

Robin leaned closer. *Echo Gate*. She hadn't heard it before, but it made her skin crawl.

"Can you break it open?" David asked.

"Eventually," she said. "But not from here."

Robin nodded. "Then we do this the smart way."

No one argued.

They all felt it, the edge of something sharp and wrong. The fight club had been a glimpse, not the whole picture. The address had been another breadcrumb. And the person holding the map had vanished through a trapdoor before the real questions started.

David stepped in closer. "The infection, it wasn't a side effect. It was the point."

Robin's voice dropped. "I know. The place we just came from? It wasn't a lab. It was a checkpoint. "It fits this Echo Gate file," Robin said. "They were studying infection transfer to see if it could alter resurrection outcomes. I wasn't just brought back. I was an experiment."

Jude's face stayed unreadable. "And we're already past it."

Robin nodded hard. "This isn't over. Not even close."

Ashley pulled the hood of her jacket tighter as they stepped into the shadows again. "Where now?"

Robin looked toward the east, where the skyline gave way to a familiar ridge of dark trees along the edge of the lake near the boathouse and the hidden entrance.

"Home," she said. "We go back. Quietly, like Jude said. Let them think we ran out of leads."

David smirked. "But we didn't."

Robin shook her head. "Not even close."

They slipped into the dark, headed back toward the Academy with one stolen tablet, two corrupted files, and more questions than they knew how to ask.

They moved through the quiet streets, keeping to the shadows and avoiding main roads. The boathouse came into view, its silhouette a stark reminder of the hidden world beneath.

Jude waited for them, his face impassive. He said nothing as they slipped inside, merely nodding as they passed.

Once inside the hidden entrance, Jude finally spoke. "There's a briefing scheduled soon. You all need to clean up first."

His gaze swept over them, noting the signs of their recent fight. "Get rid of any evidence of bruises, cuts, or torn clothes. Use the med bay if you need to but don't speak to anyone. We can't afford suspicion right now."

Robin glanced at her scraped knuckles and the tear in her sleeve. She caught Ashley's eye and saw a bruise forming on her friend's cheek.

"He's right," Robin murmured. "We need to be careful."

David nodded, already moving toward the med bay. "I'll grab some supplies. We'll patch up here before heading to the briefing."

They retreated to Robin's dorm room, the night orb on her desk humming quietly, casting a muted blue over the bunker gray walls. Phoenix perched on the edge of the bed, his feathers puffed, with one eye on the hallway.

Ashley stayed on her feet by the door, a firm grip on the tablet. "Keeping this puts us on someone's radar. Cadets have vanished for less."

Robin didn't argue. She stripped off her jacket and slumped onto the bed, her Hellhound mark still tingling faintly. Her skin hadn't stopped buzzing since they left the address. "We're not uploading it. Not yet. We just hold it. That's all."

"Like that's going to stop anyone from noticing," Ashley said, setting the tablet down on the desk with care.

David closed the med kit and leaned back against the storage cabinet. "Security's tighter than usual. We need to stay off their radar."

Robin leaned forward, elbows on her knees. "Then we act like nothing's changed."

Ashley glanced toward the closed door, then back to Robin. "But it has. We all saw her."

"You mean Wren," said Robin.

David's voice was low. "She wasn't hiding."

"No, she was right in the middle of that fight club," Robin said. "She had been watching and waiting."

Ashley moved to the edge of the bed, her tone careful but sure. "She didn't follow us home. That's something."

"I know." Robin rubbed her face with both hands. "But I still don't want her pulled into this. Not unless she chooses it."

Phoenix let out a low rasp and shifted where he perched on the bedframe. The hum of the night orb cast a faint glow across the room, too quiet for the storm building beneath their feet.

Robin stood up. "Then let's get to work."

"That tablet might fill in the blanks," said Ashley.

"Unless it's coded in nonsense," David said. "We'll need time to decode it. If any of the instructors catch wind, we'll end up in serious trouble."

Robin stared at the scuff on the floor. "We're already neck deep. I'm not backing off now."

A brisk knock on her door ended the conversation. Jude's voice rang out from the hallway. "We're expected in the briefing hall."

Ashley shot Robin a quick glance and unlocked the door. Jude stood in his usual guarded stance, broad shoulders set and he looked calm despite the tension. The black phone in his hand glowed with patterned shapes that swirled across the screen.

He noticed the tablet under Ashley's arm but said nothing. Instead, he gestured for them to follow. "The instructors want everyone present," he announced, his low tone edged enough to put Robin on alert. "I suggest you don't leave anything behind."

Is that a warning that we'll be searched?

He led them down one hall after another, ignoring their muttered attempts at small talk. Ashley didn't push it, and David remained silent. Robin replayed the ringmaster's voice, that sly hint of laughter.

They entered the large meeting hall with chairs arranged in neat rows. Every seat was filled by cadets in hoodies and worn sneakers. Onstage, June paced, reading lines off a slim tablet. She was wearing her standard uniform of a navy blazer and cargo pants.

She cleared her throat decisively and launched into an official statement.

"We have reason to believe that unauthorized resurrected individuals have been active in Austin," she said. "We advise all cadets to remain vigilant. If you encounter any unmarked undead, report them immediately. The Academy stands firm on containing such threats."

Robin braced for mention of the fight club. None came.

The instructor kept her eyes on the gathered cadets. "We will not tolerate independent investigations or activities. Follow the chain of command. Anyone found acting against our guidelines will face disciplinary measures."

A wave of apprehension rippled through the room. Several cadets whispered to each other. Robin knew they were all thinking the same thing. The Academy was aware that something big was brewing, but they were trying to tidy it up without giving details. That was all the proof she needed that they weren't telling the whole truth.

When the assembly ended, they were dismissed. Robin slipped out the back, her thoughts moving faster than her feet. Ashley and David followed a few steps behind. Jude stayed near the stage, leaning in to speak with June in a voice low enough to keep private. His face gave away nothing, but the way he shifted his weight said he wasn't just following orders. Robin watched him from the edge of the hallway. He wasn't arguing—but he wasn't agreeing either. Not blindly, anyway. Maybe he was asking questions. Maybe he already knew the answers. Either way, he didn't look like someone planning to fall in line. She filed that away.

They made their way into a hallway corner that stayed out of the instructors' line of sight. Robin kept her back to the wall, eyes scanning for movement. Ashley kept track of the stolen tablet.

"This is going to land us in it deep," Ashley muttered, fingers tightening around the edge.

David kept his voice low. "You really think we're the only ones who've seen those resurrection logs? No chance. Someone's been running this play long enough to build a system around it."

Robin nodded once. "Then the proof's still here. Buried in this building, under layers of lies."

Phoenix swooped in low, dodging overhead lighting and a near miss with a cadet's bun. He landed square on Robin's shoulder and dropped a tiny, folded slip of paper before hopping to the nearest beam. Business as usual for him.

Robin caught the slip mid fall, unfolding it with care. Twisted black symbols stared back at her, familiar in the worst way.

Ashley leaned closer. "That look like the ledger to you?"

"It matches the patterns David flagged on the encrypted files," Robin said. Her pulse ticked faster. "Same hand."

Phoenix cawed once and shifted higher into the shadows.

"He's pointing us somewhere," she added. "Or someone's pointing through him."

Ashley sighed. "Crow mail from the Underworld. Why not?"

David nodded. "If this lines up with the tablet data, we might be looking at an old corridor—one of the wings they don't patrol anymore."

Robin's jaw set. "Then let's follow it. If this leads to hard evidence, we drag it into the light."

They kept their voices low. The air around them buzzed with too many ears. Robin scanned the nearby cadets, then signaled the others toward the nearest unused supply room. Inside, it smelled like disuse and dust.

Ashley set the tablet on a dented metal shelf. Robin added the slip of paper beside it. David crouched and pulled a pencil stub from his pocket like it was standard issue.

"Let's see if the symbols match up," he said, fingers flying across the tablet. "It's the same structure. Whoever encoded this wasn't subtle."

Ashley raised an eyebrow. "You're not hacking a game from your basement. If you mess up, they'll see it."

"I know exactly how serious it is," David shot back.

Robin let out a breath. They were frayed at the edges, all of them. "Let's keep our heads. We do this right, no one sees it coming. Meanwhile..." She looked to the map view blinking in the corner of the tablet. "We check those sealed corridors. If they kept any records of my death, they didn't leave them in the main server."

Ashley frowned. "You're talking about breaking into locked territory."

Robin didn't blink. "Got a better idea?"

David gave a small nod. "I'm in. But no mistakes."

"Phoenix can run point," Robin said, slipping the paper into her pocket. "We track the data. Find the truth. No more dodging."

They exited one at a time, smooth and practiced. Robin peeled off toward her dorm. Ashley turned toward the cafeteria and David disappeared into the training wing.

Low profile. No sudden moves. The game had changed, and this time, they were the ones drawing the lines.

Back in her dorm, Robin kept the lights dim and her movements sharper than they needed to be. Rest wasn't coming, so she didn't waste time pretending. Her Hellhound mark itched under her sleeve, a constant hum of something left unfinished.

Phoenix tapped once at the vent—light and deliberate. She opened it without ceremony. He landed on the frame, feathers ruffled, eyes locked on her like he was waiting for her to catch up.

She held up the slip of paper again, this time studying it like a map instead of a mystery. They weren't just chasing rumors anymore. Whoever encoded this wanted to be found. Or wanted her to find something.

Robin dropped into her desk chair and pulled the backup tablet from her drawer. An old model no one had logged into for months Ashley had provided. "Safer this way." She booted it cold and loaded the data Ashley had pulled. While it ran, she sketched the symbols by hand, noting the overlaps with the ringmaster's ledger and the weird entry tags buried in Echo Gate's archives.

By the time David sent a secure ping, just two dots and a slash, she had three pattern matches and a rough outline of where to look next. A service corridor under the east wing. Sealed off. Low clearance. Easy to forget. Perfect for hiding something important.

She slid the paper into a hidden pouch in her boot and texted Ashley one word: *Tonight*.

This wasn't just about her anymore. If the infection trials had worked once, they'd try again. And if the Academy wasn't running them, someone inside was making sure no one found out.

Phoenix dropped from the vent with a rustle and landed on her shoulder. She didn't flinch.

"Let's move," she said under her breath.

She gathered her gear and slipped into the hall, quiet and fast. The corridor stretched ahead, blank and unassuming. Somewhere in that silence, the truth waited, wrapped in lies, sealed behind codes and metal, but still there.

She'd find it. And this time, she wouldn't walk out empty handed.

CHAPTER TWENTY-ONE

The teammates timed their exit to the minute—right after lights out, just before the patrols shifted. The tunnels below Hellhound Academy had always whispered secrets. Long corridors sealed off by rusted gates, rooms with no documented purpose, and sealed hatches with digital locks whose access expired a decade ago. David had marked a handful on a smudged printout map. The one they were heading toward was circled twice in red marker and annotated: *NOT IN ARCHIVE*.

Robin crouched beneath a low ceiling as the three of them pressed deeper into the sub sublevel junction. Their flashlamps barely pierced the clinging humidity. She had the ring in her jacket pocket, wrapped in a layer of black cloth, and she could feel it vibrate faintly as if pulling toward something.

Ashley trailed just behind, her back pressed to the slick wall, the stolen tablet tucked flat under her jacket. She hadn't spoken in the last five minutes, her jaw tight with concentration. David moved ahead in a crouch, scanning with a borrowed Academy-grade EM tracker. The needle had started twitching two corridors back and now danced steadily toward the red.

"This is it," David said quietly. He brushed cobwebs away from a metal hatch half buried in the stonework.

Robin stepped forward. The air felt charged.

The hatch had no keypad or card reader. Instead, a burned-in sigil shimmered faintly in the dark. Phoenix, from his perch on Robin's shoulder, let out a clicking whimper.

"It's the same mark," Ashley said. "Just like the one we saw at the Candle Factory."

Robin nodded and reached into her jacket to unwrap the cloth, exposing the melted ring.

Phoenix inhaled sharply and leapt from her shoulder, circling the hatch once before pressing his beak to the sigil.

The hatch clicked and slid open on a hiss of cold air.

They stepped into what looked like a surgical theater frozen mid operation. Rows of wax molds stood waist high along the edges, each vaguely humanoid, missing pieces. One had half a face. Another had two left arms. A few were dressed in scorched pieces of Academy cadet uniforms.

"Dear god," Ashley whispered. "Wax again. Why not flesh? Unless they didn't want it to hold."

"Wax can be used as a conductor or stabilizer for incomplete soul imprints," said David, looking around the room. "It's malleable, disposable, and low reactive. It's even a binding medium for stolen fragments. Easy to imbue, and easy to destroy. Wax burns, melts, reshapes. It's perfect for life that's been pulled from its original form."

Ashley gave him a sidelong glance. "You really do your

homework. I'm guessing you were a bookworm when you were alive."

In the center was a mechanical table. Robin felt her stomach churn. Wires fed into its base and a ring shaped groove had been cut into its surface. The ring in Robin's hand pulsed once and crumbled to ash. "What the hell?"

"This is where they made them," David added in a somber tone.

"Not just made," Robin said. She stepped closer and touched the groove. "They tested."

There was a hum. A low resonance Robin felt more than heard. The air tasted like burned sugar and metal. One of the wax constructs twitched.

David pulled out his baton. Ashley drew her stunner.

The construct turned its head, wax mouth opening in a fractured O.

"It's not active," Robin said, though her heart thundered. "It's echoing. Like a tuning fork."

Ashley pointed to a board filled with cadet headshots. Most were crossed out. A few glowed faintly blue beneath the dust.

"They were cataloging," she said. "These aren't rogue creations. They're... trials."

The wax figure spoke.

A single word, in Wren's voice. "Robin."

Robin reeled back, but Ashley steadied her.

The construct swayed and collapsed, face first. As it struck the floor, a rush of air blew past them and Phoenix screeched.

A memory bloomed in Robin's mind. Not her own. Wren's. A dark room, surgical lights, the cold bite of metal restraints. And a whisper in the dark. *We don't need them all to survive. Just the right ones.*

Robin staggered.

David caught her. "You okay?"

Robin looked at him, eyes wide. "Wren put that echo here. On purpose. She wanted me to find it."

She stepped back from the table and pressed her hand to her chest. The pull was stronger here. A silent thread vibrated between her heart and something far beyond this room. It wasn't just Wren. It was older, deeper, and woven into something that had always lived in her blood.

She suddenly thought of the nights she'd watched her mother stir herbs into boiling water, whispering names of ancestors as steam curled in sacred patterns. Of her father, sitting in the garden, hands resting on the soil, listening to birds and murmuring answers only he could hear. Their gifts hadn't been flashy, but they were potent, rooted in rhythms the Academy couldn't measure.

More memories flooded her brain.

Her mother had called the gift the tether. Her father said it was the echo of belonging. They had both spoken of a time when families were more than names in ledgers. They were keepers of connection, guardians of magic that lived between worlds. She hadn't understood then, but she was beginning to now.

It was more than a feeling. It was a kind of signal, passed down like marrow, that flared when the boundary between life and death was thinnest, calling the living to remember, respond, or return.

For her mom, the tether meant staying grounded by stirring herbs, whispering names, or calling the lost home with both hands steady on the pot. For her dad, it was quieter, something he listened for in birdsong or the weight of the air.

Wren used it like a flare, leaving echoes tucked in places no one else would think to look.

And Robin? The tether didn't whisper, it yanked. When it flared, her feet moved before her thoughts could catch up. It didn't care if she was ready. It pulled her toward what mattered.

The pull wasn't a side effect of resurrection. It was a map etched into her lineage. A signal passed down. And here, surrounded by constructs of stolen life and fractured soul prints, it sang loudest.

"I remember," she whispered, her eyes shining. But there was no time for reminiscing.

Ashley moved to the back wall and brushed away years of grime. "There's a second hatch," she said.

Phoenix chirped twice and flew toward the metal plate. As he landed, it glowed softly. A sigil lit beneath his claws, one Robin had seen only once before, on the inside of Wren's old field notebook.

David glanced between them. "We going deeper?"

Robin stared at the sigil.

"Yeah," she said. "We are."

Behind them, the dead construct whispered, barely audible. "They're watching."

Robin turned back once and then followed the others into the dark.

CHAPTER TWENTY-TWO

Robin emerged from the second hatch into another corridor, this one lined with glass observation panels coated in grime. The smell of scorched wax still clung to the air, sharper down here, mixed with metal and mildew. This part of the tunnels was colder, as if the heat of the world above had stopped trying to reach this far down.

David held up his flashlight and scanned the hall. "Looks like it was an old storage wing. Maybe repurposed."

Ashley pointed to faded stenciling along the concrete. "Lab 8A. Doesn't show up on any of the maps I checked."

Robin ran her fingers along the wall. There was something about this place. The pull hummed again, not a sharp tug but a steady echo that mirrored her heartbeat. Somewhere up ahead, it intensified.

"This way," she said, stepping forward.

They passed rusted lockers and empty labs. Many were filled with collapsed shelving or broken diagnostic tables.

Old equipment lay scattered under thick dust. But one room had its lights blink on as they passed.

Robin stopped.

The door slid open silently, triggered by Phoenix's presence. He perched on her shoulder, head cocked.

Inside, the room looked untouched. A console still glowed faintly green. Chairs lined up in neat rows. The air was dry, filtered. On the back wall was a screen, cracked but functional, displaying a series of rotating schematics with soul signature graphs, reanimation profiles, and a logo Robin didn't recognize. A circle within a circle, stitched with flame.

David moved toward the console. "This data... It's new. Last accessed two weeks ago."

Ashley stepped beside him. "Someone's still using this place."

Phoenix launched into the air and circled once before diving toward a locked cabinet. He tapped it with his beak twice, then returned to Robin's shoulder.

Robin crossed the room and pulled open the panel. Inside was a flash stone.

A note sat atop it, written in blocky handwriting she recognized instantly.

Use it only if you're sure. -Jude.

David stepped closer. "What is it?"
Robin picked it up. "Something I didn't know he kept."
She turned it over in her hand. Flash stones weren't like echo stones. They didn't transmit and only the one who

made the recording could authorize a playback. Unless they coded it to a soul signature.

Which meant Jude had tied this one to hers.

"Play it," said Ashley.

Robin hesitated, then pressed her thumb to the center.

The air rippled and the light warped. Jude appeared as a ghost of himself, sitting on a bench with his blazer open and shirt sleeves rolled to his elbows. He looked tired.

"Robin," his voice came, low and stripped of its usual sharpness. "If you're seeing this, it means I trust you enough to know the truth. Or you've forced your way into places I warned you not to go."

He sighed. "I wasn't always deep in it. I came here as a recruit when I was young, thinking I was doing the right thing. Trying to make something of myself. I stuck to surface roles at first. The safe jobs. That changed after Wren disappeared."

His voice lowered.

"Yes, I knew about her even then. She wasn't part of the Academy. She was my sister. Half, anyway. Same mother, different fathers. Our mom was... complicated. She kept her secrets well. Raised us apart. Different cities, different last names. I used to think she just wanted to give us space."

He shook his head.

"But now? I think she was hiding something. Maybe trying to keep us from triggering whatever the pull really is."

The image looked directly at Robin.

"Wren and I had the same mom. You didn't. But you and Wren, the same father."

Robin pressed her hand to her mouth, reeling.

"He was the quiet one," Jude continued. "Kept out of everything. I never met him. My mom never mentioned him by name. But when she talked about him, it was with weight. Legacy, she called it. Said Wren had something old in her blood. And you've got it too. Different mothers, same fire."

He paused, letting it settle.

"My father died before I could ask questions. Your father, Wren's father, was always a question mark to me. But I think Mom believed he passed something on to both of you. Old magic that needed protecting. She never said it outright, but I think she pushed me toward the Academy on purpose. Said it would give me access. Answers. She believed the old ways still mattered."

Robin didn't speak. Ashley leaned in slightly, silent.

"Wren and I were raised apart. I didn't even know we were related until we were almost grown. Mom said distance was safety. That putting us all in the same room might trigger something too old to control. Something buried in the bloodline. I thought she was being dramatic. But now..."

He exhaled slowly.

"Maybe she was trying to keep us from lighting the fuse."

He looked away.

"It was Wren's idea to dig deeper into our roots. That's what brought her here. And eventually, me."

He looked back at Robin. "And no, we're not related. Not by blood. Just by the choices we made. And the people we lost."

Ashley glanced at Robin, who shook her head. She hadn't known.

"Wren got involved in something deep. Off books. Said she found a pattern the Academy was hiding that cadets were being resurrected with altered soul prints. Some came back wrong. Some didn't come back at all."

The image flickered, but Jude's voice remained clear.

"She tried to expose it. After that, she disappeared. No official report. No explanation. Just gone. The record says she went rogue."

He leaned forward in the memory.

"I know better. I tracked her last transmission to the tunnels under Sublevel Eight. She was onto something—something bigger than rogue projects."

Phoenix let out a low croon, watching the projection.

"The pull you and Wren share, Robin? It's not a glitch. It's old magic. Pre-ledger. The kind the Academy used to catalog, not suppress. It can connect, resonate, and protect. Or destroy. Depends on who controls it."

Robin stepped closer to the image.

Jude's face softened. "They're going to come after you. They always go after the ones who come back different. But you, you were special from the start and that threatens them. That's why I stayed. Not to teach but to watch and to wait for you."

The image began to fade.

"If you want answers, go deeper. But not alone. Trust the ones who have stayed by you."

The flash stone dimmed. Silence followed.

Ashley exhaled. "He knew everything."

David looked at Robin. "And he never said anything until now?"

Robin shook her head slowly. Her throat tightened. "He was trying to protect us."

David stepped closer, lowering his voice. "So, what do we do now?"

Robin turned to the console. The pull burned in her chest like a live wire. "We find Wren."

Phoenix flared his wings and shrieked once. Lights across the room surged, illuminating a hidden door behind the console.

Ashley grinned. "Guess that answers that."

Robin reached for the handle, and they stepped into the shadows beyond.

They didn't make it far before another door slid open at the far end of the corridor. A tall silhouette stepped through, the lights behind her casting a long shadow over the floor.

Evangeline.

She looked sharper than usual—coat zipped halfway, her hair pulled back, eyes clear and alert. She didn't flinch at the sight of them.

"I figured if anyone would find that room, it'd be you," she said, her voice calm but carrying.

Robin straightened. "How long have you known?"

Evangeline stepped closer. "Long enough to regret keeping my mouth shut. And not long enough to know how to stop what's coming."

Ashley crossed her arms. "You work for them. The Academy. Why show up now?"

"I work *near* them," Evangeline corrected. "I stopped

working *for* them the day they started rewriting the resurrection protocols behind closed doors. The same day I found out about the constructs."

David narrowed his eyes. "You knew about the Masked Circle?"

"I suspected. But they're shadows behind shadows. Everything leads in circles—burned files, misdated logs. Even your file, Robin."

Robin's heart stuttered. "My file?"

Evangeline nodded. "It was accessed the day you were brought back. Not by medical, not by Academy command. Someone else flagged it for observation. Someone I can't trace."

Phoenix let out a low, uneven croak and flew to Evangeline's shoulder. She didn't react.

"I knew Wren," she said softly, meeting Robin's eyes. "We worked together to help some of the cadets. She was trying to reach you and I... I let her into the lab. That's how she knew where to leave you the messages."

Robin took a slow breath. "So why are you here now?"

"Because there's something coming through the pull," Evangeline said. "Something old and you're the key. The Circle's not just trying to raise the dead. They're trying to open a door. And I think you're what they need to hold it open. You're the hinge."

CHAPTER TWENTY-THREE

Robin didn't flinch under Evangeline's gaze. Not this time. Not after what Jude had revealed and not after hearing her name spoken in Wren's voice by a failed construct. She'd crossed a line, and whatever lay ahead, she wasn't turning back.

Evangeline gestured toward a side chamber. "We can talk in there. It's shielded from spies of all sorts."

Robin, David, and Ashley exchanged glances but followed. Phoenix gave a single flap of his wings and soared after them.

The chamber was tight, its walls embedded with glinting metallic filaments. A handful of chairs surrounded a central projection table. Evangeline tapped a sequence into the surface, and a low hum thrummed through the floor as the room sealed with a magnetic click.

"We don't have long," she said. "I wanted to explain this before the next shift sweep. I can't protect you if you're caught."

"We're past protection," Robin replied. "Start talking."

Evangeline nodded. She projected an image from the table of a three dimensional layout of the Academy campus, overlaid with pulsing blue nodes.

"These are cadets who returned from resurrection with signs of instability," she said. "Not just mental. Energetic. Their soul signatures show irregular echoes, like something else is trying to interfere."

David leaned in. "Something else?"

"Something old," Evangeline said. "Jude was right. The pull you and Wren share isn't just rare. It's inherited and it acts like a beacon. When you came back, Robin, it activated more than your memory. It activated a frequency."

Ashley crossed her arms. "A frequency for what?"

Evangeline turned to Robin. "To attract what's on the other side."

The projection changed and a new waveform appeared, jagged and pulsing in sync with the blue nodes.

"This is what we detected the night you were revived," Evangeline continued. "It's tied to you. It's been broadcasting from your signature ever since. And now, the Circle is tracking it."

Robin swallowed hard. "So, they know where I am."

"They know what you are," Evangeline said quietly. "You weren't just pulled back, you were tethered. Echo Gate didn't close behind you. It latched on. Whatever infection they used, it didn't just bring you back, it made you a fixed point between both sides. A living anchor. And now Death can find you. So can they."

Robin's brow furrowed. "Death? What do you mean *Death* can find me?"

Evangeline's gaze didn't waver. "Not a metaphor. Not

just an end. Death is... a presence. Maybe not human, maybe not flesh, but real. The old magic treated it like a being that moves between thresholds and sometimes, watches who crosses back."

Phoenix let out a low rumble and glowed faintly. A streak of white wax shimmered down his back.

"And Phoenix?" Robin asked.

Evangeline hesitated. "He's not just bonded to you. He's a transference familiar. They were created to guide soul tethered mages. There haven't been any in over a century. But he was sent to be with you."

David placed a hand lightly on Robin's back, grounding her. She didn't shrug it off.

Ashley glanced between them and arched a brow but said nothing.

"Why us?" Robin whispered. "Why our family?"

Evangeline looked at her, and for the first time, she didn't speak as a scientist or an instructor. Just a woman who'd seen too much.

"Because your line held the map," she said. "And now the Circle wants to redraw it."

The lights flickered and the projection stuttered.

David turned. "Someone's overriding the lockdown."

Evangeline didn't panic. She shut the console down and pulled a folded envelope from her coat, handing it to Robin.

"Coordinates," she said. "To the site where the first test ring was buried. It's off grid. You need to get there before they do."

Ashley took it and scanned it into her tablet.

"You coming?" Robin asked.

Evangeline smiled, faint and tired. "I have a few more lies to feed the Academy before I can disappear. But I'll meet you there. I promise."

The chamber's outer door buzzed.

Robin tucked the envelope into her jacket. "Let's move."

They vanished into the corridor before the door finished opening, the echo of footsteps already fading.

The hunt was on.

CHAPTER TWENTY-FOUR

The sky above the test site was the color of rusted steel, pressed low by storm clouds that hadn't broken. The landscape around them was flat, brittle, and scattered with dead brush. The coordinates Evangeline gave them led to the remnants of an old industrial staging ground nearly two hours outside Academy grounds. Nothing moved for miles.

Robin adjusted the strap on her pack and crouched next to a twisted steel pipe jutting from the ground. "This is it," she said. "Right under us."

Ashley scanned the area, her stolen tablet picking up faint heat signatures underground. "Still active. Something down there's pulling juice."

David checked their perimeter. "No patrols, yet. We do this fast."

Phoenix glided low over a patch of cracked concrete and shrieked. The surface shimmered faintly as if stirred by a breeze no one felt.

Robin stepped forward and held out her hand. The pull

vibrated up her arm. Phoenix landed beside her, his claws pressing into the exact center of the ripple.

A circle of old concrete shifted and receded into the earth.

They didn't hesitate. They'd come this far. The team descended into a shaft choked with dust and the smell of scorched resin. Emergency lighting hummed to life in strips along the walls. The corridor below led to a reinforced door, covered in familiar sigils. The same ones they'd seen at the Candle Factory.

Ashley moved forward and keyed in the override. The door opened with a hiss.

The lab beyond was half collapsed but partially intact. Tables, shattered monitors, and melted equipment littered the floor. In the far corner, something flickered faintly behind a glass containment field.

Robin approached slowly.

It was Martin Kling.

He was thinner, his jacket burned along one side, an old headband barely clinging to his short, cropped hair. He looked up, his eyes sharp despite the dim light.

"Took you long enough," he rasped.

Robin stared at him. "You're alive."

He barked a laugh. "Define that."

Her eyes dropped to his left arm. It was mechanical, made of twisted fiberwire and waxed bone stitched into flesh. "Your arm... That wasn't... like that before. What happened to you? Who did this?"

Martin's expression darkened. "The Masked Circle. They caught up to me and wanted to see how much of me they could hollow out before I broke." He shook his head.

"There's no time to explain more right now. Just know, I didn't let them finish."

David stepped forward, but Martin held up his good hand to stop him.

"Don't touch the field. It's not for keeping me in. It's for keeping the rest out."

Ashley circled to the side, examining a control panel with active files.

Martin nodded toward her. "You always did figure things out faster than most."

Ashley froze. "What does that mean?"

Martin looked at her carefully. "You don't remember yet, do you? You and I... we were in the same cohort. You died first. A crash test. I died two weeks later. You came back without your memories. They kept you for observation. I ran."

Ashley stepped back, her mouth tight.

Robin turned to her. "Ashley?"

Ashley shook her head. "I've had flashes. Empty rooms. A metal hallway. Someone calling me Red. I wasn't ready to say anything."

"They took your name," Martin said. "Filed it under 'Prototype 3.' They were trying to find someone who could survive full soul detachment. You weren't just brought back, you were tested, and you survived."

David clenched his jaw. "What is this place?"

Martin gestured around. "The original ring site. They tested resonance amplification here as a way to strengthen the bond between soul and flesh post resurrection. Didn't work," he said, grimacing. His words came out haltingly.

"Too much echo. Too much bleed. The place ate most of us alive."

Robin stepped closer to the barrier. "And you stayed."

"Someone had to keep the files from disappearing. The Circle wants this place erased. I held on until someone found me. Figured it'd be you."

Ashley moved to the panel. "The files are mostly intact. They used your resurrection as a base model. But Robin's is flagged differently. Not as subject. As *anchor*."

Robin blinked. "Anchor?"

Martin nodded. "They think you stabilize the rest. Your pull isn't just rare, it's catalytic. You make the energy stick."

David looked at her. "That why they need you to open the gate?"

Martin's eyes darkened. "Exactly. And they're close. They just need one more thing."

"What?" Robin asked.

Martin hesitated. "Wren."

Phoenix flared his wings.

"She went underground trying to shield the pull and mute it from both ends," said Martin. "If they find her and use that connection to track or manipulate you, they can hold the door open."

Robin felt the ground tilt beneath her.

Ashley pressed her hand to the console. "We need to move. I can copy the files."

Martin reached through a slot in the barrier and passed a glowing shard. "This unlocks the backup archive. If I'm not here when you come back, take it to Jude. He'll know what to do."

Robin took the shard.

Martin looked her in the eye. "You were never supposed to be one of us. They picked you before you died because your family carries something they can't replicate."

Robin swallowed the rising surge of anger.

David stepped beside her, his voice low. "We'll find Wren."

Ashley nodded. "And we'll stop the Circle."

Martin gave a half smile. "Then you better hurry. I stalled them long enough. But they're coming."

Phoenix shrieked. It was time to go.

CHAPTER TWENTY-FIVE

The tunnel they'd chosen wound through a disused maintenance line west of the Academy boundary, the walls damp with condensation and etched with fading stencil numbers. Water dripped steadily from cracked piping overhead, pooling in shallow recesses along the worn cement floor. Rust streaked down the seams of old access doors, and clusters of broken conduit jutted like ribs from the low ceiling. A faint, sour electric smell clung to the air, hinting at disuse and buried systems still faintly alive. Robin walked at the front, the shard Martin had given her pulsing faintly against her chest like a warning wrapped in memory. Each step echoed in low tones, swallowed quickly by the oppressive hush of the underground.

Ashley moved with sharp precision, trailing a step behind but not with hesitation. Her eyes swept the tunnel with habitual efficiency, taking in every pipe, every seam in the concrete. She didn't bother keeping quiet. Her boots struck the floor with purpose, every step landing with clean intent. One hand brushed the scar at her neck, not with nervousness, but as if confirming it was still there, still hers. Her body language wasn't withdrawn. It was coiled, focused.

David, bringing up the rear, checked their flank every few seconds, his grip steady on the baton holstered at his side. He moved with controlled precision, pausing briefly at every intersection or rusted doorframe. His fingers tapped twice against the grip each time they stopped, a habit Robin realized she'd seen him do before. It was like counting heartbeats. He walked like someone trained to absorb bad news before anyone else could hear it.

"Prototype Three," Ashley finally said. Her voice was flat, but there was an undercurrent that wasn't entirely bitter, it was calculated. Then she added, almost like an afterthought, "If you ever see the phrase 'TWIN FLARE' etched anywhere again, don't touch it. Not unless you want what's left of your mind to burn out."

Robin blinked, caught off guard. "How do you know that?"

Ashley's expression was unreadable. "Because I remember more than I let on. Not clearly, but enough to know I've seen what that phrase does to a mind."

Robin studied her, the silence stretching. "You've been protecting us from more than just bullets."

Ashley gave a tight nod. "It wasn't time. Until now."

Robin tilted her head. "You sound like someone who helped write the manual."

Ashley didn't flinch. "I didn't write it. But I knew who did. I ran operations under them. Test deployments, field calibrations. Before the Circle locked everything down."

Robin stepped closer. "So why bring you back?"

Ashley's mouth twitched, almost a smile. "Because they didn't think I'd make it. I was a stress test. They wanted to see if wiping someone that close to the truth could still hold."

"And?"

Ashley's eyes burned. "They were wrong."

Robin slowed. "That's not who you are. That's what they called you. There's a difference."

Ashley didn't meet her eyes. "They erased my name. All I have now is what I find out in stolen records and side notes on forgotten consoles. Martin said I died first. But I'm not sure I was ever fully brought back. Not like you."

David stopped. "You walk beside us, don't you?"

She nodded once.

"Then you're back. Doesn't have to be perfect to be real."

Robin looked from David to Ashley and slowed her pace again. "What about you, David? You said you remember. I never asked what."

David took a breath. The tunnel opened slightly ahead, light filtering in through a broken access vent.

"I remember the cold," he said. "I was part of a cadet recon unit during early field exercises. We got separated. One of the instructors called it a test. Three of us didn't make it. I was one of them."

Robin listened quietly. David rarely spoke this much unless he had something sharp to add.

"I remember bleeding out beside a cracked concrete barricade," he continued. "And I remember waking up in the infirmary with someone else's heartbeat. Nothing lined up right for days. The sky felt off. My hands were colder than they should've been."

Ashley looked up, her jaw set and eyes hard. Not vulnerable, but angry, determined. She wasn't unraveling, she was reigniting. "Why didn't you ever tell us?"

David shrugged. "I didn't want to make it real, and didn't want you looking at me the way they did."

They reached the surface moments later, stepping into a windblown clearing littered with shattered synthetic fencing. Tall grasses, brittle and pale from lack of sun, rattled against twisted metal posts. The sky overhead was a bleached gray, sagging with low cloud cover that made everything feel suffocated. A few blackened trees leaned at odd angles near the perimeter; their bark peeled back like scorched skin. The outpost Evangeline had mentioned stood ahead, squat and battered, blending into the surrounding slope.

Robin approached the sealed door and held up the shard. Her steps were deliberate now, slower, more grounded. She paused just shy of the threshold and scanned the frame for traps out of instinct, then advanced the final step with a breath she didn't realize she'd been holding. The shard vibrated against her palm. Phoenix circled once above, then descended in a slow spiral.

The door released with a groan.

Inside, the lab smelled like melted circuits and old ozone. The walls were paneled with dull titanium plates, each etched with fading Academy control marks. Dust coated the consoles like a blanket of ash, and the ventilation system gave off a constant, pulsing hum that felt too slow to be natural. Debris crunched beneath their boots.

Scorched data pads, shattered glass, and the melted remains of a coffee canister long rusted through. Terminals blinked on low power. One flickered to life automatically as they stepped closer.

Ashley went straight to it, her fingers flying across the dusty interface with practiced urgency. She leaned into the screen, shoulders squared, her movements fluid and sharp despite the grime. "Martin embedded coordinates in the shard. Also tagged a file labeled TWIN FLARE."

David stood guard by the doorway, eyes on the landscape beyond.

Robin moved to the far wall. Symbols had been carved there, older than the Academy's symbols. One looked like a version of the sigil Phoenix had left near her bed.

When she reached out and touched it, a pulse rolled up her arm. It wasn't painful, but grounding.

A memory flickered of the lake and Wren's hand. A tether of light.

Robin exhaled sharply.

Ashley turned from the console. "It gets worse. One of the logs from the Academy system says your death was pre-approved."

Robin froze. "By who?"

Ashley held up the tablet.

David stepped closer to look. His face darkened. "Jude."

Robin said nothing. She just stared at the screen, her mouth slightly open.

Ashley shut the console down. "We bring him answers, and he better have his own."

Phoenix clicked softly.

Robin nodded, the shard cool in her grip again. They were done waiting.

CHAPTER TWENTY-SIX

The wind had shifted by the time they reached the edge of the ridge overlooking the Academy's restricted vault sector. Below, squat concrete bunkers stretched like buried teeth, ringed with chainlink fencing topped in rusted coils of razor wire. The vault buildings were plain, utilitarian, and half swallowed by the earth in a deserted part of Del Valle, just outside of Austin, as if the Academy didn't want anyone to remember they existed. Even the light seemed reluctant to touch them, leaving them a cloudy gray.

The wind had shifted by the time they reached the edge of the ridge overlooking the Academy's restricted vault sector. Robin crouched low, the shard pressed to her chest beneath her jacket. The glow had dimmed since Martin passed it to her, but it still pulsed faintly, like a compass buried under layers of memory.

Ashley knelt beside her; her eyes locked on the security tower just below. A thin scar ran along the side of her neck, mostly hidden beneath the edge of her collar. Her fingers never stopped moving to adjust a strap, brushing phantom dust off her knees, or flexing and curling like she had to keep something from shaking loose. "There's a blind spot in their motion sensors. Thirty-second window."

David adjusted the strap on his rifle, his movements quiet and deliberate. Robin had already learned that he always checked his gear twice, sometimes three times. He was reliable and consistent. A low twitch ran through his fingers when things got quiet. A tension he tried to mask but never quite could. "We hit the archive room first. Then the pods."

Phoenix hovered above them in low, silent arcs, scanning. His waxy wings didn't flap so much as flex, moving like molten paper in slow motion. The feathers along his spine shimmered with faint blue tracings, as if he were drawing invisible lines through the air. His eyes, bead-like and ember colored, darted between heat trails no one else could see.

Robin nodded. "No backup. No room for mistakes."

Ashley gave a grim smile. "Wouldn't be a mission if we didn't break a few rules."

They moved in silence, slipping past the perimeter, through a patch of scrub and into the sub vault entrance to a recessed hatch half hidden behind a broken wall of ivy covered stone. The tunnel beyond was cool and damp, lined with oxidized piping that pulsed faintly with redirected power. The air smelled of old coolant and concrete dust. They were surprised to find that Evangeline was waiting just inside.

She held up a hand before they could speak. "Don't waste time. I rerouted the patrol paths for twelve minutes."

"You're here," Robin said quietly. "You came."

"I always planned to." Evangeline met her gaze. "You need to see what they did."

She led them through a narrow hallway lined with cryo sealed lockers, some filled with a cadet, the metal walls insulated and humming with latent energy. The floor here was grated steel, echoing every footfall with a hollow clang. Overhead, yellow tinted tubes flickered weakly, casting the cadets' faces in a sickly wash of light. Many were empty, their status panels blinking red. But others glowed steady blue. Robin counted twenty-six in total. One of them hummed with a familiar frequency.

Phoenix flared his wings and hovered beside it. His talons gripped the edge of the locker frame with sharp precision, and the glow from his underbelly intensified in a steady pulse. He turned his head once toward Robin, then back to the pod, neck moving with uncanny avian elegance. He was a sentinel in flight.

Ashley approached slowly. Her hand trembled as she wiped condensation from the nameplate.

The name wasn't hers. But the face inside the pod looked like it could have been.

"My sister," she whispered. "They said she never made it through training. That her body was unrecoverable."

David stepped forward. "She's not gone. Just paused."

Evangeline touched a panel. "These are the first recall units. The Circle flagged them for extraction, not recovery."

Robin turned. "You mean... to build new constructs?"

"Or host vessels," Evangeline said. "For whatever's trying to push through from the other side."

Ashley swallowed hard. "Can we wake her up?"

Evangeline hesitated. "You can. But she may not be the same."

Ashley stared at the glass, jaw clenched.

Robin moved down the row seeing more faces. Some she recognized from old class rosters. One that made her freeze.

The cadet inside wasn't a stranger, not entirely. Robin didn't remember his name at first, just the way he used to pace before drills, muttering jokes to himself to cut the tension. He'd been in one of her early training cycles. Quiet, but observant. He had a scar over one eye he never explained and a habit of watching the exits in every room like he didn't trust walls to keep anything out. His name came to her slowly. "You're Michael Roe," she whispered.

There were rumors back then that his quirk wasn't just reflexes or enhanced hearing. Some said he could sense echoes left behind after spells, that he could 'hear magic' even after it dissipated. Others claimed he was pulled from an early recall experiment that didn't quite fail, just... changed him. He was transferred in quietly after something classified went sideways, and no one ever found out from where.

He looked unchanged like they'd just frozen him mid breath.

Phoenix clicked, then let out a low, uneasy trill. As his wings twitched, a faint frost shimmered along the edges. Thin veins of pale blue ice began threading through the translucent wax. When he flapped, the air rippled with a whisper of cold, like a door opening from far below. His tail curled tighter beneath him, and he hovered higher, drawing small figure eights in the air like he was tracking a signal only he could feel.

The console beside Michael's pod blinked with red symbols. Robin scanned them quickly.

"This one's been altered. Not frozen, just stalled. He's been active."

David glanced over. "A test subject." He stepped slightly in front of Robin without thinking, shoulders tight. His eyes lingered on Michael, but then looked to the rest of the pods, narrowing slightly. "We don't know who, or what, is coming out of those. We need to be ready."

Evangeline nodded. "They used the ring's early resonance model on a handful. They tried to find more anchors besides you, but none held and most fractured."

Ashley backed away from her sister's pod. Her eyes were dry but blazing.

"We wake them. All of them. If they're already compromised, we have to know."

Robin nodded. "Do it."

Evangeline input the override. One by one, the pods hissed and slid open.

The room filled with a low hum as the cadets began to stir. Frosted glass panels fogged and hissed open, releasing sterile steam into the vault air. Each pod let out a high-pitched whine as it unlocked, the sound bouncing off the hard walls like the start of a storm.

Robin watched Michael's eyes flutter open, her fingers tightening reflexively around the edge of the pod. For a moment his eyes were clear, then clouded. He whispered, "They're watching from the ring."

Robin leaned closer. "Who? Who's watching?"

But he was already convulsing.

Evangeline hit a stasis field, freezing the feedback loop before it could spread.

Ashley knelt beside her sister's pod, murmuring something too low to hear. Her sister didn't stir.

Robin turned to Evangeline. "We need to destroy this place."

Evangeline hesitated. "There's something else. A secondary ring that's experimental, mobile. It's been moved offsite. My access ends here. You need the ringmaster. He's been running tests in the city. Someplace underground."

David's expression darkened. "The fight club."

Robin clenched her jaw. "He's back and he's next."

Ashley stood slowly. "Then let's finish this."

Phoenix chirped and launched skyward as the first pod fully disengaged behind them.

The recalled were waking up. And the reckoning had begun.

CHAPTER TWENTY-SEVEN

The tunnels beneath the city carried heat and vibration like nervous breath. Robin moved fast, the scent of rust and ozone sharp in her nose. Phoenix glided ahead, his wings silent, save for the occasional whisper of underworld frost trailing in his wake.

Ashley walked at her right shoulder, her face grim but alert. David was at her left, scanning sightlines and shadow gaps, his baton drawn and humming faintly.

They weren't alone.

Robin felt it before she heard it. There was a pulse in the back of her skull, like someone whispering her name through water.

"The signal," Ashley muttered. "It's getting louder."

Evangeline's earlier map had led them here to the remains of an abandoned train transfer station deep under downtown Austin. It was part of a collapsed metro expansion buried decades ago. The walls dripped with condensation and old rails curved away into the dark.

"He's using the mobile ring to boost resonance," Robin said. "That's what Phoenix is tracking."

Phoenix dipped suddenly and let out a low shriek, talons flashing.

"Left!" David shouted.

They ducked into a half fallen control office as something shimmered in the open corridor. A burst of spatial disruption, like the air had been torn sideways.

A figure stepped into view. Not the ringmaster, not yet.

It was another construct. Wax fleshed, stitched together with cords of pulsing blue. Cadet armor twisted into something ceremonial. It wore a half mask of cracked porcelain and carried a baton like David's but fused with arcane metal.

"That's new," Ashley said dryly.

Robin stepped forward. "We test its stability."

David frowned. "You sure?"

"If it breaks easy, the ringmaster is desperate. If it doesn't, we need to know what he's building."

Phoenix screeched just as the construct lunged.

The fight was fast and dirty. David blocked high, Ashley rolled low and fired a burst of low-frequency stun, and Robin slid in with a strike of her resonance infused pick. The construct absorbed the hits like clay.

Until Phoenix dove.

The familiar struck with both talons, releasing a burst of blue fire edged in frost. The mask cracked, and the construct let out a noise that wasn't cadet or Circle.

It collapsed, twitching, then evaporated into smoke.

"It wasn't bound fully," Robin said, chest heaving.

Ashley wiped a smear of wax off her arm. "They're

rushing the process. Trying to force resonance into unstable vessels."

Robin looked ahead and the signal in her head sharpened into a direction. She pointed, "There."

They moved through broken gates and collapsed debris, into a wide atrium filled with scaffolding and noise. The floor was littered with fractured tiles and scorched cables, some still sparking faintly in the gloom. The air smelled like burnt wax and ozone. High above, half collapsed catwalks swayed gently with each pulse from the ring. A low hum resonated through the metal support beams like a heartbeat echoing underground. At its center stood the ringmaster.

He hadn't changed much. Same dark coat, same too pale face that looked half melted and regal. He smiled when he saw them.

"Well, well, well. The dead walk fast these days," he said.

Robin stepped forward. "Stop the ring. Now."

"Why would I?" His smile grew. "It's already awake. Just waiting for the anchor to step inside."

The platform behind him pulsed with light. Energy arced in fractured halos along the ring's inner edge, casting warped reflections onto the rusted walls. The ring emitted a low-frequency hum that rattled Robin's ribs and made Phoenix's wings jitter with reflexive cold. Arcs of blue flame circled a metallic ring mounted on rails. Cables fed into it from every direction.

Ashley stepped up beside Robin. "You think we're here to watch?"

"You're here to choose," the ringmaster replied. "We don't need all of you. Just one of you to open the way."

David tensed. "Then we'll make sure you get none of us."

The ring flared and constructs emerged from behind machinery, their silhouettes jerking unnaturally through the haze. Each one seemed stitched from multiple sources with different uniforms, armor plating fused to raw flesh, limbs moving with a mix of mechanical efficiency and magical tremor. One dragged a length of chain across the floor, the links hissing like steam as they passed. Three of them, each in partial armor, one dragging an electro chain behind it.

Robin reached for her shard. It was time to break the ring.

CHAPTER TWENTY-EIGHT

The constructs moved like storm surge; fast, chaotic, and brutal. Robin ducked as the first chain came whipping toward her head, the metal tipped in something that sparked against stone. Ashley launched a flash burst that scattered two of the attackers, and David moved with practiced precision, baton meeting chain in a blinding arc of kinetic force.

Up close, they looked wrong. Not just wax and armor. They moved with twitchy hesitation, as if being dragged between two commands. One had a cadet badge fused into its chest plate. Another's lips moved, mouthing a name no one there recognized. Robin felt a wave of cold pass through her as realization hit.

"They're half souls," she muttered. "Pieces of cadets pulled back without anchors. No wonder they can't hold form."

Ashley gritted her teeth. "Resonance without consent. They built these things from echo traces and leftover energy. That's why they scream. They don't know if they're alive."

Phoenix dove again, frost trailing off his wings like torn silk. When he struck one of the constructs, it let out a cry that didn't belong to the dead or the living—a distortion that hurt to hear.

Robin gritted her teeth. The platform was powering up behind the ringmaster, and she could feel the pull now as a physical pressure, tugging from her ribs like a chain she hadn't known was there.

"He's syncing with the ring!" Ashley shouted. "He's using your signature as the final tether!"

Robin stepped forward. The ring responded with a shimmer of blue light.

"Not today," she whispered.

She drew the resonance shard from her jacket. The shard, gifted by Martin, pulsed to life with a low whine as she held it high.

Phoenix screeched and landed on her arm, the tips of his talons freezing her sleeve. For a moment, they stood at the edge of the ring's activation platform, the light drawing in toward them like breath.

Then a voice cut through the din.

"Robin!"

"No!" It was Wren.

She dropped from the scaffolding above, landing in a crouch that cracked the floor. Her hair was tied back, and a wax burned jacket clung to her frame. She had a baton in one hand and a resonance tag in the other.

"You always show up at the dramatic parts," Robin said.

"It's a family trait," Wren replied.

Ashley and David regrouped as more constructs poured

in. Wren threw her resonance tag into the center of the ring. It detonated with a sound like collapsing glass.

The ring stuttered and the ringmaster's expression twisted from confidence to fury. "You can't stop it!" he bellowed. "It's already begun!"

Wren was already beside Robin, placing a hand on her arm. "You're the anchor," she said, "but you don't have to carry it alone."

The pull surged between them.

Robin gripped the shard tighter. The glow spread up her arm, met by a matching light from Wren's hand. Where their skin touched, a web of silver shimmered and etched itself into the air.

Phoenix lifted off and circled the ring, his body shedding snowflakes that never reached the floor.

"Who's directing him?" Robin asked under her breath.

Wren didn't look away. "You already know. The pull runs both ways and someone on the other side has been watching since the beginning."

The ring began to fracture, cracks spreading across its outer edge as the tether refused to stabilize.

The constructs howled.

David hurled one into the scaffolding. Ashley locked another into a feedback loop using her handheld emitter.

The ringmaster backed away, his eyes growing wide with fear.

Robin took a breath, pressed her palm to the shard, and let the pull extend.

She felt Phoenix respond, not with a cry but with silence followed by a message in the form of an image. It was a pair of eyes watching from the other side of a silver wall with a raised hand. It was all part of a connection forged, long ago.

Robin opened her mouth. "I remember," she said.

The ring shattered and the force blew outward, throwing constructs like paper. The ringmaster vanished in the wave with a scream, just as the light faded leaving only an eerie stillness.

Phoenix landed on Wren's shoulder and chirped once. There was no frost this time. Only a soft shimmer of gold under his feathers.

"That felt permanent," Ashley muttered.

David nodded. "We need to find out where the rest of the energy went."

Wren looked at Robin. "And what it woke up."

CHAPTER TWENTY-NINE

The team regrouped in one of the surface tunnels just beyond the blast radius. The atrium behind them lay in ruin, choked in smoke and fragments of shattered resonance. Whatever magic had powered the ring was gone now or moved somewhere else.

Robin sat on the broken remains of a rail tie, the resonance shard cooling in her palm. Phoenix perched beside her, wings folded tight, a gold beneath his feathers that was dimming to pearl. He hadn't made a sound since the ring broke.

Ashley finished patching a shallow cut on David's arm with one of the last sterile strips from her med pack. "We need to talk about what just happened," she said, not looking up. "And what we saw in that ring."

"Half souls," Wren confirmed. She leaned against a cracked support beam, arms crossed. Her jacket was still scorched from the ring's backlash, one sleeve torn near the shoulder. A faint burn mark traced her jaw, half hidden by soot and old freckles. Her eyes, once warm amber, now held the sharp clarity of someone who had seen too much and come out burning brighter for it. "They were pulled from cadets who died but didn't fully leave. The Masked Circle tried to bind fragments of their soul signatures to constructs. But the resonance destabilized. It always does."

Robin looked at her. "They knew it wouldn't work?"

Wren gave a dry laugh. "That was the point. Failure gives them more data. They don't want resurrection, they want replacement. The Masked Circle believes souls are currency. That with enough fragments, you can stitch together something... better."

David frowned. "Better for who?"

"For them." Wren pulled a folded piece of scorched parchment from inside her jacket and held it up. It shimmered faintly with runes. "I stole this from the lower archives before they wiped them. It's part of the original ledger. The one before the Academy took over back when the Masked Circle had a name."

Ashley raised an eyebrow. "Which was?"

"The Order of the Masked Circle of Reclamation," Wren said. "Originally formed to reclaim magical inheritance lost during the collapse of the old bloodlines. Only now, they've turned it into a crusade."

Robin took the parchment and turned it in her hand. The script shimmered with her touch.

"They marked me."

Wren nodded. "You and anyone like you. Anchors with resonance strong enough to hold a thread to the other side. That's why Phoenix came to you. The pull in your family line made you a beacon. You lit up the second you crossed back over."

Robin clenched her fist around the parchment.

Ashley looked from Wren to Robin. "Then what do we do now? We've shattered their ring, but they're still out there. And they know Robin's the key."

David stepped forward. "We hit their remaining infrastructure. Hard. We burn their access points and sever the data trails."

"And we find the rest of the ledger," Robin said. "Before they do."

Phoenix lifted his head. One amber eye blinked slowly, and a single shimmer of frost flared along his wingtips. It was a reminder that something behind the silver wall still watched.

Wren stepped closer. "Then we start with the name. And we find every place they ever tried to hide it."

Robin stood. "Let's go dig up what they tried to bury."

CHAPTER THIRTY

The northern vaults beneath Hellhound Academy were sealed by three layers of reinforced sigils, half fused to the old infrastructure and shielded by legacy wards no one had bothered to update in decades. The hallway leading down to them was narrow, lined in corroded copper sheeting that pulsed faintly with residual magic. Dust clung to the walls like ash.

But the parchment Robin held shimmered the moment they reached the outermost gate.

Phoenix floated ahead, his feathers pulsing with a faint blue frost. He landed on the edge of the gate's frame, talons curling against the cold metal. The sigils flared and the door opened.

Inside was a forgotten archive; not digital, not even magically indexed. Scrolls, ledgers, and engraved metal sheets lined narrow drawers stacked to the ceiling. The air smelled of dry parchment and something older, something metallic. A long workbench stood at the center, cracked and pitted from time. Cobwebs draped the overhead beams, and faded boot prints crossed the stone like ghosts of those who came before. Dust coated everything.

"This is where they started," Wren whispered. "The Order kept their earliest records here. Before the Academy swallowed them. Before the resurrection protocols were even formalized."

Ashley moved carefully, running gloved fingers over one of the drawers. "There's no surveillance down here. The Academy didn't want anyone finding this."

David paced the outer walls, his eyes alert. "And the Masked Circle didn't want it destroyed, either, which means it still matters."

Robin stepped into the center of the room and opened her hand. The parchment glowed against the archive's ambient hum. One drawer slid open by itself.

Inside was a half engraved plate. A symbol of the mask-within-a-circle and beneath it, there was a name etched in the same ink that shimmered on Phoenix's wings.

"What is it?" Ashley asked.

Robin traced the name. "A member ledger. A founding record."

She read the names aloud. Some were long forgotten and some were suspiciously familiar.

One of them was Jude. Silence fell again.

"He wasn't marked," Wren finally said. "But his name being here… they must have chosen him. Not to kill, not yet, but to use. The Circle needs living subjects to test how far they can push resurrection and control. Jude must fit their profile."

David's jaw tightened. "And he walked away."

Ashley turned to Robin. "So why help us?"

Robin stared at the name. "Maybe he wanted out. Maybe he slipped the net before they could finish what they started. Either way, we'll find him and ask him."

Phoenix let out a low warble and tilted his head toward the far end of the chamber.

There, etched into the stone, was a second circle. It was crudely carved, like someone had done it in a hurry with a piece of a broken blade. The lines were uneven, and the edges rough, but the shape was unmistakable. It pulsed faintly in time with the air around it, as if the rock itself remembered being cut. Not the Masked Circle's mark, but something deeper and raw, etched by hand.

A message beneath it read, *The ledger is never closed.*

Robin stepped forward and pressed her hand against the symbol. The stone beneath her palm was cold and slightly damp, and the carved lines felt deeper than they looked, like the edges had been worn down by time or something trying to escape. The pulse beneath it echoed softly into her bones, like a heartbeat answering back.

Phoenix rose into the air, slowly at first, then with purpose. His wings stretched wide, catching the low, ambient light and throwing fractured gold patterns against the ceiling. The frost along his wingtips glittered faintly, but it was tempered by a new hue. The quiet fire of something returned.

She felt it again. It was the pull. Not painful, not urgent, but steady. It was a promise.

David moved to her side. "This isn't over."

Robin nodded. "It never was."

Wren whispered, "What still breathes can still fight."

Robin looked at her friends. "Then we keep breathing. We keep fighting. And we finish what they started."

Phoenix flared his wings.

Behind them, the archive lights dimmed. The air thickened, taking on a stillness that felt older than language. Somewhere between the stone and the silence, the temperature dropped a few degrees, and the smell of old earth and colder things drifted in. Beneath their feet, the stone floor trembled almost imperceptibly. Somewhere, deeper than the vaults, something else stirred.

THE STORY CONTINUES

The story continues in book two, *Dust to Dust,* coming soon to Amazon.

MARTHA'S NOTES

APRIL 23, 2025

Spring in Austin: The Garden Awakens (And So Do the Weeds)

Spring in Austin is like a grand performance—and I am cast as the lead gardener in my own little backyard. One day, the yard looks like something from a Disney film where everything has gone to sleep, and the next, everything is green, growing, blooming and in need of attention. The garden doesn't just wake up; it throws open the doors, cranks up the music, and invites every living thing to the party.

The weeds are the first to RSVP, of course. They must have a built-in alarm clock because the moment the temperature shifts from "chilly" to "pleasant," they launch their hostile takeover. One day, I'm admiring the first brave little blooms, and the next, dandelions are popping up here and there. It's like they wait for me to look away before they spring up overnight.

Little secret though – I let them stay for a while because

they're the first feeding system of the season for honeybees and patience and timing are two of the big deals about gardening.

The tomato plants, on the other hand, are the drama queens of the garden. They make an entrance every year in the raised beds like they've just returned from an epic journey, which, in a way, they have. They grow tall and wide, climbing onto trellises meant for other plants until I cut back the suckers, and occasionally attempting to strangle a neighboring pepper plant in their enthusiasm. It's the only way to get a good tomato outside of southern New Jersey or Hanover County, Virginia.

And then there are the squirrels, feral pigs and raccoons. The joys of living just on the edge of a ranch, which I actually love. These big and little bandits are already plotting their summer raids. I see the squirrels, tails twitching, eyes scanning the yard like seasoned burglars casing a bank. They hang upside down from the bird feeder to eat the sunflower seeds. I envy their core muscles.

Despite the chaos, there's something undeniably magical about watching the earth wake up. It's a reminder that even when things seem dormant, they're just getting ready for the next big bloom. That feels like a metaphor for life, doesn't it? We all go through those slow, quiet seasons where it seems like nothing is happening. But under the surface, things are shifting, growing, and preparing for their moment in the sun. Growth isn't always obvious, but it's always happening.

Gardening is a lot like writing, too. You plant ideas, water them with attention (and occasionally tears), and then hope something wonderful grows. Some stories take root quickly, pushing up toward the sunlight with enthusiasm. Others need time, resting beneath the surface until just the right conditions encourage them to break through. And sometimes, just like in my garden, weeds show up and demand attention.

In writing, those weeds come in the form of self-doubt, distractions, or the occasional plot hole big enough to fly a plane through. (Inside joke just for Mr. Anderle. Let's see if he notices.) One day, you think you have a perfect scene, and the next, you realize it's strangling the entire story like an overgrown vine. The trick is persistence, taking breaks, asking for help – in other words, balance. Keep pulling the weeds, keep tending the soil, and eventually, you end up with something beautiful—or at least something that won't completely embarrass you when it's time to share it with the world.

And then there's the waiting. The hardest part of both gardening and writing is the in-between time, the stretch where nothing seems to be happening, but you have to trust that something is. I can't rush the tomatoes any more than I can force a story to unfold before it's ready. It's all about patience, trust, and maybe a little bit of bribery in the form of good compost or strong coffee.

Of course, there are days when I stand in the middle of my overgrown yard, feeling completely overwhelmed. The weeds are winning, the plants are growing in all the wrong directions, and the squirrels are probably laughing at me from the safety of the trees. On those days, I remind myself that not every battle has to be won in a single afternoon. Some gardens—and some books—take time. And if all else fails? There's always pizza delivery and an evening spent admiring the garden from inside the house.

Ultimately, spring in Austin is a gentle and beautiful time of year full of hope and new beginnings. I'll keep digging, keep pulling weeds, and keep planting new ideas, because you never know which one might turn into something amazing.

And as for the all the critters, including the bull frogs and tree frogs and fire ants and snakes of every kind? I suppose they're part of the process, too. But I'm keeping my eye on them. More adventure to follow.

MICHAEL'S NOTES

MAY 27, 2025

My Slightly-Too-Quiet Writing Lair
(For Now)

First off, a massive thank you! Not just for picking up this story and diving in, but for sticking around to read these ramblings in the back. You folks are the reason I get to do this, and I appreciate you hanging out with me for a bit.

Occasionally, I like to think about, or at least share, how we authors occasionally (and sometimes accidentally) stumble upon ideas. It's not always a lightning bolt moment; sometimes it's more like tripping over a plot bunny in the dark.

So, LMBPN is working on a new series right now. It's a little bit of a twist on a familiar trope and a little bit inspired by a YouTube video.

I think I might have mentioned in another author note somewhere how I've got this dream for my office. I'm picturing windows that aren't just windows. I want them to have the ability to show me completely different scenes.

And I'm not talking about just sticking a poster on the wall, folks. I'm dreaming of windows that can display, say, a live feed from a mountaintop, making my office look out onto some epic vista.

Or, even better, imagine all my windows showing the vastness of space, stars glittering, nebulae swirling... Hell yeah!

Now, I've actually looked into this. I did a fair bit of research to see if those new LED sheets, the thin plastic-y ones you see on TikTok, could do the trick. Turns out, if you want decent resolution – and trust me, you do, because pixelated space just isn't the same – it gets real expensive, real fast.

I crunched the numbers for my windows – they're about 28 inches wide and nearly six feet tall, and I've got three of them. Minimum, and I mean *minimum*, we're talking somewhere between $5,000 and $6,000. Ouch. That's firmly outside my budget.

And that's *me* saying it's outside my budget, without even running it by the Queen – my wife. Even I know that's a non-starter. (Happy wife, happy life, right?)

So, with my sci-fi window project on the back burner (for now... a man can dream!), I realized I could repurpose my TV. For about three years, that thing has sat dark most days of the week. Lately, though, I've started playing YouTube videos – you know, the ones with hours of music and cool, looping atmospheric scenes.

It's surprisingly nice.

One I've been digging shows this city, almost completely dark, with just this eerie light coming up from the streets far, far below, and little flying cars zipping

MICHAEL'S NOTES

about. It's incredibly impressive, and I can't quite tell if it's all 3D rendered or what.

But when I get up close to the TV, with its crazy good dot pitch, I can see tiny little windows in the buildings.

And that's when my little author brain starts whirring. What's going on behind *those* windows?

Then I'm looking at this video, and I start thinking... what if this isn't just any city? What if these towers I'm seeing aren't like the ones in New York or Chicago or London? What if these are *mega*-towers, soaring 300, 400 stories tall, housing a quarter of a million people each? Just massive.

(Yes, I did some back-of-the-napkin calculations on what that would entail. It's mind boggling.)

And then, like a scene from that Judge Dredd movie (the Karl Urban one, not the other one... though both have their moments), I imagined: what would it look like if one of those colossal dreadnoughts – we're talking over a kilometer long, capable of inserting troops into 50 stories of a building at once – suddenly appeared in a city like *that*?

(Snapping my fingers mentally in my head. Try it, makes these authors notes seem way more impressive.)

So, that's the spark! We're working through the story right now – it'll go through editing and all the usual fun stuff – but it's all about that.

What happens with the politics, the shift in power, the legal nightmares... and what if this dreadnought is crewed by a bunch of untouchables? Because, of course, I had to have that in there. A crew that's all about doing what's right and damn the tangled politics they've just flown into.

That's how this story idea came around. I was watching

a YouTube video, my mind wandered, and I thought about a classic trope: the lone battleship, usually out in the cold, dark of space. And I thought, what if I take that trope – the lone battleship, the dedicated crew – and drop it smack dab into a cyberpunk future with these colossal, Judge Dredd-style mega-buildings? And, for political reasons (because there are *always* political reasons and I am a cynical author), it's the only ship of its kind there.

It's shaping up to be a wild ride, and it should be coming out in the next two or three months. Be on the lookout for it. I really hope you folks like it. And there you have it – a little peek into the sometimes bizarre process of how a series gets born.

Until the next book, keep those pages turning!

Ad Aeternitatem,
   Michael Anderle

PS: For more behind-the-scenes stuff, sneak peeks, and the occasional odd thought that pops into my head, don't forget to subscribe to the MORE STORIES with Michael newsletter HERE: https://michael.beehiiv.com/

PSS: What kind of crazy view would *you* want your sci-fi windows to show? Let me know! I'm always up for new daydream material.

OTHER SERIES IN THE ORICERAN
UNIVERSE:

THE LEIRA CHRONICLES
CASE FILES OF AN URBAN WITCH
THE EVERMORES CHRONICLES
SOUL STONE MAGE
THE KACY CHRONICLES
MIDWEST MAGIC CHRONICLES
THE FAIRHAVEN CHRONICLES
I FEAR NO EVIL
THE DANIEL CODEX SERIES
SCHOOL OF NECESSARY MAGIC
SCHOOL OF NECESSARY MAGIC: RAINE CAMPBELL
ALISON BROWNSTONE
FEDERAL AGENTS OF MAGIC
SCIONS OF MAGIC
THE UNBELIEVABLE MR. BROWNSTONE
DWARF BOUNTY HUNTER
ACADEMY OF NECESSARY MAGIC
MAGIC CITY CHRONICLES
ROGUE AGENTS OF MAGIC

OTHER SERIES IN THE ORICERAN UNIVERSE:

OTHER BOOKS BY JUDITH BERENS

OTHER BOOKS BY MARTHA CARR

JOIN THE ORICERAN UNIVERSE FAN GROUP ON FACEBOOK!

CONNECT WITH THE AUTHORS

Martha Carr Social

Website: http://www.marthacarr.com

Facebook: https://www.facebook.com/groups/MarthaCarrFans/

Michael Anderle Social

Website: http://lmbpn.com

Email List: https://michael.beehiiv.com/

https://www.facebook.com/LMBPNPublishing

https://twitter.com/MichaelAnderle

https://www.instagram.com/lmbpn_publishing/

https://www.bookbub.com/authors/michael-anderle

BOOKS BY MICHAEL ANDERLE

Sign up for the LMBPN email list to be notified of new releases and special deals!

https://lmbpn.com/email/

For a complete list of books by Michael Anderle, please visit:

www.lmbpn.com/ma-books/

www.ingramcontent.com/pod-product-compliance
Lightning Source LLC
LaVergne TN
LVHW091717070526
838199LV00050B/2435